Siân Vidak

Hope of Ray

Siân Vidak

First Edition: January 2021

Copyright © Siân Vidak, 2021

All rights reserved.

ISBN: 9798593564566

This is a work of fiction.
Names, characters, places, businesses, organisations, and incidents are either the product of the author's imagination, or are used fictitiously. Any resemblance to real persons, living or dead, locations, or events, is entirely coincidental.

Cover design copyright © Siân Vidak
& Violet Vidak, 2021

Contents

1. Sophia 1
2. Jacob 33
3. Pom 41
4. David Pomeroy Walker 59
5. Diana 72
6. Helen 75
7. Hope 83
8. Sophia and Jacob 97
9. Helen Elizabeth Bramwell 104
10. Ian Henry Keatan 109
11. Ray 118
12. Judy 130
13. Lucy 141
14. Maribel 150
15. Roo 174
16. Robson 187
17. Faith and David 194
18. Noël 201
19. Reuben-Ray 212
20. Leanna 220
21. Augustine 222
22. Sophia and Ray 227
23. Jimmy 247
24. Joanna 253
25. Christopher 256
26. Raymond Albert Bramwell 260
27. David 262
28. Hubert Parry 274

Siân Vidak

Dedication

He stole my heart, my body, my soul.

Chapter One

Sophia

I stood up - legs like jelly, well, more like a trembling gelatinous mess, in absolute honesty.

I stood up, hollow, numb with agony; my stomach was knotting, I could feel my rectum cramping, I was gripped with nerves. It was as if I was six years old again, the weight of the world upon my shoulders; I was that shy little girl playing Mary, only this wasn't a rehearsal.

I couldn't get the words out; in what seemed to be an ever descending reality; the teacher wasn't there to prompt me, I couldn't escape the fact that this wasn't the Nativity, it was my life.

The words moulded into a large mess, I kept staring at the paper – wishing, hoping, he was going to walk into the Chapel, but nothing. How could he? When the harsh reality was right there. He was cold, in the box, as I clumsily attempted to articulate about the love of my life, all the while our children sat in the pew, unable to comprehend that Daddy was never coming home, and all they had now was his picture staring back at them.

Our story had me illustrated as this strong, formidable woman, today I was about to crash and burn. I just wanted to hide in my bed and pretend I was a fairy, doing all the silly voices to my babies, as I read their favourite story. The story I read today however, was one I never wanted to open the pages of again.

I was smacking back down to Earth with a crashing sensation, as I now used all of my reserves to fulfil my last wifely duty. I couldn't survive under this facade of strength, I knew for us to survive now, as a family of five, and for me to ride the storm of four children, five years old and under; I would have to admit my vulnerability openly.

This, running through my mind for what must have been seconds, felt like hours, I looked down at the paper for inspiration once more. Nothing. It was still a blur, the sea of words were just a black hole.

As I looked up, I drew a breath; the wave of colour, worn to honour him, gave me the clarity I needed, this was my final chance to tell him I loved him, with everyone else to share the emotion with me, the people who had taken time out of their day to show my family sympathy and respect.

I closed my eyes, and went right back to the beginning...

I was in my early twenties once more. I had finished secretarial school and had a good job; I had achieved good A levels in English and Maths. This lead to me working for the Saunders family, they were one of the local power families within the town, the town being Fremmington Ayshe, where I grew up. My parents knew the Saunders, and everyone in general knew everyone else's business. Nothing was sacred.

I worked hard and had integrity, I knew much of the scandal within the town, but I enjoyed my job, so decided 'ignorance was bliss' in regards to the local gossip mongering. I'd love to say I played hard and drank like a fish, like a stereotypical twenty-something, but I'd be deluding myself.

I was a little bit of a tease, especially with one Jacob Saunders. I was of reasonable height, slim, with curly brown hair, highlighted with natural red tones. I was always a smidge flirty, and with office-style 1950's chic, it worked in my favour, especially being in a predominantly male industry.

Miss Sophia Hardy, that was me.

Hope of Ray

It was March 1st, I was inundated in the office that day. I really didn't know my arse from my elbow. I can remember my workload still to this day.

- Press release on the new development,
- Pay three invoices,
- Post our bills,
- Ring around the timber companies and source new timbers,
- Check Jacob's flight details; his flight was from City and West Airport, flight number AXG346J to Lamezia Terme Airport. His departure time was 1300hrs.

I was easily distracted when Jacob was in the office; he was six foot three, with a broad frame. He was the third son to my boss, Christopher Saunders. Jacob had this deep, lionhearted personality, which went beyond those hazel eyes, the swarthy skin against the slicked-back chestnut, shoulder-length hair. He had a finely contoured body; muscular, apparent was his sportsmanship.

As soon as he walked through the door, his presence would just take over. He was a man's man, and I just fanaticized about him grabbing me hard, pressing me up against the wall, taking control. But, Jacob Saunders was my boss, only, not in my head... he was my little plaything, he could do anything with me, and my thoughts weren't always so innocent.

I had been in the office all morning, my jobs didn't seem to be depleting at all. Then, in saunters the ever so dishy Jacob, complete with rugby attire. Oh my goodness, I was in heaven. It really didn't take a lot for my imagination to run wild. The thoughts got pretty hot and steamy, I was a total sucker for strong thighs, I found them ever so sexy, and a total turn on, and Jacob was no exception. My eyes were drawn to his upper legs, every fibre of muscle perfectly formed.

As he assumed his usual stance, with one knee raised and resting on the corner of my desk, my eyes drew away from his pulsating thigh, across to his crotch, where his shorts pulled tight across his package. Jake had a little shuffle, my eyes wandered up his torso, his body was commanding the room, I tried to ignore the flushing feeling he was causing me to experience, it's a cliché, but our eyes met, and I could feel the sexual tension rising.

The door swung open, with a verbal, "Knock knock!"

A rather posh one granted, but seriously, "Knock knock"? And, why didn't you wait to be invited in?

There he stood, this burning orange, ginger-haired man, slightly shorter than average, with a hairline creeping back. He was well dressed, wearing a check shirt with multiple blue tones and contrasting red, casually, yet smartly, paired with dark jeans, and he had on boots, almost like cowboy boots, I'd never forget those boots.

"Ready Jacob?"

"Yep."

Jacob grabbed the plans, in the tubes, laid on the coffee table, and walked out. Ray following, he did however, give me a glance, as if to say, "I'm not normally that rude, but he's off and I need to follow, so please don't think ill of me", as a silent apology.

And there it was, my first encounter with Ray.

I was still totally present in Jacobs shorts, although his habit of just walking out of the office, without the basic attempt of manners to say goodbye, wound me up slightly, I have no doubt it was a deliberate ploy on his behalf.

My bubble of wanderings got a sharp pop. In flew Jacob and Ray, they were talking about pre-season training, how they had to focus away from the pitch momentarily, and start hitting their core strength hard.

Already I was lost; from the whole conversation, I picked up that weeks one and two would focus on an aerobic fitness base, and apparently, this was going to be the underpinnings for the rest of the programme.

They both enthused about training, and reminisced how they had both racked up various injuries over the years. It would seem that, through rugby, Jacob and Ray had known each other for a good few years.

Throughout the conversation I kept quiet, I decided to listen, learn and pretend I knew nothing, maybe I would find out if Jake was attached. Ray went on to mention his wife Helen. She had been on a wine tasting weekend with her work. Jacob didn't mention any spouse.

While they were man gossiping, I heard a couple of names I recognised, my ears pricked up; I was nosey, but knew blabbing would lose me my job. I heard every rumour, on and off the pitch, to do with the club; it was a masculine form of bitching, they were one step away from pulling hair. Frankly, I didn't care that Pete was cheating on his wife, although, having never met Pete, I did now have a very low opinion of him. He was seeing a new, younger, bird behind his Mrs' back; Jacob scoffed at this, while Ray just gave the disapproving tone of, "He'll get caught, he always does."

From this, I had deduced that Pete was a regular naughty boy, and his wife always took him back. Their gossip didn't improve much, but I did now know that Kev was obviously going through a crisis, he had bought a new sports car, and was trying to attract a different type of woman, now that he'd divorced.

I was rather busy, looking at a new pair of shoes, the inane babblings of that pair had been somewhat distracting to my "real" work. The shoes were peep toe, with a cute kitten heel, covered in floral silk.

There he was, over my shoulder, making a very Jacob witty quip at my expense.

"So, are they for the office, or the bedroom?"

I really did fancy him, but I didn't want to be obvious, though my reaction was totally the opposite, more of an 'in for a penny, in for pound' kind of attitude.

"Either for you... where shall we try first, the bedroom or the desk?"

Jacob smirked and nodded his head, as he pulled back away from me.

My verbal incontinence made me want to burst into a ball of flames and fall on the floor in ashes.

Ray cracked a smile. I tried to carry on with my work.

"This is Sophia, Sophia this is Ray, he is our contractor. And more importantly, a VERY good friend, see you look after him."

We shook hands and did the pleasant, "Hellos".

I glanced at the clock, I needed to head out; I picked up the daily post and my purse, and headed out the door. Most people my age had a picture of their boyfriend, or besties in a photo booth, in their purse; I had a picture of my darling Pom.

When I got back to the office, Ray had disappeared; I braced myself for a reprimand, I wasn't sure yet if Jacob had a sense of humour, it was only

Jacob and me. There were two desks, mine was by the window and was modern in look, Christopher's was very traditional, dark wood, with built in drawers, and green leather on top. Jacob would always commandeer his father's desk when his dad wasn't there; it was almost infantile, as if to say, "I'm the boss". This type of behaviour reminded me of a little girl walking around the house in her mother's shoes.

"Missy Hardy."

"Yes, Mr Saunders?"

"Your behaviour earlier... was... hilarious! I really didn't expect that reaction from you. Are those shoes for work or pleasure?"

"How about **your** pleasure?" I retorted.

At this point, I decided I had been pretty forward; Jacob hadn't really had an active part in the business until now, so I had never worked with him, now the barriers were down, I suppose it seemed like the right time to make my position perfectly clear. It seemed so exciting to be flirting with an older man; I felt my behaviour was out of character, for all I knew he had a wife and kids tucked away at home, with the family dog called Rover. I was being a risk taker, and was likely to get burnt, but I had no duty to anyone but myself, as a selfish early twenty-something.

"Jacob, I fancy you, you are stunning, so, if you want..." I gave a cheeky grin and raised my eyebrows, "...those shoes are for your pleasure."

I stood up from my desk, turned off my monitor, put on my coat and grabbed my bag. I went over to Jake, leant over so my lips brushed his ear, and his eyes caught a glimpse of my cleavage, and softly whispered, "Good night."

Slowly, I stood back up, and left for the evening. I didn't look back, to me that was enough to leave him wanting more, hopefully I piqued his interest.

The following day, the day that paved the rest of my life, every twist and turn that evolved, the crossroads I would experience more than once, taking the wrong road, and trying to navigate back to the right journey.

The office was fraught with deadlines and the impending visit from a bureaucrat, over the new buildings.

"Missy Hardy, come with me." Jacob commanded.

"Pardon?"

"We're going on a field trip Sophia, so grab your stuff and let's go."

I was so excited to be out of the office finally, and going on a trip with Jake, but really, his sucky tone of voice was not needed.

We could have our pick of what company car to take, but Jake decided to take his white van. I opened the door, and got in; I had to wade my way through a never-ending mountain of magazines in the foot well, and empty food wrappers, this clearly wasn't a man whose wife packed him a lunch. Sweeping the seat clear of screwed up crusty dirty shirts, I negotiated my pencil skirt up, shimmied across as best I could without looking clumsy, and buckled up.

As we backed out of the drive, I looked at Jake, he was wearing a pair of steel toe-capped rigger boots, with rugby socks rolled down, peeking out the top of the boots, shorts and a tee, it was blue with some sort of dog motif on it. He finished his look with a grey-blue anorak that had seen better days. I just smiled; he still oozed this sex appeal somehow. We drove, I decided it best not to engage in conversation until he initiated it;

yesterday I could have made a right you-know-what out of myself, I had no idea how the land lied today.

We headed out past the manor house on the edge of the town, as you turned left, into the manor, there were two cottages that mirrored each other, just after the first cattle grid, they were like chocolate box cottages, picturesque and beautiful. We headed out on the Wimpleton Road, down towards the ford by the post box and bench, into Merton Major. The family had land under development on the edge of the village, and had permissions for five new dwellings; there were strict conditions about the sympathies it had to pay in order to blend in with the existing buildings, the roofing tiles though had been somewhat of a sticking point.

Apparently, I was there to take notes, what a bunch of...

He put the ladder up to the first floor window and said, "Up you go, I'll hold the ladder firm while you go on up, and then I'll join you."

He had a smug look on his face, like he anticipated I would decline and be all girly about it. If Jacob Saunders thought I was going to climb a ladder in my shoes, he was very much mistaken! I bent down into my bag, fumbled around for a few seconds, and produced a second pair of shoes; although I only ever wore low heels, they were killer heels, killing the soles of my feet. I always had a spare pair of flats in my bag, mainly for the walk to and from work, so Jacob's challenge for me was no mean feat.

I slipped one shoe off - grabbing Jake's arm to steady myself on the uneven ground, he tensed his arm, and I could feel it pulsing. I was ready to climb the ladder, no one was going to defeat me; I had this internal conflict, where I would compete with my own standards and never show weakness on the outside. Being young, it was easy to push myself a little further, I had no idea that, in the years to follow, this would become my worst enemy.

My bottom was on the larger side, and would move independently from the rest of my body, I made sure Jacob followed it up every step.

We were all alone in the new cottages; they weren't cottages yet, just an empty concrete and brick shell. There were a few sheets of plasterboard, piled on the floor, and made watertight by a green tarpaulin.

Jacob took command of the scenario; for once, I wasn't feeling so sure of myself, there was nothing, straight down the line this was business. I was writing down his dictation, half the time he had his back to me, he felt cold, no... anything. I took the cue to be quiet.

"Look here Sophia!"

I was commanded to look at the specification plans that Jacob had rolled out, on the top of the plasterboard sheets, which he was now using as a makeshift table. He was crouched down, in this almost caveman-like stance, I tootied down beside him to look, my pen and paper poised ready. I slipped my bag handles off my shoulder, and dropped them to the floor, next to me. So there I was, next to him, not even a few inches separated us. I was a size 12 yet had all the right curves; it wasn't through a lack of hard work though. It had taken me years to battle the fat / thin drama, and now I realised health was huge, I had waged war on the comfort eating, and defeated the fridge picking.

Jake had a hardened exterior that day though; we just looked at those plans. I could see this immense body out the corner of my eye, his hand lifted, I felt it touch my knee.

In amazement, my head turned, it felt like I was doing a slow-motion impression of an owl, our eyes fixed onto each other. He ran his hand up my thigh, it was a gentle moment, he just grazed it with his hand. Slowly, still in contact, we stood up. Instantly his hands started to run over the side of my hips, the tips of his fingers drew up my body to the back of my head, where he clenched my curls. I went on to tip toes, letting him lean in, our lips pressed, it was that easy.

He walked me backwards, while still kissing me, his hand still entwined in my curls, the other wrapping around me, pulling me closer into him. I was aroused, I could feel this tingling sensation throughout my body, he pressed me hard against the wall, Jacob was tugging at my curls, as the tension grew the tugs became harder, his pelvis pressed firmly against me. He released his hands from around me, unclasping my hair; his hands were now free to hold my cheeks, as he continuously pecked my lips.

My nails ran up and down his back, right down his buttocks; his lips were starting to wander down my neck, inch by inch. It was very much a classic movie scene. My hands ran over his chest, he pulled back, took both my hands and 'cuffed' them with one thumb and index finger, raised them above my head, in an almost crucifix style position; I looked at him, drew a breath, panting, my skin feeling tacky with the heat.

"Alright then mate, speak later."

Jacob pulled away; he was like a rabbit in headlights.

"Who the hell is that?" I whispered.

"Damn, it's Ray and his blokes."

Ray had turned up, with two of his workers. With that, the moment of passion was over; the trouble was, we were both left piqued with arousal. I felt like I could explode there and then, I wanted more, was this going to add to the chase though?

We carried on like nothing had happened, passed the time of day with Ray, and that was it. He didn't speak to me, just switched on the radio, he felt cold again. The moment on site felt surreal, and I couldn't really digest what had occurred, it was fanciful, it didn't happen to girls like me. He dropped me back at work, and disappeared.

Disappeared to Italy! My head was buzzing with confusion, he quite clearly didn't like what he saw, he'd acted on impulse and now regretted it, I was sure. He got caught in a moment that had erupted from flirting; I shouldn't have led him on. Jacob was now safely hidden away in Italy; we had no means of communication, although it wasn't like he didn't know where I worked, and my hours. Three weeks it would be, and March 2nd was the last time I saw him.

The fantasy of him built, I had no idea why he was in Italy and I couldn't mention too much to Christopher, it would make it too obvious.

"Ah, I see we are still waiting for a postcard, you'd think he'd tell us he was alive." I'd quip.

His father had his nose in the paper, while sat at his desk, he'd turn the page over and ruffle it, and to remedy this he'd shake the paper away from him.

"Ah lass, that son of mine has never done a thing he was told, he was going to order my landscaping bricks from a manufacturer, and get them shipped over for me. It was a week's job, with travel in that time as well, quite why Jacob thinks three weeks, at my expense, is needed I'm not sure."

Christopher had a slight northern accent.

Jacob was older than me, seventeen years older to be precise, but that paled into insignificance, I felt consumed with every thought of him, and every "What if?" It was ridiculous on reflection, we'd had one semi-intimate moment, and now I was away with the fairies. I was desperate to see him.

I had decided, no matter what I was feeling, I was not going to lie down and be walked over, so as far as I was concerned, he could broach the subject, if he so wished. Well that was the plan anyway, but like all good plans, there was a possible down fall.

There it was, March 25th, Jacob's return date, and my day off. I contemplated what to do; mother was due to head into Wimpleton for market day; should I offer to take her and Pom? At least I knew we'd be having bangers and mash for tea; that was one certainty. I tried to get him out of my mind, and filling my day seemed like the best solution. I checked his flight; it was on time to land at City and West for 0830hrs.

Mother had made my breakfast, just like I was still five years old; she was fussing about doing her usual day-to-day jobs. By this time I had usually left for work, but was in no doubt, this was her behaviour every day, not just when I was home to hinder her routine. I was clock watching, while having to hear a tale from yesterday's Ladies Circle. Brenda had become a Grandmother, for the third time, this time it was from her youngest daughter, Sarah, who had just delivered her first child, a boy, named Harry; while Gary, Brenda's son, was married, and their youngest was now three. I was genuinely happy for Brenda; she had three healthy grandchildren, and was clearly happy about this, by sharing her good news. What my mother forgot, with all this feel good talk, is that I had never met Brenda, and likewise, that extended to Sarah and Gary too.

My phone started ringing; I leapt up, excusing myself as I went out of the room. I pressed the green button.

"Can you pick me up? Please, can you meet me at the Airport? I've cancelled my lift home; I want you to meet me. Sophia, hello... Sophia, speak to me."

"I'm here, I'm here. Why me?"

"The way things were left, it wasn't right what I did. Please, I'm sorry."

His tone was desperate, wanting, almost begging, forgiveness.

I perched on the edge of my bed, I dragged my blanket over my knees and hugged the corner with my spare hand; it was like a default setting.

"Jacob, I..., I..."

"Go to the office, pick up a car, well you know what my favourite choice is and drive to me, take the petty cash and fill up, ring me when you decide what to do."

I just managed to piece the last sentence together, as the incoherent airport tannoy system went into overdrive with announcements.

He'd hung up, I could feel the desperation in his voice, and I knew I'd go running; he deliberately cancelled his ride home, just so I'd taxi him in his favourite Volvo; but were his intentions just to recreate the other week, or of true remorse. I'd only know if I went to meet him.

He had taken the first step, so I guessed that was a positive, I knew instantly what I was doing; I knew how my feelings had been for three weeks. I went and made my excuses to mother, and told her not to worry about my dinner, as I had to make a trip for work. She knew I loved my job, and didn't question it, this wasn't the first time I had worked overtime as a "taxi service" for the Saunders for social events, they paid great overtime rates and this would be no different in my mother's assumptions.

I wasn't going to dress up for him, especially as I was travelling quite a distance, I wanted comfort over looks. I scraped back the untameable mess into a ponytail, threw on some jeans and a tee, I went for my favourite boots, they were equestrian boots, not that I had ever even sat on a horse. I flicked the mascara over my lashes, and that would be the sum total of effort. Was it me, testing to see if he was just all about looks, or if he was interested in me for personality as well? I guess I was testing him, and this would be a clear indicator of his intentions.

I got to the office, left a brief note saying I was going to rescue Jacob, and that the car hadn't been stolen. I could see it now, pulled over on a stretch of motorway in a stolen car. I took the four-by-four. I could drive this one, and did on a regular basis when in Fremmington Ayshe, it was good on country roads, and had lots of boot space, I had no idea what luggage Jacob had, so anything small just seemed silly to entertain.

On the road, I called him; the boom of the road combined with the Bluetooth connection, meant I had to do the shouty thing. The phone rang and rang.

"Sophia?"

I was trying to play it cool and casual, I didn't want to make an idiot of myself and get hurt, although at this point it was a little bit late to worry about such things.

"Hey you, what time did you land? I'll be with you in about an hour, give or take."

"As soon as I landed I rang you, so a couple of hours ago, I guess. I'm having some food, oh God, please tell me you had food before you left, or am I going to have to buy you brunch?"

He made me giggle, and feel like every anxiety I had induced myself, when I could have just said no, went away.

"My mother had lovingly cooked me boiled eggs and soldiers; just don't even go there, you enjoy your bacon sarnie."

"How did you know I had a bacon sandwich?"

"You're a creature of habit, crispy bacon, on brown bread, no butter, and brown sauce; although it is criminal to have brown sauce, bacon and tommy kay are the correct combination. I have walked, every Friday morning for the last 18 months, to collect the Friday order, or did you think the bread fairy brought them to site for you?"

"Tomato ketchup? Tomato ketchup? Why? We need words when you arrive. I'll see you in a while, bye."

"Bye."

The rest of the journey went well, I was happy and things seemed relaxed. I sang my little heart out until I turned off for the airport, in my head I was on an L.A. tour of my greatest hits.

I pulled into the airport, that Audi, a speedy then slam the breaks on kind of driver, who had been in front of me for part the journey, was now doing some kind of 'in and out of the parking space correcting dance', they were infuriating. My stomach had started knotting and I felt sick. I'd suffered all my life with this type of stage fright, though Mrs Crompton, of class 3C, wasn't there to prompt me today.

I parked, got out, and locked up. I called Jake, just like I promised, I was shaking as I pressed the buttons, I was going to see him, and although everything was hunky-dory on the phone, the chemistry when we met could be totally different. I kept walking towards the terminal's automatic doors, my stomach didn't just rumble, it bubbled and burned. I went through the doors, he answered.

"I'm here, by the information desk, I've just arrived. Where are you? I'll come and meet you, I'll find you."

"Stay on the line, I'll make my way to you, don't move."

What was he playing at? I could hear the screeching of his chair against the tiled floor, as he pushed it in, I could tell he was still in the restaurant by the clinking of china on china, and cutlery shuffling across plates, in the background.

"I'm here, by the main doors."

I stood still, feet feeling almost glued to the floor, I kept twisting and turning round, looking all over, hoping to catch a glimpse of him.

"Where are you Jake, I'm still stood here, I haven't moved, I can't see you."

"I'm on my way." he insisted.

"But where are you?"

I sounded, with that last question, pathetic and whiney.

"I'm right behind you, turn around."

I turned, and there he was, the man in black. Black casual shirt, black chinos, with Chelsea boots.

"Hey you."

I let out this breath of relief.

"Good trip?"

"Yeah; good. I'm sorry."

"Leave it." I scrunched my face up in a ball. "It's not the right time."

I smiled, to let him know everything was OK, and I led him to the car, I didn't say much, now wasn't the time for it, and I very much felt that it would be airing my dirty laundry in public.

He had a small flight bag, and that was it; haggard brown leather, the creases each telling their own story of travel, and his past. A past, no doubt, filled with grazes and blemishes.

He held out his hand, the background noise was such a bellowing and booming tone, that any chance of conversation was non-existent, the wheels of the jumbo jets, gliding small distances above our heads, felt almost touchable. The gesture, of Jacob offering to hold my hand, was one of warmth and openness. Awkward had faded away, onward had presented itself.

I took his hand, his giant shovels just dwarfed me, as he did with his whole stature, he gave my hand a reassuring squeeze, in that pulsing style of one, release, two. We then interlaced our fingers. For every giant pace he took, my tiny little feet shuffled about two or three extra paces. We danced our way through the terminal car park, with a giant pace, shuffle, shuffle, shuffle; do-si-do-ing around the many cars and pedestrians with 'head-up-arse-syndrome'. Getting back to the car had the usual trials any car park offers, only exacerbated by my own self doubt, was he just being polite in the terminal because he had an audience?

As we approached the four-by-four, complete with the SND 451 C personal registration plate, I had to do the usual handbag fumble to locate the keys, with one click, Jacob and I would be caged for the next couple of hours. He took control; he was definitely one of those leader types.

"I'll drive sweetie."

"You're the boss."

He opened the driver's door, after throwing his bag on the back seat. I had already sat in the passenger seat, I was twisting from the waist to buckle up, and he was just raising his left side onto the seat.

"Jesus Christ, how small are you?"

"All good whisky Jacob, all good whisky."

The driver's seat made a whoosh and click noise as it was adjusted to maximum, all the mirrors were altered, his seat belt slung over his shoulder, but not yet clipped in, he leant over and spoke softly, "Thank you."

I felt vulnerable, the office girl wasn't really the true me, I think I had adopted that style after my secondary school education, and the bullying I endured. Everyday being told I was ugly, I just longed to be accepted, and Sophia Hardy was, in all honesty, too much of a tease, when really, she just yearned to be loved. Loved by people who were acquaintances, by all accounts, being loved by her family wasn't ever an issue.

I moved towards him, pressed my cheek against his, placing a small peck upon it with a, "Welcome home." whispered.

We drove in silence; then we drove with mindless conversation, not one mention of his trip, three weeks away and not one story or report of the weather. There was still a great big elephant in the backseat, so to speak, that was being ignored. Before we hit the motorway, there were several A roads, with rolling agricultural fields, waterways, and solar farms.

I could feel my cheeks burning in rage, as my thoughts were all about addressing the outstanding issues. I had this monologue in my head, and now it was the do or die moment, where I decided to release my verbal incontinence once more.

"Jacob, let me finish this before you say anything, please; the Sophia that day in the cottage, and the Sophia you see in the office, they aren't the real me. It's a defence, for the last three weeks I have analysed every moment, and questioned it all, and although elements are me, it's not the person I really am, does that make sense? I was bullied at school, and I guess in the working world, I just wanted to fit in, so I got witty. I'm just an extreme, magnified version of myself. I go home at night, to my parent's house, I have never lived alone, my Mum cooks my tea and washes my clothes. I spend every Sunday with my Granddad. The flirtiness is just a defence, I don't like to drink, but do under peer pressure. I sleep in my single bed, with my teddy bear and blankie. I'm not what you think. I'm boring, dull in fact!"

I left it there, I had nothing else.

His reply was one of simplicity. "OK."

My internal voice was screaming, "What? You reply to me spilling my guts out with, 'OK.' Wow, you are a cold arse, I hope you go back to Italy, and I never see you again."

We hadn't even reached the motorway, the thought of the duration of the journey in silence was not one I desired; I tapped the dial on the radio. The nasal timbre of the presenter came on, it was one of those golden oldie type segments, I hadn't an issue with that, I was brought up on this music, so I enjoyed a quickstep down memory lane. In essence, my musical taste was one of a middle-aged frump.

Charlotte, from Bromley, has emailed in with, 'Can you wishing Steve a "Happy Anniversary, I love you, as do the boys, Shane and Tyler."

I couldn't recall the song, it was something abstract.

The song was catchy, but I wasn't going to enjoy it out of protest, Jacob on the other hand, tappy, tappy, tappy, on the steering wheel, with his thumb, while remaining in the perfect ten-to-two driving position. How could one person push so many buttons and evoke every emotion possible?

There was a succession of songs, that my soul associated with my childhood. Before I could stop myself, I was singing. The song was a happy place for me, as soon as I realised I'd dropped my barriers I could see a wry smile to the side of his face in my peripheral vision, reactionary as I was, I flicked the radio dial back off.

I could still hear tappy, tappy, tappy, or so I thought. Glancing over to the dash, the left indicator was flashing, he was going the wrong way! All I wanted to do was go home and never see him again, granted that would be hard considering we worked for the same firm, but Christopher would give me a good reference, I was sure.

"You're going the wrong way; you stay on this road for another 8.6 miles." I harshly snapped.

"OK."

"OK? Are you even listening to what I am saying?"

"OK."

"O-fucking-K, O--K? Wow! You certainly are piece of work, I drove all the way up here for you Jacob, well more fool me."

He never raised his voice once. "Sophia, why don't you just hush?"

"It speaks! 'Hush'? Out of interest, Mr Saunders, Sir, did I pick you up as an employee, or, we'll assume, an acquaintance doing you a favour?"

"Sophia, just hush."

I could feel the emotional involvement hitting a crescendo, and I was finding it hard to keep control, the angered quiver in my voice, however, gave it all away. He just remained composed, whilst I ranted.

About three quarters of a mile down this road, he indicated left into a car park, my assumption was that we were turning around and heading back towards the A road we had just left; he parked up. Through a sparse tree line, when I say 'tree line' I mean four trees, there stood a crisp white building, quite fresh and newly painted, the classic thatched roof, everything that personified a country pub.

"Why are we here?"

He had stopped, put the hand brake on, turned the ignition off, and unclipped his belt; he turned towards me, leaning on his left side.

"Why are we here?" I repeated.

In that moment, I felt so unsure, but of what I had no idea.

"Sophia, just hush." He placed his index finger on my lips, gently he pressed. He then proceeded. "Please let me finish."

I nodded, and he removed his finger from my lips, he shuffled in his seat and relaxed his shoulders back.

"I... I'm... sorry. That day in the cottage, I freaked out, I mean, you're in your early twenties, and I didn't want to be inappropriate, like some middle-aged office lech. You are beautiful, and can have your pick of the men, you're something of a handful, and you have so many attributes. I felt it that day, I know it's a cliché with the term 'spark', but you're in your twenties and I'm, well I guess old. I was worried, in the moment we'd get caught up, and then you'd regret it, making it awkward. You work for my family for Christ sakes. And I still want you."

"So I work for your dad, he pays my wages; he pays yours too, Jacob. KISS ME! If you still feel it, then great, if not, then we drive home and avoid each other in work, at all costs. KISS ME!"

Oh, wow. Time paused as I savoured his taste, it was sensational. In that moment my ovaries skipped a beat, flashing through my head was the wedding, babies, family holidays, and even the dog we had, it was a golden retriever.

A furious vibration started. "Shit, it's my phone."

I did that in-the-car-seat-crab-contortion, as I wiggled my phone out of my back pocket.

"It's your dad, I'll have to answer it, he, well you know what he's like."

Jacob nodded, with the look of, 'Please act like everything is normal'.

"Hi Christopher."

"Is he there? Did you really go running for him? My goodness, you are valued in our team, however, on your day off, with no promise of pay for overtime, you can say no girl."

"Well, I felt sorry for him, and in all honesty, I wanted to drive your car, so I couldn't say, 'No' really." I replied, a little tongue in cheek.

"Put him on, I want words."

I screwed my face up as I squirmed and handed my phone over.

"Hey dad."

"You arrived then? Take her to lunch, you take her to lunch and bloody foot the bill, you tightwad; you best give her tomorrow off too, with all the running around she's done for you."

Chris had hung up, not giving Jacob the chance to respond, he did this a lot, it was his way of saying his word was final.

"Well, let's go for lunch then, you must be hungry? Let's go and sit down, just you and me. When we get back home, we'll have no chance of going out without someone knowing us."

"OK."

We walked, hand in hand, into the Claythorn Arms. You couldn't even see the pub from the road side, I'd have had no clue that it even existed.

To this day, I can remember what we ordered: I had apple juice, and Jacob had cranberry; he ordered a 12oz rump steak, with the works, including blue cheese dressing. I had a classic Ploughman's, it was my favourite.

We sat in the lounge all afternoon, drinking tea; several pots were poured. We didn't really stop holding hands or cuddling, the Queen Anne floral wing back, was most accommodating. I can't recall the words; I just remember my jaw aching from smiling so much.

The night had started to draw in, and the pub was filling with locals.

"Huh, have you seen the time? We need to head home, I guess? I'm happy to drive in the dark, if you're feeling tired from your flight."

Jacob was far too relaxed, "Let's stay, spend the night with me, here, you don't have to work tomorrow."

I didn't even hesitate with my answer, I nodded. I hoped I hadn't come across as cheap and easy.

"Just give me five minutes to make my excuses to mother." I gesticulated five, with my hand held up, like a statue, and waved it.

I told my mother we had broken down, we would stay the night; I would be home at some time tomorrow. I hated lying to mother, I knew in time, if things were more than these 48 hours, I would tell her, but for now, I just wanted quiet.

We went to book in for the evening, the landlord was a stout Welshman named Taft, Jacob and I approached the bar, to ask if he had any rooms available.

"Excuse me; do you have any rooms for this evening?"

"Can I assume you'd like a double?"

He shuffled under the dark wooden counter top, to find his booking-in diary; he placed it on the top of the worn varnish. "Can I take a name, or shall I just put it under Smith?" he quipped.

Jacob scoffed at him, and announced, "We are, in fact, Mr and Mrs Saunders, so put it under that."

Mrs? Mrs Saunders? He said, "Mrs Saunders"; I calmed my thoughts, and just went with it. I could see Jacob was trying not to lose face at such comments, it was bizarrely cute.

The night was simplistic, I lay wrapped in his arms with his t-shirt on; strangely it had a panda on it, which went well with my very little pants. I nuzzled into his bare chest, he had a fair amount of hair, it was sexy and a turn on, it was masculine. It also had the odd fleck of grey.

He ran his fingers across my forehead and into my hair, well as much as you could, before the jungle of curls consumed it. Jacob was very open, we just lay it all out bare, he wanted, one day, to settle down, two point four children, and the dog, but he wasn't there yet. He also guessed it wasn't where I wanted to be in the immediate future.

The following day together was beautiful, we did the tourist thing in a local hot spot, Miltonbury Cathedral was steeped in history; I had read about it years previously, its architecture was of Romanesque and Gothic styles, it was built between 1089 and 1499. It hosted vaulted ceilings and soaring stained glass windows, behind a high altar.

I loved to read, I spent many hours with my nose in a book. Little did people know that my handbag was so large to fit in all my library books, my card was worn and dog-eared at the corners.

The acoustics of Miltonbury Cathedral were like nothing I had ever heard before. Jacob stood in the western part of the chancel, between the nave and the sanctuary. He took a deep breath in, and began singing Psalm 23, "The Lord is my Shepherd".

"The Lord is my Shepherd; I shall not want.

"He makes me lie down in green pastures…"

Jacob's full and rich baritone reverberated through the entire Cathedral. He had an incredible voice; I didn't expect that, it took me off guard. A man of the cloth was stood up; he applauded Jacob after he finished the first verse.

"What a voice you have, would you sing something else?"

"I can manage Jerusalem?"

"Well, I shall play the organ. How about you, can you sing young lady?"

"Oh, me? No, no, no…"

"She can, I've heard in the office, when she thinks she's alone." Jacob insisted. "Sophia you lead and I will join you."

I was so nervous; I hadn't sung for anyone since the spring concert of my fifth year of secondary school. The smell of the polished wood was distracting me, Jacob's voice was intimidating in all honesty, and I couldn't stand up to the scrutiny.

"And did those feet in ancient time," I timidly began, somewhat embarrassed, before Jacob joined me, bolstering my faltering confidence.

"Walk upon England's mountains green?" We sang together, my reassured voice finding strength alongside Jacob's.

By the time we had finished, and I let out a breath of relief, it dawned on me, we had harmonised without any struggle, it was a natural dynamic.

We held hands and giggled our way around the rest of the Cathedral, in disbelief at our performance, we'd even drawn a small crowd of spectators. We were ourselves, away from the norm; with no interfering eyes, we were just a couple.

The journey home was full of apprehension, what would the working relationship be like, or was this it now, and work would always be awkward. We pulled off the dual carriageway, on to the flyover, turning right over the bridge, into the top end of town. My stomach was now in overdrive, that acute sensation to release my bowels washed over me. I started to clench. Pulling into the yard, after weaving around parked cars down the main street, I could see Christopher locking up.

Christopher was an astute man, very intelligent, he had worked hard to establish his business and nurture its pristine reputation. In all honesty, things had come a lot easier for Jacob; he could be a loose cannon, as he had been for the last 48 hours, and his father would always be there to pick up the slack.

We both got out; I looked over to Chris, who was stood still at the door, the key still in the mortise lock, his fingers pressed either side of the key. Jacob had moved around to my side of the car, and now stood next to me. We wanted to kiss goodbye, it felt incommodious, with Chris as a bystander, more so inappropriate; Chris was not only Jacob's father, but also my employer. I glanced back over to Chris; he gave us the nod, a nod of approval. Rather than being totally brazen, intuitively we gave a lingering kiss to the cheek.

"See you tomorrow." Jacob softly spoke.

I didn't hang about; I headed out of the yard for the short walk home. Jacob, I knew, was in for the third degree from his father, not in an interrogating way, more a 'What's going on? I didn't expect this to happen'.

"Night Chris." I cheerily chirped, as I, near as damn it, skipped out of the yard.

At home, my dinner was waiting on the table: sausage and mashed potatoes, it was, of course, accompanied with onion gravy and peas. It was, however, a day late this week. The host this evening, as usual, was my mother. I knew exactly how Jacob's evening was going, as my mother had twenty questions lined up for me too.

Mum was typically old fashioned; she was the wife, serving the homestead, and raising children, while dad was the one to 'bring home the bacon', my childhood was incredibly traditional. As she poured a brew from the teapot, adorned with a tea cosy she had knitted, she let the tea flow into her china cup, with delicate primrose motif, gently resting on the saucer.

She casually enquired, "So how was work? Especially with Jacob, he's not as hard working as his father, is he? Christopher has always worked hard, he and your father are about the same age, they were at school together; they both used to be delivery boys for Slades, back in the day."

My mother had this terrible habit of asking questions, then immediately blathering on with mindless facts, not actually allowing the person to answer. I sat there, waiting to see if she had any further statements, before I answered, and then came the second phase of intense rambling.

"Of course, Jacob was a nightmare in his teens..."

"Oh, really?" I squeezed in, between her breaths, with a curious tone I tried to play down.

"Oh yes, he was the rebel child; his older brother's, Luke and Daniel, went to school and university with no problems, hence they have good careers, with prospects of promotions. I mean Luke has a lovely wife, and a little one, he settled down well. Daniel is a wonderful teacher in...? In...? Um, let me think..."

Mother was quite gushing about his brothers, the dread about what was to come next brought on a minor sweat, my hairline, on my neck, was starting to itch.

"That's it!" She clicked her fingers triumphantly in the air, "Awkley, he, Daniel that is, teaches at Awkley. Moving very well up the pay scale, he's management, head of year, I believe. Jacob dropped out of uni', he went through a bit of an 'organic' stage." My mother was never one to be politically correct.

"He started painting; he's talented no doubt, sold a fair few, several years ago now. That's how he got to buy his cottage, you know where it is; head out of the town and take the left up towards Knowling Hill, once you get to the crossroads, head towards the Manor House; tucked in, just behind the hedges, after you get to the first cattle grid, are two

Game Keeper's cottages. He lives in one of them. Your Nanna was in service at the Manor, for his Lordship's Grandparents.

"He went to Crawford for uni', I think, well that aside, Christopher went up one weekend, to visit. He found Jacob in a right state, no money, no food, not a clean cup in the place, but all this beautiful art around him. Chris bought him back home immediately, and Jacob has worked for his father ever since. I think his father's guiding hand has probably kept him on the straight and narrow. Oh, I tell a lie, there was that summer when he went AWOL, turned all nomadic; he was gone for several months. Poor Chris simply struggled on, and when Jacob finally returned home, he just carried on like before he went walkies. He's a good father like that."

She finally paused her monologue about Jacob, turned and clenched my hand, gave it a little wobble and said, "Well darling?"

I took my platform, now mother had clearly indicated she was finished.

"He was lovely, I didn't really know him, outside of being one of my bosses and the flimsy working relationship we had, which is cold at times, but he is lovely. We had pub lunch, you should have seen the portions; they were obscene. Then I spent the afternoon drinking tea with him, and laughing to the point my jaw was achy. He's um, asked me on a date."

I tried to play it all casual; I struggled, when actually I wanted to be a bit gushing about him. I slipped that in at the end of the conversation, nonchalantly.

"A date? Well, when? I mean; I suppose he must be grown up now, and under his father's positive influence." Mother was now squirming, and quite clearly trying to remove her foot from her mouth.

"Do you hear that, Roo, our Sophia has been asked out on a date, by Chris Saunders' youngest lad, you know? Jacob."

Father had a wonderful way to deal with mother; he'd wander into the kitchen and shuffle a couple of objects about, acknowledging what she said, all the while looking at the clock. He'd never sit down, as that would mean committing to a conversation on the mindless tripe my mother spewed.

He'd always say, "Ah sweetums, that news article is about to start, I should really watch it, it could affect us long term." before slinking out again.

Well, this familiar scenario started to play out, just like normal; he shuffled in and mumbled, "Jacob, ay? He must be a grown lad by now, isn't he a teacher?"

"No, that's the older brother, Daniel, head of year in Awkley Academy."

"Ah yes." he said, head down, munching a soft toffee he had taken from the sweet bowl on the work top.

Mother decided to add in a thoughtful detail or two to dad, "Jacob went through an artist phase; he has Keeper's Cottage, on the edge of the Manor estate, up past Knowling Hill."

"Oh fancy. So the boy, he's what, a couple of years older than you Sophia?"

I could feel my buttocks soldering to my jeans, as I sweated profusely, waiting for the eruption I assumed would come next. "Well dad, he's more than a couple of years older than me."

Dad scoffed, "Age is just a number; I mean, look at your mother and me, eight years is perfectly fine."

"Dad, it's **considerably** more." I emphasized the 'considerably'.

"Well, what's ten years? I mean, thirty is nothing these days."

Dad had gone with a modest two years on his eight year gap to mother. I was dreading the next sentence, I'd never dated a man before, and this was different to the silly boys I had dated at school.

"He's 37! I know it's extreme, but it's only a date." I blurted.

Mother started to backpedal on all previous statements, "I suppose he must have grown up, and grown as a person, matured even, since his days as an artist, being under his father's guiding hand has clearly helped. He has his own home, he seems much more stable. Much better than those scruffy oiks your age, with their laddish behaviour."

On that level of acceptance, I decided to scarper; I did a very loud yawn, making my excuses to exit. "I think I'll have an early night, I'm exhausted."

Chapter Two

Jacob

Working life hadn't changed too much; I had taken on many new roles. I spent more time with Jacob in a professional capacity, being more hands on and less of a glorified tea lady. Although, bacon sandwiches on a Friday was still very much a 'must have'.

Chris was openly approving of us; it was a huge relief not have him against us. Apparently, I was a calming influence on his son. Jacob's mother was OK, in exceedingly small doses; she was divorced from Chris, from her behaviour, you could clearly understand why. Chris positively voiced his happiness about the subject. She would just make sniping comments, and be inflammatory.

The classic one, I remember, was at the Christening of Luke's third child, Amy. We'd all travelled for the weekend, to celebrate, we naturally shared the car with Jake's father; his mother had made her own way, luckily for us.

At the Church, after the ceremony, the official photographs began. Luke innocently asked for a photograph of, "Uncle Jake and Aunty Soph, with Amy." His mother was sour that weekend, her relationship with her tennis coach, or some such, had just fallen through, and now no one was allowed to be happy. Upon Luke's request, she piped up, "Huh, 'Aunty', they're not married."

Jake always tried to appease her moods in situations like this, so she didn't show them all up, he'd always try and reply with humour, "Thank you mother, I'm working on it, just give me time."

I tended to ignore her; it wound her up more when she couldn't get a rise out of me, being decorous was far more important to me. Besides, I wasn't the only partner she hated, Daniel had turned up with his girlfriend, and Heather wasn't favoured either. No one was good enough for her boys, and she made that abundantly clear.

After the Christening, and after Luke had called me 'Aunty Soph', Jake and I knew we were getting serious. My parents didn't bat an eye that Jake was seventeen years my senior. Jake lovingly consumed my mother's fruitcake, telling her what a wonderful cook she was, even on the occasions when the cake was more miss than hit. He'd listen to my dad waffle on for hours about politics, the state of the country, and how they should just drop the Great from Great Britain, as there was nothing Great anymore.

He pandered to them slightly; it made life a little easier. When mother had an armful of shopping, she'd very often pop into work, on the off chance I was free, or to ask if I wanted chops for tea. Mother's cooking had a very limited repertoire, she and dad were stuck in a routine, but it worked for their marriage. The route back up to their house was deceptively steep; Jake would run her home in the car, if he was able. He'd carry her shopping in, placing it on the kitchen table. Mother thought he was a complete gentleman.

Jacob's cottage was quaint, it was a typical expectation of a Keeper's Cottage, it was authentic, Jacob had chosen to keep it simple and it was so easy to fall in love with his home.

On the edge of the Manor Estate, Keeper's Cottage was just after the first cattle grid. It mirrored an identical cottage on the right hand side of the drive. Jake's was on the left, it had old iron railings, vertical supports, with the rails evenly spaced running horizontally. A large wooden post held the latch to the farm gate, hinged with two industrial hinges on the left hand side, it opened inward onto the driveway of stone chippings.

Dull grey chippings, created paths around the four small flowerbeds, they were edged with cobble bricks in a glazed brown effect. The flowerbeds had so much potential, but they were rustic at best, a couple of miniature bushes, heather and lavender, and there were some remains of, what might have once been, rosemary. It was a clear indicator that Jacob was not a horticulturalist.

The thatched roof extended down, making part of the porch roof, held up with weathered, wind-battered timbers. A welly boot rack stood under the hall window, there was room for four pairs of boots, there stood Jacob's size 13s, alone.

The windows didn't match, all single glazed, the living room window was six panes of glass, each no bigger than A5 in size, set into white glossed timber. Upstairs, the glass panes, half the size again, were encased in flaking varnished timbers.

The kitchen was my favourite place to stand; it had petite windows, one over the Belfast sink, it was just four panes, in the classic square formation, the light filtered in allowing you to enjoy the sky's colours at any time of the day. Washing-up was always interesting, very often, after placing the last bowl on the split wooden drainer, I'd turn to the single, narrow window, at the rear of the cottage. As I wiped my hands, the dairy herd would be in the field adjacent to the boundary of the cottage gardens, again it had the iron fencing continuing around the perimeter.

Most evenings now, I didn't know where I'd be sleeping. It had gotten to the point that I had asked mother not to cook my dinner, as I didn't want her wasting food. It was a turbulent time in my life; when I was at home, mum still did everything for me, I was her little girl, and I don't think she knew how to cope with me transitioning into an independent woman, rather than being reliant on her. When I was with Jacob, we were equal partners, and decided jointly how we ran our domestic situation.

I had one constant in my life, and that was not going to change: my Grandfather, Pom. Every Sunday, I picked him up at 10am, ready for Church. He so desperately wanted to go, I'm not sure if it was the social aspect, or Pascal's Wager.

He had been widowed since I was eight; I don't really remember my Nanna, she's more a picture than a person.

I had my own key to his yellow aluminium, two-part, double-glazed, frosted glass, front door. I'd open the door with, "Taxi for Pom", and there he'd be, sat in his arm chair, with a lace doily on the headrest. His cup and saucer was set on the nest of tables, ready for his return, and on the other side, my Nanna's place laid bare.

His aged body was slowing down, it took considerably more effort to raise himself from the chair than it used to, more often than not he'd take my offer of an arm, to help him up. He squared up his tie, and then his jacket; he always wore a suit and tie, on a cold day a jerkin was on underneath. His walk was more a shuffle than a stride these days.

In the kitchen, over the drainer was a mirror, next to the door. The cupboard opposite contained Pom's shaving mug, keys, and hair lacquer. Before we left, he'd comb his hair one last time, and spray some lacquer. Being a young man in the era of The War gave Pom the edge, he always, even in his eighties, got up early, at first light. He'd shave at the kitchen sink, old school, with a mug and bristle brush. I loved how his routine had never faltered, for sixty years.

Sunday had become the day of unrest. Once Pom and I had been to church, I always stayed with him, it was our time. We'd do the tea and biscuits thing, avoiding two specific women in the congregation, they were as thick as thieves, we hadn't a clue who they were, but they always seemed to be in everyone's business. Then we'd head back to mum and dad's. Mother would always be serving as we got to the door. She was, in this case, fabulously punctual. Roast chicken and all the trimmings; every third Sunday of the month was topside and Yorkshire puddings, to add diversity.

At two o'clock, I would make my exit, ready to pick Jake up from the match, and we'd spend the rest of the day together, but not before I'd left mother's with a slice of fruitcake for him.

Jake hadn't played the previous season, due to injury, so this was the first season I'd got real exposure to the game. Naturally, Jake was the butt for much of the ridicule this season.

It was the second match of the season, the first one finished on a jolly lads' pub-crawl; this time though, I'd have to enter the clubhouse and retrieve him.

I spent my days with builders, so I really had little fear of entering. I walked in; first of all, I noticed Ray, heading over towards him was going to be the most logical idea. He acknowledged me, with a wave and nod, simplistic, yet warm.

"Hi Ray, where is he?"

"Where's who?" I heard Jake's tones from behind.

"Ah, you! Good Game?" I turned around and tapped his chest with my index finger. "How is the injury? Do I need to take you home and nurse you?" I had that glint in my eye.

Jacob stooped down to peck my lips, and as they pressed mine, the roar of, "Oi Oi!" erupted in the club, as the lads raised their glasses.

"Pete's on his way to being wankered then." Ray announced to Jacob and me.

"Raymond! We have company!" an unknown woman reprimanded Ray.

A smidge embarrassed, and my cheeks on fire, Ray introduced me to his wife, Helen.

"Helen, this is Sophia. Sophia, this is Helen."

This petite lady turned around, with shoulder length, mouse brown hair, highlighted.

"Hi Sophia, Ray told me you were hoping to pop in. So you're the one settling down this rebel."

"Hmm, it would seem, rebel; you're not the first to describe him as that." I replied with a smile.

I could also see Jacob dying internally, so he shifted the topic pretty swiftly, turning to Ray, "Can we talk shop for two minutes please? Your team should be in by Wednesday. I will have final confirmation Monday a.m. from the planning department, and the roof will finally be on." Jacob sounded all authoritarian.

I was not the Tea Girl any longer. In fact, I had been replaced, and had the pleasure of fully training my successor. She was a very sweet girl, called Joanna.

Monday came, and Joanna was flying solo for the first time; I was in the office when the call came in. It was the planning department; they had refused to let Jacob and his dad proceed, until they could renegotiate roofing tiles, again. Poor Joanna, I could see she was about to shit a brick.

I'd heard everything. When she started her sentences with, "Erm, erm, Jacob...", I knew she was dreading passing the message on.

"I'll sort it, is he in the Chapel?" I volunteered, knowing I could placate him, or alternatively forgive his chuntering.

This was part of the business I'd never really gotten involved in. I headed out of the office, I wasn't going to interfere with current proceedings, just assess the state of play.

Typically, Chris was away, he had taken a cruise, with a lady friend.

I went in the side door of the Chapel. The back room had its door shut, I knocked.

"Who is it?" Jacob replied.

"Jacob, it's me, can I come in?"

"I'm with a client at the moment, enter if you wish."

I entered quietly, I asked as softly toned as possible. "How long are you going to be?"

I was acutely conscious that there was dead body laid out, but I wanted to be respectful.

Jake looked flustered, he even sounded it. "I just need to dress the hair, I have clothed Mrs Brown, and once her hair is finished I can ring the family. My dad normally does the hair and make-up. They want to view the body tomorrow."

"What needs doing? Are you to curl or set the hair, and then dress it? May I help you?"

"Really, you'll help? Have you seen a dead body before, aren't you worried?"

"Jacob, I have seen you and your dad bring numerous body bags back to the Chapel. I have slept many nights, when you are on call, and woken up to an empty bed. These are people who can't hurt me."

"OK." He was totally perplexed by my offer.

I walked in, washed up, and put on a disposable apron and gloves. I'd had plenty of practice setting hair; I had been a Saturday girl in a salon.

"Thank you. As you seem to be a natural at this, when the family visit, can you be in the Chapel of Rest with them? Dad is normally 'Front of House', so to speak, and I think you'll offer a great level of empathy."

"Ok, I'll be there. Speaking of empathy, please don't shoot the messenger; the authorities won't give the go ahead, apparently renegotiations are needed over the roof."

I finished up, and scarpered quickly. I still don't know how that played out to this day, he curbed his anger and frustration well; either that or his dad slipped the council a back-hander.

Chapter Three

Pom

After my transition day, from secretary to undertaker, I went home every night to Keeper's Cottage.

I'd cut the bread every morning on the larder cabinet drop leaf, and hang our smalls on the old hooks above the fireplace; the fire was always prepared, ready to be lit when we got home, before we left in the morning.

I had gone on some undertaking courses, and now I spent my life 'on call' with Jacob. Every day, I made our lunch, we worked unsocial hours some days, I guess we just had a mutual understanding, and acceptance. Life seemed to be in the fast lane, birthdays seemed to come round quicker each year.

We spent social time with Ray and Helen, and the occasional Sunday at the Rugby Club, though Jake had begrudgingly hung up his boots. His aging body didn't agree with the up-and-coming young lads any longer. His knees had been gammy for months, the physicality of the job, and a couple of hard tackles, had left Jacob with his right knee strapped up for longer periods than ever before; he took it as a sign that he should be a spectator, rather than participant. Ray hung his boots up when he and Helen had decided to start a family.

Ray and Helen were expecting a baby. After a long struggle, Helen had miscarried three babies - all boys, each and every tragedy was earth shattering. Every time they shared the joyous news, we barely had time to celebrate, before we mourned their loss. It was heartbreaking. I'd have done anything in my power, to give them their dream. The months of heartache had crept into years, then one day, they finally got their 'miracle baby'. Their excitement was adorable to watch, how could you not be happy for them, after all the trauma, I always kept a little strength in reserve, and held back. I couldn't bear the thought of Helen being torn apart once more.

Ray and Jacob spent hours planning and battling the National Park, on yet another building project, this time in Fremmington Ayshe, on the west end of the town. I got to spend lots of time with Helen, we were inseparable. We went baby shopping often. The love she had for her unborn child was evident by her desire to provide everything they could ever want in life. She cared for her unborn child by doing everything by the book, so they arrived safe and well. She was just beautiful as a pregnant mumma. Her strength was admirable.

Our relationship had evolved over the years; the first day I met her, in the rugby club, and she reprimanded Ray for his language, I thought Helen was a terrible prude; getting to know her, she was nothing of the sort. Out of the four of us, she had the biggest potty mouth. She was so well humoured, and normally the instigator to any of the shenanigans, we as a foursome got involved in.

Helen and I became close, I trusted her, I didn't speak about my relationship with Jake very often to people, but I knew 'Helly' wouldn't break that confidence, and she never did.

Focusing on new life with Helen and Ray, sharing their adventure, was a privilege. We knew well before three months; and when Helen was about 22 weeks I got to feel the baby kick, it was one of the most exciting moments. Very often Jake got that look from Ray, "Your turn next mate."

One Saturday afternoon, I'd just locked the Chapel door, and turned to walk to my car, there stood mother and father. Their arms linked, when I say linked, it was more like father was supporting her.

"Tell her Roo, I can't."

"Sophia darling, it's Pom, he's, unwell, he's had a stroke. Mummy found him in bed when we visited. It's not good. Come on, we'll take you."

Dad ushered mother and me to the car. I didn't speak. I couldn't speak. I was stupefied at events. I had only spoken to him on Wednesday, to arrange church this week. He was fine last week; he showed no sign of illness.

My parents left me alone in the side room, to say my goodbyes. Goodbye... I felt like I'd been pelted with a million ball bearings. This wasn't happening, my pain couldn't be real. The room was clean, white and cold; there was no warmth of home, which is where I wished we were, having tea. The ward noises echoed, and people bustled. The clock tick – tick – TICKED! It's all I could hear, nothing but tick – tick – TICK.

Mother came back in with a doctor. He started a sentence with, "I'm very sorry"; did they get taught that at medical school? The, "I'm very sorry, but..." speech.

I held Pom's hand. He was going to die; the fire that engulfed his body was not contained rapidly enough, and now his broken and burned shell was to be left until the fire was completely exhausted.

"I'm not leaving."

"Pardon." My mother queried sternly.

"I'm not leaving. You come into this world with your mother to greet you. Leaving the world with someone who loves you by your side completes the circle." I was forcefully adamant.

"Sweetheart, that's a very honourable sentiment, but, no."

"Judy, our Sophia is more than equipped to cope, more so than you or I, let her make the choice." My dad's voice was always one of reason.

"Thank you mum, I'll call you when it's time. Jake will pick me up, and we'll take care of the rest."

My mother kissed Pom goodnight for the final time, she left sobbing, cradled over my dad's handkerchief, to muffle the wails. Dad had mother clutched just above both elbows, steering her out of the room. It was 6 p.m., and I sat down for the long night ahead. I only heard the tick – tick – TICK!

Pom laid there, oxygen mask on, yet motionless. His breathing was raspy, I'd seen the breathing changes before with work, I wasn't scared, angry more so, that we wouldn't get to spend any more of our life together. He'd never get to sit at the top table on my wedding day, or hold my children. Nursing them, how he once nursed me. It was cruel and unfair.

His breathing alternated between loud rasping and quiet breathing. He had a death rattle. He could no longer cough or swallow, the secretion of saliva pooling in his throat was causing the rattling noise.

Towards the end, he took a breath periodically; he'd inhale, followed by no breath for several seconds, and then have a further intake.

I knew he hadn't long, I went to the nurse's station, "Can I ring my parents? Cheyne-Stokes breathing is here."

The nurse looked taken back by my comments, as she dialled for me.

"Mum, it's time."

I said no more, I couldn't. I let the phone go, walked back into the room, and perched on the edge of my seat. I took his hand and wrapped both of mine around his.

"Pom, I'm back."

He gasped. The fire was extinguished.

Death was not to be feared. I sat with him for 45 minutes, until Jake arrived.

"Sophia, your husband's here, we've buzzed him into the building."

Jake embraced me, so I felt secure, I howled into his jumper. I pulled myself off him and gave him the nod. He was just brilliant, I was quite clearly capable of my job, only this time it was a little too close to home. So he took the lead.

"I'm assuming, with it being the early hours of Sunday morning, we will be waiting for all the paperwork until p.m. on Tuesday? We will call then to see if the body can be released." Jacob said, with professional confidence.

The confused nurse was tripping over her words, "Sir, if you or your wife call the funeral directors tomorrow morning, they will liaise with you as to the process."

I started gesticulating with my finger, between myself and Jake, to indicate we were... with a, "No, no, no."

"My wife and I are the undertakers, it just so happens this time it's personal." Jacob gave clear clarification.

We were buzzed out of the ward, and walked the empty, darkened corridors of the hospital. For security reasons, only the main entrance was open, so we followed the red line in the dim light, until we found reception, where we exited into the dropping temperatures of the morning.

As overwhelmed as I was, going home was also a relief.

"You called me your wife." I mumbled, in my daze.

"I know I did." Replied Jake, matter-of-factly.

"But we're not."

"Sophia, is now the time to pick over the smallest of details, after your ordeal? You're heartbroken and tired." He said, with the most honourable intentions.

"Jake, death invokes so many emotions, we see it every day. Death, ultimately, brings the juxtaposition of my best friend having her first baby in a few months, into rather a harsh perspective."

"So what, my darling, are you saying?"

"I don't know, I'm tired, I'm emotional. Let's go home. I want my cup, a decent cuppa, and a shower to wash away the day."

I spent the rest of the journey glazed-over. Out of the window, all I saw were colour changes. I didn't recognise any landmarks, as the tears lay a frosting over my pupils.

Then, there we were, Keeper's Cottage. I was home. I remembered the first time I brought Pom here for tea. He just cooed. Joanie, his sister, had a little thatched cottage in South Devon, and he romanced about his visits there in the 1950s. He told me of how she had pheasants dance across her garden, and that, from her front door, up on the horizon, you could see a faint light from the saw mill, and silhouettes of the stags.

Pom had a tiled fireplace, it still functioned, but it was very nondescript. The fireplace at Keeper's Cottage was somewhat larger, gigantic stones, with oak lintel and slate hearth, the penetrating heat warmed our whole cottage.

We had a fireguard-come-seat, it was brass, upholstered in oxblood red leather, creased and worn. Of an evening, after we got home, I'd sit there and watch the flames catch, trying to take stock of the day.

Some days were horrific, just taking in a beautiful, yet simplistic, part of life acted like therapy.

When we came home, after work, Jacob lit the fire, while I put the kettle on the Aga. I'd put the washing on, and start to lower the clothes airer above the fire; the airer was a cast iron frame, with wooden slats. We lived in such a high-speed world, especially with our jobs, that going back 50 years elicited the most enchanting calmness in our home life.

When I first moved into Keeper's Cottage, there was a sofa in front of the hearth, it was lovely for us, we'd snuggle up, it was the perfect size for a couple.

Pom found it very difficult to get down to, and up from, our sofa. He had become such a regular visitor that I decided a fireside chair, with high legs and a high back, would be much more suitable for him. He loved his chair; I'd hear tales of how his sister Joanie had two such fireside chairs, that she would sew small rounds of fabric by hand for hours on end, making them into mats. In the evenings, her husband would read the paper beside the fire, after a hard days graft. He was a farmhand and milker to the Lord of the Manor's prized herd.

I could only desire magic in a relationship the way Pom described Joanie and Bill's marriage. Sadly, Jacob and I were thrust into a career, and a modern world, that made this lifestyle unattainable, I was envious. My grandparents long life together was a relationship goal I had always wanted myself, I yearned for that, yet Pom never spoke of their marriage like Joanie's, it was endearing when he reminisced about his big sister.

Joanie had left home at the outbreak of World War Two; she had become a land girl. She had moved to the south of the county, and not returned home after The War, she had married her first love, and settled there with him.

Pom used to say to me "You're just like her you know, Joanie I mean. Oh yes, I can see my sister in you."

Jacob and I walked through the front door. It was blue, with two rectangular panes of glass in the top half of the door, with dimpled frosted glass. I walked into our living room, and dropped my bag off my shoulder, just letting it fall to the floor, with no regard for what was in it.

I stood in the doorway, looking at that chair. The autumnal coloured leaf pattern blurred, as I caught sight of the rainbow, crocheted blanket folded on the arm, Pom loved a knee blanket, and it was one my grandmother had made, they were always bright and cheery, made out of odds and ends of left over yarn. One day, when I went to Pom's house, I found him under their bed, digging around for the blanket; he was fussing, wanting to bring it to ours.

I reluctantly walked over to his chair; I perched on the edge of it, just like I'd done hours before hand in the hospital, and stared at the blanket. I stroked it a couple of times. I clutched it in both hands, and drew it up to my nose. I drew a deep breath. It was him. His smell was on it. He was with me on his darkest day. His smell made me feel safe; I was relieved to be at home, finally comforted by him.

"Sophia, darling, I have to leave, I've another call out."

By this time my nose was sore, red and blocked by the hurt and pain of my sorrow, my leaking eyes had wept until they stung.

I looked confused, I pulled the blanket away, "But where's your dad?"

"He's gone away, with his lady friend, umm Emily I think it is, for a... long weekend."

A wry smile crept across my face at the thought of Chris wooing a woman.

"I'll come with you; you can't go out on your own."

"Go and shower, wrap yourself up warm, and sleep, my darling. I will be fine on my own. You need time to digest what has happened."

"Jacob, I spend every day surrounded by death. In a day, I can be part of two or three families lives, each one, by their own merit, heartbreaking, some worse than others. I don't go home and sleep it off after every encounter."

I went to the cupboard, put on my suit and with that 'no arguments given' demeanour, we went to our pick up. Jacob knew, by my adamant tones, I would be professional by every measure. I knew, as I went through the evolution from office girl to undertaker, this wasn't a job, it was a way of life; just like farming, seven days a week, any time of the day or night. Death had no limits.

We took our private ambulance, and headed along the country lane towards Wimpleton. From our home the lane was always laden with mud and manure, shreds from the hay bales, and potholes filled with puddles. It didn't matter how many times we hosed it down at the yard, the ambulance was always dressed with mud spatter; when we took the road to Wimpleton our poor ambulance always looked like it had been on a rally track.

Wimpleton was, by modern standards, pretty backwards, like most places in the county. The town was steeped in old tradition, every market day the main street would be closed, while the farmers brought their livestock into the old cattle market. I'd always been fascinated by it as a child, and couldn't wait to go into Wimpleton shopping, with my mother and Pom, in the holidays.

We'd always visit 'Maggy May's Sweets and Treats'. The sweet shop was shelf after shelf of jars filled with sweets, it was magical as you watched them unscrew the lid, and scoop the sweets out into a paper bag that was already on the scales, counterbalanced by small metal weights.

Pom would have a pound of boiled sweets; his favourite was rhubarb and custard. He would also buy a bar of dark chocolate, and every night, after his supper, he'd break four nubs off the bar, placing them on the nest of tables, he'd nibble his way through them throughout the evening. Four was the perfect amount, he'd tell me, as the chocolate was so rich. When I went, he'd ask me if I would like any sweets, white chocolate buttons were my favourite, especially when they had sprinkles on them.

There would be stalls, selling homemade produce, honey, jam, chutney, cured hams, and meats straight from the farm, wonky carrots, and potatoes, still muddy. I loved to carry my basket, like my mum, and fill it with all our treats.

Even now, as an adult, where possible I liked to head over on market day, Jacob would always make time for me to do so where practicable. If I hadn't been for a while, a special treat would always be a small selection of cheeses, maybe three or four, an artisan loaf, farmhouse being my favourite. You could make great doorstops out of it, and add the accompanying local ham, and onion chutney. A ploughman's was always a welcome sight at the dinner table.

Driving through Wimpleton, market square was a distraction before we arrived at the Caunter household. Luckily, with it being a Sunday, we had managed to park right outside the house.

There was nothing worse, and more undignified, than having to remove a body, with upset relatives and distraught family, than to expose them to curtain-twitchers while they are wheeled down the road. We always liked to operate a more discreet service, wherever possible.

We arrived to find the out-of-hours doctor there, to verify the death. From a formality point of view, it would be easy, Doctor Prichard, although on an out-of-hours call out, was the family doctor to Mrs Caunter, and was a partner in the surgery she attended. He knew the deceased, and verification of her being Mrs Phillipa Caunter, and confirmation of her death, was stress free.

She was an elderly lady, who had been under the care of the doctor in the last two weeks. Her health had been deteriorating with age. It was still, however, an awful and painful time for her family. We were greeted by her daughter, Gloria; she was the next of kin, and she was distraught. Her immediate family was there; children and grandchildren.

We had gone in and done the introductions, we would need to speak to the doctor, checking all was well, before removing the body. We'd need to do a risk assessment, signing off all the relevant red tape, which in this day and age impinged upon us. When people were at their lowest, we had to show compassion, without fear of reprisal. This part of the job was not something we wished to expose the family to.

Jacob and I had developed a routine, which, we hoped, sheltered the family from such bureaucracy, and could provide them with a high level of integrity, we prided ourselves on it. I would sit down with the family, make them a pot of tea, I'd provide them with all the vital details, whilst Jacob would politely absent himself, taking care of the rest.

The family sat in the living room, puffy-eyed and clearly wanting to support each other through the terrible experience.

"First of all, I am so very sorry for your loss. While Jacob speaks to the doctor, I need to run through a few essentials. I will make it clear right now, we WILL NOT remove Mrs Caunter until you are all ready, you can take your time."

The look on their faces, after I said that, was usually one of relief, you could see them getting anxious, fearing that they are going to be in here, while Jacob sneaks the body out.

"Because the death was expected, and your mother has been under a Doctor's care in the last two weeks, and Doctor Prichard knows your mother, it will be a simple process. Once you have obtained the medical certificate, with cause of death, you can then proceed to register the death at the Registry Office."

People always feel overawed, so it has to be broken down into small digestible sections, death leaves a person heavily distracted.

"You will have five days, by law, to register the death; there will be no coroner involvement. Next, you will need to make an appointment with the Registry Office, registering the death is free, and it will take you about forty-five minutes."

A young lad gesticulated that he wanted to ask a question, he was very reserved in his demeanour.

"Who needs to register Grandma's death?"

I smiled at him, "What's your name?"

"It's. It's. It's Arthur." He stuttered.

"Well Arthur, you can register the death, if you are related to the person, or you were with the person when they died, or you live at the place where the deceased person does, or if there is no known relative available to register the death, and finally, if you are instructing the funeral director."

There were four people in their fifties or sixties sat in the room, I guessed they were all children to Mrs Caunter.

"Do you have your mother's medical number, birth certificate, and marriage certificate to hand? They are useful to take with you to the Registry Office as well."

The mutterings of which sideboard they were filed in, or were they in the box under the bed in spare bedroom, had begun between the siblings.

"Right, I must tell you, the death needs to be registered in the district in which it occurred. You will need to provide the date and place of death, their full name, and any other names they went by. Their date and place of birth, their relationship status, for example married, or widowed, or civil partnership, and their usual address. Other details needed, will be those of any surviving spouse.

"If memory serves, didn't we do Mr Caunter's funeral, back some two years ago, he passed away at St Cuthbert's."

"Yes, that was father, but you never visited us then, I don't recall your face dear." said Gloria, a kindly lady, now sat quietly in the corner of the living room.

"No, it wasn't me, my father-in-law, Christopher Saunders, and Jacob, who is upstairs; I believe were in attendance. The last point I must tell you is this, whoever registers the death, will need to have their details recorded. Does anyone have any questions?"

"Well, I suppose we start planning what we want next, do you remember what Dad had?" This must have been Gloria's younger sister asking, it wasn't uncommon to see people go into overdrive, they had all started to talk over each other with their suggestions. I gave them a minute or two, to work it out of their systems, it was always better to let them vent, it was a coping mechanism.

"Ladies and gents, for today, we do not need to make any rash decisions; I will leave all instructions for registering Mrs Caunter's death, here on the table."

Jacob had come into the living room, he gave me the nod. He stood in his morning suit, with pinstriped grey trousers. Getting trousers for Jacob was always a trial; he was so tall that I very often had to take the hems down for him. He had a white shirt, with black tie, and his black tailored jacket with tails.

"If you have finished, please could I excuse Sophia, if you could remain here for the moment please."

I had to go and see the body for myself; I needed to be aware of the health and safety. We had agreed on the removal method and signed off the forms, we liked to keep a comprehensive record.

Mrs Caunter had died in her bedroom, in her nightdress. Those last moments in her home, she deserved the right to dignity. I pulled the duvet covers over her, just like she was asleep. Her family was invited to say a final goodbye, before we left the house with her.

The hardest part of seeing your loved one leave their home, was seeing them leave in a black body bag, the lasting vision of them being wheeled out of the house. We had taken a conscious decision to wrap the body in a shroud; it would not leave such a deep scar when they left the house, we hoped.

Once the family had all said goodbye, we would ask them if they could go downstairs and wait for us to complete the removal. We always suggested they might start to think about readings between themselves, it worked quite well as a distraction.

The family was cooperative; we had removed her body into the ambulance. Once any body was placed in the ambulance, protocol was never to leave it unattended.

I went into the family, inviting them to the door as we left. Before getting into the vehicle, I would bow my head in respect. As we drove away from the house, in the mirror, we saw the all too familiar scenes of a family holding each other as they sobbed, it was always far more pleasant to see scenes of love and unity in the mirror, rather than division and anger. We never spoke on those journeys.

After going to the Chapel, and putting Mrs Caunter's body in the refrigerator, I was ready to drop. At Keeper's Cottage, I came home to the same routine as I normally would after a call out; today was, in many respects, another day at the office; but it had an edge on it, I was hurting.

I'd had several calls from my mother, I'd had to ignore them, I felt like a bad daughter, this was my mother's hour of need and I had sidelined her. I returned her calls; the conversation had to start with nothing other than an apology.

"Hi mum, I'm so sorry I've missed your calls. We literally got in the door and got a call out. I wasn't ignoring you."

Mother's face was quite clearly bunged up from crying, she sounded like she had flu.

"You went on a callout, Sophia, are you mad? Did you hear that, Roo? She went on a callout. Anyway, sweetie, you can't have got any food prepared, come to us for dinner. We can make some arrangements, and you can have your Sunday roast, just like normal."

I didn't hesitate to agree, what was the point, in times of death people craved normality more than ever, and who should I be to deny my mother that desire. I should understand more than most.

"Give me a couple of hours, to at least shower and have a nap mum, please. Could we have a three o'clock sitting?"

I placed the phone on the table and walked away, I started to cry, but I don't know what set me off. Jacob picked up the phone.

"Judy, it's just starting to hit her now. We'll join you for three. I'll look after her, I promise. See you then."

I sat back in his chair; Jacob came over, sat in the second chair and placed his hand on mine.

"Darling, what set you off?"

"I was just thinking about Mrs Caunter; she got to die at home, with her loved ones around her. Pom didn't have that luxury, I'm just feeling angry, his death was in an anonymous room. It was a failure on my behalf; I should have suggested palliative care at home, so that his death was comfortable and somewhere familiar. I know this stuff Jacob, and I neglected to address it."

"Sophia, hush, his death was so rapid; we had no time to prepare. Go and shower the day away. I will make you a cup of tea. You are not on call as of now, you're sleep deprived, and in no fit state to help another family. You held the Caunters together with the utmost level of professionalism, and I am so proud of you. Now is the time for you to be on compassionate leave. No arguments."

Hope of Ray

I didn't have the strength to argue; I got up and headed to our bathroom. The bathroom was next to the kitchen, I never locked the door, it just being the two of us. Jake followed me into the kitchen and flicked the kettle on.

I'd put the shower on to warm, he brought my tea in and sat on the stool. While he watched me shower, he asked if he heard me correctly, "Did you refer to my dad as your father-in-law today? That meaning I was your husband?"

"I did, why? Are you suggesting we should be husband and wife?"

"Why change what we have? Although I don't think today is the day for such a decision, I don't know, I love you, your strength and beauty, this morning proved that."

I didn't pursue it anymore, he left the bathroom, and I think he hoped I would cry to myself, letting the heartbreak and pain out. I got myself together after a good nap; I'd rolled myself up in the covers and slept it off. When I woke, my face felt heavy, like it does with a hangover. I'd forgotten we had to go to mum's; I just wanted to relax, and take stock of the last twenty four hours; I had to be the dutiful daughter though.

When I got up, Jacob wasn't home, I yelled his name a couple of times, I opened the front door, the car was missing, though that blasted bike was parked by the fence opposite, then I found a note on the kitchen table, which read...

> *"Gone for ice cream and chocolate,*
> *because you need comfort food,*
> *be back in time for your mum's*
> *x x x"*

While my ever-loving Jake had supplies, which he was stashing in the freezer for later, I was pacing, and rubbing my hands together, I was just one step away from saying "Out damn spot!" All I wanted was to get to mum's, because the sooner we got there, the sooner we could leave. She would likely go into overdrive, bombarding me, I know it would be meant without malice, but I wasn't ready for it.

Surprisingly, mother was mellow, all things considered. Dad had plied her with a couple of sherries, for medicinal purposes, it had worked a treat, he should do it more often, she was calm, and not highly-strung, for once.

Jacob was his usual charming self, he kept reassuring mother like he would any bereft child. She was in agreement, because she was clueless to arranging a funeral, that it would be best if we took the reins.

I'd made a promise to my mother; we'd take care of Pom. Jake had aired his concerns to me privately that I had tunnel vision about Pom, that my conflict of grieving and being the funeral lead, were causing him to worry. I was close to breaking down, and he made it perfectly clear, regardless of our relationship, he would pull me off the case if I couldn't handle it. I loved and hated him in equal measure for that. How dare he...

Chapter Four

David Pomeroy Walker

Pom had made it back to our beautiful little chapel; he was ready to be embalmed. I had, along with Jacob, embalmed many bodies, preparing them for viewing. This time I felt conflicted, I felt composed and capable, however, nervous and anxious too, would *I* be able to fulfil my duty?

Emotions ran high in plenty of cases. The worst preparations I had ever experienced were for the funeral of Marcus, his neck bruised from the noose he had around his neck. His father refused to see his body, his father's words were, "He's a bloody fool!" his father's anger made him come across as devoid of emotion. His mother, Gillian, was adamant she wanted to see her baby one last time. I spent hours trying to conceal and blend out the markings on his neck. He'd cut his life short, I couldn't have his mother scared permanently.

Strangely, it didn't surprise me when we got the second call to Bracknell Farm, for a second suicide, in a matter of months. I was heartbroken for Gillian; life was too much living without her only child, she sought to reunite with Marcus, her only option a shotgun. That bastard husband of hers never even paid his last respects to her. I think, in some odd way, I understood her motives.

Pom had been taken out of the refrigerator, and removed from his body bag, which was hospital issue, he was ready for embalming. It was agreed I would lead, but, at any time, if I was unable to perform my job to the highest of standards, Jacob would take over, no arguments.

Jacob, ever the professional, questioned my methods before I even dared touch Pom, assessing my capabilities before I started. I loved him for that, I forgave him. His integrity was faultless.

"Sophia, talk me through your kit."

"I have disinfectant, for cleansing the body, formaldehyde, incision tools, fluid drains and suction pump. Cavity fluid, cotton wool, eye caps, petroleum jelly, and incontinence pads, not forgetting the suture kit."

I pointed to each tool on my trolley, clearly demonstrating I knew what I was doing.

"Before you start, where are you going to make your incision to begin?"

"Mr Walker is in the supine position, he is lying horizontally, with his face and torso up, as opposed to the prone position, his placement is correct for this procedure.

"I will make my incision in the brachial artery, when I need to commence with that part of the process. Before this, I will make an initial evaluation of Mr Walker, such as lividity, rigor, and intravenous injection sites."

I was very forthright in my answers to Jacob, he had to be certain, and, truth be told, I was confirming to myself, that I was capable; I was riddled with self doubt. Calling Pom by his formal name was my way of trying to play down the emotional enormity I was facing.

"Sophia, I'm satisfied you are more than capable to complete your duty."

He sat back silently and observed. Delicately, I started to cleanse Pom's body with disinfectant, it was almost poetic, I spent every Sunday taking him to Church, like his loyal disciple, and now I served him one last time. I was John the Baptist, and he was Jesus. I washed him with the delicate flow of water, he was my God, and this was our River Jordan.

I was ready to locate his brachial artery, ready for my first incision. My hand was shaking, I pulled away momentarily, I needed to compose myself, I tried to put the emotional connection to the back of my mind; I exhaled, ready to attempt it one more time.

It was worse now than before, I couldn't do my job correctly, and it would be irresponsible of me to carry on. I could see Jacob; watching. Noting every micro expression I made. I put the scalpel down.

"I can't, you need to do this for me."

I ripped my disposable apron off, pushing the bin pedal, dumping the waste as I left. Jacob followed me into the Chapel of Rest.

"I've failed Pom." I sobbed.

"No Sophia, no you haven't, don't ever think that. You were courageous enough to admit you couldn't do it, and if I know anything about Pom, he'd admire you more for your honesty."

He kissed me on the forehead, "I will complete the embalming; I don't deem you fit to carry out your duty, with every will in the world. I am now taking over as your superior. You may 'sit in' only, until the process is completed."

I walked away, knowing it would be far more painful being a spectator. While I felt a failure, I understood that we could not afford personal issues to cloud our judgement, especially in such a sensitive business. Truth be told, I was relieved. I had faith in Jacob.

I didn't enter into the Chapel again that day; I was to be on the other side of the fence, as a grieving relative. The next time I saw Pom, was the day before his funeral. My mother and father would join me, for one final goodbye.

His maple coffin, with matt finish, simple yet elegant, complete with golden handles, housed dear Pom for his final journey, his coffin lay open to greet us.

Mum had chosen a suit, the one he wore every Sunday for Church. A navy blue jacket, double breasted, with four buttons, the top one still hanging on by a thread. His matching trousers, grey socks. Very often, the toes had been darned; he had a 'make do and mend' mentality. His black shoes always polished for Church. His white shirt, crisp white, never greying. Underneath his jacket was his woollen maroon waistcoat, with matching tie.

Jacob had taken care over every detail, even his hair was lacquered back. I think, in some ways, the scrutiny and pressure from me was worse than attending to a family member.

My mother fell to pieces; my dad had a firm grip of her, propping her up, supporting her aching body. I silently let the tears leak out, as I looked over every detail, I could feel Jacob's nerves as he waited for my comment.

I encouraged my mother to say her final goodbyes, she apprehensively edged towards him, and hesitantly, she kissed his forehead.

"Sleep well, Daddy."

My father tapped Pom's hand. "I'll look after her David."

I placed my palm on top of Pom's cold hands; I'd do anything to feel his soft hands once more. His skin always felt silky and fragile. I leant in and gave him one last kiss on the forehead. I didn't fear it, placing my hand on his cheek. "Until we meet again, Pom."

I left with my parents. Dad ushered mum out; leaving the room, I looked back at Jacob, who mouthed, "I love you." to me. I knew what was to come next, I was not ready to see the lid of his coffin screwed down, that was one part of the job I didn't enjoy, it gave a finality to life. It was now boxed forever more.

Because of modern standards of the undertaking world, thanks to manual handling regulations and red tape, it was recommended that coffins and caskets be wheeled into ceremonies on trolleys, where possible.

We arranged that Pom would be in St Laurence Church, before his mourners arrived, I hated it when they were wheeled in, it was so impersonal and it lacked the final rite of passage, a tradition that showed respect to the dead.

It was certainly a different vibe to the funerals I normally attended. The congregation was relatively full, plenty of his fellow Churchgoers there. It was always a pleasant sight to see the congregation evenly spaced, rather than the family isolated at the front of the Church, it broke down barriers.

Jacob led, with Toby and George following behind him, to in front of the coffin. They all bowed their heads, and then made their way to the back of the church. Mother and Father followed, and I was the last person to walk down to Pom. I was wearing a red dress, with a navy blue lace overlay; it had red trim and a red waistband, tied into a bow at the back. I wore it with black shoes and tights. I felt naked not being in my usual morning suit. I stood, paused, and genuflected, biting my lip, trying not to cry, and then I took my seat next to my parents.

His order of service was very classical: John 14:1-3, 2 Corinthians 1:3-4. Reverend Michaels spoke of his interactions with Pom, how he was an avid Churchgoer, who had bravely stepped up when his country needed him, in World War Two, where he was in the Devonshire Regiment. He read a eulogy, on my mother's behalf, that she had written. She regaled a tale from her childhood, her and Nanna had met Pom from work one day, they were going for a walk, and Pom had requested a second set of shoes, so as not to muddy his work shoes. Nanna had brought him two **left** shoes; my mum recalled how he moaned all the way round. I could hear his moaning as if he were sat next to me. We sang, "The Day Thou Gavest, Lord, is Ended", and "All Things Bright and Beautiful". I had sung these hymns time and time again, today they meant so much more to me, and it was the first time I had sung them for a loved one. Jacob's voice always carried over everyone else; he enhanced both the tone and volume for the whole congregation, wherever we worked.

The day had drawn to a close, after a wake in the Church Hall, where teas and a light lunch were offered. I was overwhelmed by the events of the day, and I arranged to take a couple days off. I needed some down time, before I made myself ill, I couldn't afford to burn myself out, with Jacob leaving on Friday, for his annual three weeks in Italy.

"What a day sweetheart, you did your Pom proud today. You did me proud, I love you very much." Said Jacob, as he was packing his worn leather bag, ready for his departure. I lay on our bed, hollow, reliving the day over and over again; I must have walked down the aisle, and genuflected, fifty times. Why couldn't I keep it together to embalm him? My thoughts raced. I'd let myself down, and by not fulfilling my duties, I'd regret it for the rest of my life.

I erupted into tears; Jacob stopped his packing and sat on our bed, giving me his undivided attention. He managed to decipher my inaudible wail of broken sentences, while I sobbed my way through. I told him how I regretted not being able to embalm Pom; Jacob kindly pointed out that I acted with the upmost professionalism, by withdrawing myself, and that was far more commendable.

I withdrew for the next two days, trying to relax; having a break was definitely needed to recharge my batteries. I managed to complete the first book I had read in a few years, life had certainly taken over. I hadn't read for such a long time for pleasure, immersing myself into another world was therapy; the escapism gave my body tranquillity.

I was due to go back to work on Thursday. Jacob came home on the Wednesday evening with a case file I needed to read; for a family of three, a young couple, in their early twenties, and their two year old daughter. They had lost their lives to carbon monoxide poisoning. The landlord of their home had not maintained the property, especially the boiler, and he had been charged with manslaughter. I had some recollection of this hitting the local news, a few weeks previously. They had suffered at the hands of a silent killer.

"I need you to handle this while I'm away, bring yourself up to date, and make contact with both families tomorrow, to liaise."

I'd glanced over the particulars, instantly thrusting it back into Jacob's hand with great ferocity.

"NO!" I replied and walked away.

"What do you mean, 'NO'?"

"I mean 'NO!' Jacob. As in, 'NO', I'm not doing it!"

"But I go away on Friday."

"And I mean NO Jacob, what part of NO don't you understand? I'm not ready to return, after what feels like a personal trauma, with Pom. I've had little to no compassionate leave. I mean NO, end of!"

"That's beyond selfish Sophia, I thought better of you."

"Don't emotionally blackmail me, Jacob Saunders. Yeah, I'm selfish, that's me all over. Tell me, who was the one who came to collect Mrs Caunter's body with you after a personal bereavement? I can't recall who it was... oh yes, it was ME!

"I tell you what, if I'm that selfish, maybe I should just dump you right in it; tomorrow morning I'll go and see if Jimmy Powell has a job for Little Miss Selfish, clearly this isn't working.

"Maybe you should sleep in the spare room tonight!"

I retreated to our room, throwing his clothes out on the landing, slamming the door, and making it perfectly clear I didn't want to speak to him that evening.

Jacob left for work, without a goodbye, on that Thursday morning. I was angry with him, but surely he wouldn't leave for Italy without making up; I was now feeling incredibly guilty about my reaction.

I set about cleaning my act up; I'd make it into work, albeit late. Show willing. I was struggling to come to terms with Pom's death, busying myself had been a temporary solution, to muddle through. Could Jacob recognise I was struggling, maybe forgive me?

A red car pulled up on the drive, it was Helen, and I guessed Jacob had called her for backup. I opened the door, left it open, and went to pop the kettle on.

"Hi Hels."

"Hi, thought I'd pop in, see how you were doing."

"Hels, don't be so transparent, you text me less than two hours ago, remember?" I lifted my eyebrow at her.

"Ok, bang to rights." She conceded.

"What did the arse tell you then?"

"'The arse', as you call him, is genuinely worried about you; he rang because of your reaction last night, over a new case he wants you to work. He's worried it's out of character, and he thought you'd talk to me. So...?"

"He wants me to lead the funeral of a young family, who died from carbon monoxide poisoning. When I told him 'NO', he had the brass balls to call me selfish. I'm not ready. Cards on the table, Pom's death has ripped me apart, I'm struggling to come to terms with it."

"Are you getting ready to go to work?" Helen queried.

"Yeah, I thought I'd better show willing."

"Well, what a total tool he is, don't go in. His dad can deal with it, you need to rest up. Start back on Monday; make it abundantly clear how you feel. You, of all people, know bereavement is a strange thing.

"I'll be having words with Jacob!" she forcefully declared.

Helen knew the way to my heart was chutney and cheese, on farmhouse bread. She'd bought all the necessary supplies for lunch; it was such a mummsy thing to do. I loved the way Helen could get to the root of the problem; she was always objective in her council, when it came to Jacob and me.

Jacob returned that evening, with his tail between his legs. He was apologetic, he even sounded remorseful. His father was going to take the lead, while Jacob was away on his annual three-week trip to Italy. His dad had been slowly removing himself from the day-to-day running, to allow a smoother transition for Jacob to take the business over fully.

Every year, Jacob took his three weeks R and R, always to Italy. In that time we never made contact, it didn't seem weird, I'd become accustomed to him doing this, even before we were a couple. It was how he took stock of his life and, I guess, helped him keep an even keel with life as an undertaker. His dad did similar, he took an extended annual leave; it must have been what the Saunders did.

Jacob and I pieced back together the shattered relationship, we knew we had both been reactionary. He knew I wouldn't leave Saunders; as I loved the flexibility of working there. Although I got on well with Jimmy Powell, and we had worked together on rare occasions, Jacob knew Jimmy and I differed too much in our work ethics and visions. Jim was always black and white; he followed the textbook to the letter, while I was more accommodating in my approach. Families had to heal, letting them feel in control, and included, at such times was huge. Breaking down barriers was important to me. Society is very diverse, plenty of people are moving away from traditional, religious, funerals; especially the younger generation, it was becoming more a celebration of life. Jim Powell struggled to accept diversity; that not every ceremony would now be in a Church or Chapel.

It was agreed I would return to work on Monday; Christopher would be more hands on, while I took lighter duties until I was ready. I realised this was Jacob's olive branch; I took it, knowing he departed in the morning.

We made arrangements for his return, it was now a tradition of sorts; we'd meet at the airport and spend the evening reliving our first night at the Claythorn Arms.

The morning he left, we said goodbye, in a loving manner, it felt forced on my behalf, maybe even disingenuous. I wondered if spending the weekend away, before my return to work, would be beneficial. I questioned my thoughts, why did I have to squeeze my respite into a weekend, I'd had a week off by default, while he could vanish for three weeks, no questions asked. Why had he been so reactionary to me needing time to get myself together? He had that luxury every year.

Maybe Jacob wasn't the person for me; he had plenty of positives, he was a good undertaker, he worked hard, and was committed to his vocation in life; apart from those sacred three weeks a year, when he must not be disturbed. The three weeks never bothered me, until now. It was a very one-sided policy, and it was making me agitated.

If Jacob and I confronted the issue, we could potentially end up parting, going our separate ways. I lived with him, in his house, I'd have to leave. I didn't want to face the prospect of moving back home, to mum and dad's, it was an option, but not one I was desperate to use. I decided I would pop into Merton Major, to the letting agents, check out my options, just in case Jacob and I weren't compatible for a future together.

Helen had invited me over for dinner; I think she had taken pity on my dinner for one option. When I got there, having greeted my favourite pregnant lady with: guacamole, cured bacon, and ice; she had the most random cravings, Helen cut straight to the chase, she was soft and gentle, with the girl next door look about her, however, for the people who really knew her, she loved them hard. She would move heaven and earth, she could be cutthroat when she thought they were about to screw up. Helen protected us all like a Mamma bear.

"Why are you looking at moving out of Keeper's Cottage?"

"I wasn't." I shrugged it off, hoping Hels would drop it.

"Don't insult my intelligence, you were seen. Tori Atherton was in the letting agent at the same time as you; she rang me, wanting the gossip on that, and I quote, 'Hotty at the undertakers, and his girlfriend, apparently they've split up.' According to her."

"Oh her, looks like she has just finished primary school, we met her here once, at a barbeque, when you worked there, she was a Saturday girl, no wonder she was smiling at me."

I was caught. Helen and Ray let me pour my soul out. I felt awful, Ray and Jacob were friends, yet here I was slagging him off. Ray and Jacob had known each other since their teens, playing rugby together, Ray probably knew Jacob better than anyone.

"Jacob just needs time, it is his way to keep on going, he's shite at showing emotion, always has been. His time away is to allow him to cope with real life. It's like therapy for him. Just like you girls vent by seeking solace in each other, Jacob seeks solace in the hills of Italy. Granted he needs to pay you the same respect, in allowing you the same privilege, but backing him into a corner, to explain his actions, will only make it worse. He'll feel stupid and withdraw over it."

Ray continued, "You know what a total fool he was towards you, before he finally told you how he felt, and I guess that was a clumsy mess when he did.

"Jacob won't forgive me for telling you this, we were about fifteen, playing rugby, it was a league match. He was angry a lot! His parents hadn't long split up. This lad took him down with a hard high tackle, and Jacob started beating him to a pulp. He blackened his eyes, split his lip, his mouth pooled with blood. I'm guessing his dad, Christopher, smoothed it over, nothing more came of it.

"Jacob battled his anger for a couple of years, then he found painting, Art College was a release for Jacob, to explore his emotions creatively. He fell in love with Italian culture, the artists in particular, Michelangelo,

Raphael, Botticelli, and Caravaggio. Giving him this freedom, and respecting his need, makes him a better man; the man who swept you off your feet."

Ray had so eloquently explained parts of Jacob that were still in darkness to me, he had thrown light on Jacob, and I trusted Ray's judgement.

Jacob's return was one I was excited for; I had blown up a situation out of all proportion. I knew I loved Jacob, why wouldn't I, he understood me, everything we worked for was as a partnership, and I needed to remember that.

At the Claythorn Arms, we always re-enacted the day we first went there. We would have the same lunch; I'd have the classic ploughman's, Jacob the 12oz rump steak. The afternoon would always be spent drinking tea by the fire, laughing at each other's anecdotes of childhood. When we turned in for bed, we'd spend the evening wrapped in the sheets, reaffirming our bond with each other. We would never have sex on those evenings, we'd just touch each other, smell one another, it made our relationship more sensual, not everything had to be based upon lust, and the carnal relations between a man and woman.

Chapter Five

Diana

"What's that darling?" Jake asked.

I was obviously doing my scowl, with the 'what are you writing to me for?' look, a look I quite often threw in dismay at work, when red tape type letters fell onto my desk. This time, it had landed on my doormat, at home.

"Hmm?"

"Darling, what are you scowling at?"

Jacob was leant over the back of the sofa, looking towards me, in the doorway between the living room and hall.

"It's from Chaineys and Daulton."

I wandered over and dropped the tri-folded letter on his lap, without saying another word. I walked back to the kitchen. I wanted to busy myself. I was in total dismay. Jacob came in; I assume he had read the letter through, to be fully informed, before he made any comments.

"Did you not know, Sophia?"

"No Jacob, I knew all along, which is why I am now stood here bloody shaking in total disbelief, yep they're all key signs of someone fully in the know!" I sniped at him.

"I'm trying to help, sniping at me, isn't going to find a resolution, I'm trying to support you."

"I... I'm... sorry." I said, as I broke down into tears, leaning against the sink worktop, my head bowed down, looking at the floor, Jacob held out a tissue. He nudged my head back up, using his finger like a crook, driving the tip of my chin back up.

"He never mentioned it to you? Just left it with Chaineys and Daulton?"

"I guess so, what do I do?"

"Ring your mother; she'll know, I'm sure."

So my only option was to ring mum, I really hoped she knew what was going on, or was I about to deliver a bombshell. I could only anticipate they had contacted her too, I pressed the last three digits on the key pad, 4, 1, 8. It rang.

"Hello, Hardy residence."

"Hi mum, it's me."

"Hello darling, you'll never guess what I had today; it was a letter from Chaineys and Daulton."

"Ah, yes, that's what I was ringing about." I paused; hoping mother would fill in the rest.

"So, you got the house then? Well, it only seemed right when he suggested it, he was worried he'd offend me, but like I said at the time, you'd need it more than me. Your father and I were lucky, we got on the property ladder, but your generation never stood a chance. So I was thrilled when he wanted to leave it as a gift to you.

"And when the time comes, you'll have our house too. It'll make a terrific pension fund for you sweetheart."

"Mum, you knew all these years, Pom was going to leave me the house, and you said nothing, why didn't you tell me?"

"Well, it wasn't my place."

It wasn't her place to tell me, but yet she tells me everyone else's useless business.

"When did Pom make his will?"

"Oh that's easy, he made it the summer after your grandmother died, maybe six months after." Mother was certain about that.

"Mum, I know Pom wasn't a rich man, and as I now own his home, I shouldn't quibble, but why has he left £800 to a lady called Diana Hinkley? Another £500 goes to Marjie Hinkley, and if she is dead, to pass it on to Diana. Who are they? He never mentioned them."

"Umm, he knew Marjie from when he was posted in the War, apparently her daughter, Diana, was like a God-daughter to him.

"Look darling, your father's tea needs serving. Don't look back; you have been given a wonderful future. You deserve every happiness. The dignity you gave Pom, on his last journey, I couldn't thank you enough for that. This only seems fair. Look the spuds are crisping. Love you."

With that, mother put the phone down. I didn't have to relay our conversation to Jacob, mother's voice always carried on the phone.

Chapter Six

Helen

The 9th of January, Helen's waters had broken in the early hours of the morning. I got a text from her, she was so excitable, it was 5.45am. Nothing had happened by 8am, she was advised to keep moving, to bring on labour.

All day I kept looking at my phone for updates. Ray was at home, quietly beside himself, pacing the kitchen, when I popped in on the lunchtime. Helen was getting the odd twinge but nothing regular. She was her usual self, her favourite topic of debate being, had Jacob asked me to marry him yet?

"So, has he done it yet, you know, popped the question?"

She had this terrible habit of waiting for me to put my lunch in my mouth, so I couldn't reply straight away.

"When you say 'Pop the question' do you mean... 'Darling, it's Tuesday, shall we have steak?' Then no, he didn't ask that either."

She was moving about, attempting sexy circles, I happily informed her that she looked like a whale, and I'd ring Greenpeace.

I couldn't stay long; we had to pick the body up of a homeless man, from the hospital mortuary.

"Right you, I'm sorry, I have to go. The next time I see you, you'll be a mamma, and I can't wait to meet her, Helen. I know you're going to be a wonderful mother. I love you Hels. Call me if you need anything."

I gave her an almighty cuddle and kiss; I left her doing pregnant lady lunges, and popped into the kitchen.

"I'm off; call me if you need anything. You'll do great Ray, you both deserve every happiness. Although, you might want to go and stop the great whale from lunging, she's going to wreck the place!" We both scoffed, and off I went.

By afternoon tea break, she was finally on her way to the hospital. I was so relieved for her. I'm not sure Ray knew what to expect. Jacob had a message earlier in the day, Ray was shit scared, and had no idea what to do. He was a first time dad, he wasn't meant to know what to do, or how to react, so he could be forgiven for being scared, and overwhelmed, at a baby arriving.

At 7.59 p.m., I'd got a text at home, by some luck, saying she was on the labour ward and five centimetres, so she was in established labour. Jacob and I sat by the fire, waiting for news on baby Bramwell's arrival. It was so quiet and calm, we hadn't really had much time of late, just sitting together was perfect.

"Do you think we'll ever have a family, I mean babies?" I asked.

"Hmm, one day, but don't you want the marriage part first? It doesn't bother me either way, if we get married or not, why fix something that isn't broken, besides we're run ragged most days now. I mean this is the first time we have properly sat down in ages." Jacob rambled.

He continued, "Why don't we take the time to train up the two lads, George and Toby, so they can go on call and handle the paper work, with dad having semi-retired, it would make sense."

"OK." There was no argument from me; we had been on call, seven days a week, for months, with no rest. Marginally reducing our working week, to progress our home life, seemed like a good thing to do. I was twenty-six, nearly twenty-seven, and had plenty of years left to bear children.

Jacob was forty-three, men fathered children well into their seventies, so all things considered, Jacob was looking pretty youthful.

I'd had no updates on Helen when we turned in for bed, at 10.30 p.m. I knew, hopefully by morning, I'd wake to find a text telling me all was well. The alarms had gone off like they did every day, I'd tossed and turned all night, anxious of news, the first thing I did was grab my phone. There, waiting for me, was a text, time stamped 3.03 a.m.

Baby Hope Elizabeth Bramwell born at 2.54am weighing 7lb 1oz.

I was so excited for them, it was a precious moment. I didn't reply back, I knew I'd speak to Ray as soon as it wasn't an unsightly hour.

Having spoken to Ray, I learned that Helen had a pretty rough time; it wasn't the fairytale birth she had desired. Hope had become distressed; her heart rate had dipped whilst Helen was having contractions. Poor Helen, she had been at it for hours, her emotional exhaustion, and the physical strain her body was under, she had become beaten. The doctors and midwives had decided the safest option, for both mother and baby, was an assisted birth, Helen had gone to theatre, for a forceps delivery.

Ray was now an authority on forceps delivery; informing me that one in every eight babies was delivered in such a way in the UK. Helen had received a minor tear, which meant she'd had a few stitches. Helen didn't care about her pain, it was a small price to pay, her baby was now here in her arms, safe and well. Hope had slight bruising to her face, but she was safe, like Helen said, the bruise would fade.

Ray thought they may be home by tomorrow evening, all being well. I arranged to see them that evening, if they were up for visitors, and offered to bring them dinner, by which I meant pizza, my dinners were so basic this was a better option.

When I went over, the following evening, Jacob came with me. Apparently, him and Ray had finally grown up, one was a father, the other a businessman, he joked. It was a far cry from their heady rugby days.

Helen looked as though she had been out for a night on the town, according to Jacob, in his tactless observations. Her eyes were black; she looked deprived of all energy after her ordeal. She was sat in the chair, with a blanket on, as she was feeling cold. It was a chilly January evening outside, but the house was toasty warm, I'd taken my cardigan off, it was that hot, as the heat claimed the room. Beautiful Hope was in her bassinette, next to her mother.

"Can I Helen? Can I hold her?"

I scooped Hope up into my arms; she had tiny wisps of red hair on her head.

"Crikey Ray, she'll have more hair than you by the time she's one."

Ray rubbed his balding head, as I walked over to Jacob; sitting down next to him, he put his arm around my shoulder.

"Hello Hope, I'm your Aunty Soph, and this is Uncle Jakey."

Ray came and perched on the arm of Helen's chair, he looked at Helen before continuing.

"On that note, would you do us the honour of being Hope's guardians? We're not religious, but we want to acknowledge her birth in a more casual way than a Christening."

We both agreed instantly, knowing that, if we were ever in the same position, Ray and Helen would be our choice, to guide our children.

Helen was nodding off; the last couple of days had caught up on them, they both needed rest. Helen wasn't looking great, she looked like she had a bad bout of flu, the way she was holding herself in the chair. We bid them goodnight, wishing them a restful sleep, if that was at all possible with a newborn.

Our phone rang at 1.10am on January 12th; it was nothing unusual, we both stirred, as we always did. Jacob sat on the side of the bed, ready to start dressing; our mourning suits were laid out, as they always were at night.

I never expected to hear his voice on the end of the line, I hit Jacob to stop what he was doing, and I passed him the phone, I couldn't quite comprehend what I'd been told.

I heard Jacob speak, his words were inaudible, Jacob put the phone down on the bed; he looked at me, his eyes stunned and welling up. "Oh no, Jacob, tell me I heard him wrong, he's got it wrong, tell me he's got it wrong!" I was almost hysterical before I'd finished my sentence. I'd lost it, screaming at Jacob from the other side of the bed.

"She's dead. Helen's dead. My darling, I'm so sorry."

"She can't be, she just had a baby, they have it wrong."

I was in shock, feeling angry, I had no details, no reasoning, she was Hope's mummy, and she wouldn't leave her like this.

Ray had gone, with Helen and Hope, in an ambulance to St Cuthbert's, many hours before, he had no means of getting home, so we went to pick him up. We were familiar faces at the hospital; the nurses lead us straight to Ray. He was sat next to Helen's bed, Hope's empty car seat next to him.

Jacob didn't want me to go with him to the hospital; he thought I was better placed to wait at home. Strangely, I understood his caution, with my reaction to Pom. But that was not his choice.

He was in a side room, the door open, even though it was the dead of night; Helen lay motionless, and Ray was staring into space. He didn't even hear us enter the room, I touched his shoulder, and he didn't flinch, just kept his focus forward.

"Ray, it's me."

Ray turned to us, his face was swollen, his eyes red, he opened his mouth, but no words came out, he let out a mighty howl; that noise would haunt me. Falling into my arms, I still had no clues as to the events that had unfolded, it was clear Hope was with him, but there was no sign as to her whereabouts.

I ordered Jacob to go and find Hope, and find out what had happened, if possible. Ray couldn't communicate, and I just held him close, in my arms. I didn't want to let go of him, because as soon as I did, I had to face the harsh reality that my best friend lay dead in the bed next to us. As I consoled her widower, knowing in a few minutes time his newborn baby would be in his care, all the while he was riddled with instant grief.

"Sophia." Jacob beckoned me out of the room.

I sat Ray back down; I was scared he'd fall down if I just left him.

"Hope is on the maternity wing, being fed and cared for at the moment, we need to take him home, he can't sit there indefinitely."

"He won't leave her, you know as well as I do how strongly he loves Helen, you go and reason with him, he's your best friend."

Hope of Ray

I asked the nurses if I could sit in the family room, whilst we waited for Hope, I arranged with them that I'd stay the night with Ray and look after Hope. The nurse kindly showed me into the room, I broke into a wail, she'd left me too; how on earth would I cope without Helen being there for me?

Hope was brought to me, fed and changed, that had bought us a couple hours until she would need more milk. Helen was breast-feeding her. It was suggested we got some formula, and acted upon the suggestion rather quickly.

An hour and a half after arriving at the hospital, we finally convinced Ray to leave Helen's side, he was a fragment of the man he was the last time we saw him.

We took him home, to his house in Merton Major, after a silent car journey, he walked in the door and bypassed Hope, straight up to his room. I wanted to go and comfort him, but Jacob told me to leave him.

I asked Jake, "Can you go out for baby formula? There's nothing here for Hope to drink, not even a bottle in the house, get newborn stuff, and some cold water sterilizers, I don't know what else to do."

Jacob set about running to the supermarket; we were still clueless as to what had happened. About 10 minutes before his return, Hope started to cry, I'd been sat there, looking at her, feeling helpless and underprepared for what the next few days would bring.

I held her in my arms, comforting her, her tiny little soul that would never know Helen. I kissed her tiny cheeks, trying to reassure her that someone was here. But I wasn't Helen, I didn't feel, sound or smell like her. Ray came and sat himself in the chair, he was hollow.

"Sepsis." He mumbled, almost imperceptibly.

"What Ray? Sorry, I didn't hear you."

"Sepsis, she died from sepsis, that's what they said, her symptoms were masquerading as flu, according to the doctor."

"I don't understand, she was fit and healthy, she'd just had a baby."

"I was told sepsis doesn't discriminate, you can be fit and healthy one day, and dead the next."

Jacob returned with supplies, I set about preparing bottles, we shut our selves away in the kitchen, to make plans to cover tomorrow, as it was obvious that Ray was in no fit state to be left alone, especially caring for a newborn.

"He told me, while you were out, Helen had sepsis; I just don't understand how this has happened. We'd only seen her a few hours before, she seemed fit and well, maybe tired and flu-like, but I put that down to giving birth."

"Sepsis, is known as the silent killer, Sophia, it is unpredictable, rapid, and can go undiagnosed, it has no clear signs or symptoms. I read a leaflet on it once, it can kill in twelve hours, within six hours you could be feeling incredibly sick, every hour you wait for treatment the mortality rate increases by 10%, without antibiotics."

"And now it's fucking claimed the life of Helen, leaving Ray and Hope alone!"

"Stay here with them, as long as it takes, I'll take care of work, you support them, in any way they need it. Stay a couple of nights, he can't be alone. I'll drop over some things for you later.

"I'm so, so sorry Sophia, I don't know what to say."

"Hug me tight and don't let go, that's more than enough."

Chapter Seven

Hope

I had been at Ray's house for nigh on a week. He was beside himself. He was a first time father, and heartbroken. This should have been a wonderful time, where his world had been turned upside down by a bundle of joy; instead, it was blown apart and devastated with Helen's death. At two days old, baby Hope had become motherless.

Ray was sleep deprived; he couldn't cope with the demands of caring for Hope, and finish the job at Beckworth Heath safely. He had to finish, or he wouldn't be paid, the foreman and developers at Meadow Ford Mews were somewhat devoid of compassion.

His eyes were black, he looked emotionally beaten. I had no doubt that, over time, as Hope slept better, he would look and feel better too. For the moment, I was sleeping on the sofa, and doing night feeds every two and a half hours. I felt so much pain and sorrow for her to never know her mummy. To never know the woman, who was desperate to love her unconditionally for all of time.

Every time I soothed and comforted Hope, I'd tell her a story of Helen, and what a beautiful friend she was; it was my way to cope, getting me through the heartache I felt. I held her tight and wept. I couldn't do it when Ray was around, he needed my support. In my job, I had seen men crumble with death, when it was my best friend's, it was personal. I had never seen a grown man howl with such anguish, I couldn't let him down by showing my hurt; I had to be as upbeat as possible to see him through.

I'd noticed Ray had become distant from Hope. The midwife had visited early one morning, Ray was still in bed, he'd finally slept longer than a couple of hours, so I left him to rest, to heal his emotional wounds, they also needed care and attention. I mentioned his behaviour to the midwife, how he was seeming to reject Hope, or blame her for Helen's death, he'd become despondent. The midwife arranged for a doctor to visit him, and suggested, with Ray's consent, I take Hope out for the day.

Jacob and I were the only 'family' they had close by, his parents had emigrated 20 years ago, and were on standby to get flights over. In my opinion, they seemed like total whackjobs; I mean, who leaves their child, at any age, in need like that. They were totally unempathetic. They had a holiday to Tonga next week, how dare Ray inconvenience them.

Helen's parents had passed away many years before, when she was in her teens; they were geriatric when she was born, and she'd always anticipated losing them young, though she didn't expect them to go while she was a teenager. Their car careered off a sharp bend, on an icy road; they ended up in the river, no one was about and they were trapped, dying a tragic death of drowning. Helen had been away, skiing with the school, on a half-term excursion.

I left the house with a shopping list for Hope. She'd had to go on formula; I thought a couple of premade milks would also be prudent while Ray established a routine. It was bitter-sweet loading her into her pram; she had never been in it before, and her scritching showed her disgruntlement. The first time she'd take an adventure out of the house was with me, not her mum. I felt like I was betraying Helen; I wrapped her baby up warm, in blankets she had chosen, and I took her baby out to "show her off" to the world. I would dirty the wheels on its maiden voyage.

I walked the three miles from Merton Major into Fremmington Ayshe; the fresh air was bound to help us both. I had to go into the office; I'd pretty much abandoned my working life to be the best friend I could be to Helen, in life and death. Jacob was unbelievably supportive; he carried on being the face of our business, and helped the Bramwell's wherever possible. He'd clearly learnt from the harsh lessons Pom had delivered, about my emotional state.

Ray needed to get out of the house, or let it out and vent at someone other than me. I was going to suggest Hope came for a sleepover at Keeper's Cottage, and Jacob head over to Ray's with some beer, men open up to other men differently. I'd have Hope for a couple of days longer, then Ray would have time to engage with her, he was her daddy, she needed him and, deep down, he was going to need her. Her innocence was going to be the therapy he needed.

I'd gotten to the village green in Merton Major; Hope had stopped fussing and was now settled. Village life meant nothing was ever private for long, people knew of Helen's death, they pushed cards through the door, and neighbour's curtains twitched at the comings and goings; their morbid curiosity led them to want a glimpse of the poor, tragic, baby Hope. I'd stopped to read the parish notice board; and then it began. Two women, retired I guess, in their early sixties, skittled across the road as soon as they saw me.

"Hello dear, oh there she is, poor little thing, such a heartbreak."

Their heads, all the while, tilted slightly to one side, nodding condescendingly. I know their intentions were meant well, but their delivery was somewhat devoid of sincerity.

"How is he? Is he coping? At least he has you for support. Of course she was such a wanted baby."

I smiled, and stayed quiet, while they babbled relentlessly at me. I intended for them to get it out of their system, so we could get on with our day. However, we'd stopped, and now more, how can I put it, nosey, old, inconsiderate bats, came over. They meant no malice by their comments, but the filter didn't quite work, and their level of insensitivity meant they got the wrath of my hurt. I'd tried my hardest to bite my tongue, for the sake of our business, as well as for my friend's devastated family.

"Aw, bless the little sweet cherub, so sad."

"Helen died of blood poisoning, didn't she?"

"No, it was her heart." The lady gestured, "No", by shaking her finger.

I stood in shock at the total lack of censorship; they prattled on as if I wasn't even there.

"Well, was it blood poisoning?" They asked and looked at me.

"It's believed it was sepsis." Another added, before I could answer.

"Well sepsis is blood poisoning." Said another voice from the gaggle.

"I suppose you and your fella will be adopting her now, he's not going to want to see her face every day, reminding him of his wife."

I was horrified, angry, and nauseated, at such comments from people I didn't even know. I bit back.

"I beg your pardon? Why would I adopt her? Hope has a perfect, loving father, who, in his time of need, has allowed his friends to help. And NO, blood poisoning is NOT the same as sepsis. Good day ladies!" I barked, fiercely; striding away before the interrogation committee of busybodies could unruffle enough to compose a reply to my outburst.

I power-walked the rest of the way, to channel my anger; thankfully, Hope didn't even flinch at the shouty me in the village.

When I got to the office, I was a smidge flustered, as I'd brooded the entire journey; I was hurt by the comments and embarrassed at how they'd treated us. Joanna was on her own; she was a great girl and really sympathetic; which, in our profession, was a very good attribute to have. I walked in agitated; she greeted me with, "I'll pop the kettle on."

I sat in our comfy family lounge area, off the office. I fed Hope, she guzzled a whole three ounce bottle, and then I winded her, she was a little fractious.

"Sophia, your tea is going cold, can I hold her? Then you can drink your tea, maybe even enjoy it."

"Thanks Joanna. Where's Jacob? I came to speak to him; I'd forgotten why I was even here."

Joanna put her arms out for Hope. "He's on a call out."

"Do you know where, and what it is?"

"No, he took the call himself, and left with George." Joanna was swaying Hope, and she was peaceful.

The phone rang again, the landline was always turned up deafeningly loud, with it being a cordless phone, and three or four of us using it, the handset had a habit of wandering.

"I'll get it, just to do what I would normally be doing... magic!" For once it was on the desk, where it should be.

"Good afternoon, Saunders and Son."

"Hello, it's Gemima, from the district council, can I speak to Mr Jacob Saunders?"

"I'm sorry, he is out the office at present, may I help?"

"No, I must speak to Mr Saunders, or superior staff, about the matter in hand; I'm not able to leave a message with a receptionist." Gemima had that insistent, officious, and self-important tone.

"Well Gemima; I'm Sophia Hardy, I'm second lead to Mr Saunders, how may I help you?"

"I'd like to confirm the funeral arrangements for the vagrant you picked up, from St Cuthbert's, on January 9th, you may also know him as Ian Keatan. He is due to have a pauper's funeral; I can confirm the council has traced no family, so we, as a council, will fulfil our statutory obligation."

Gemima had really got my back up, but I strived to remain professional.

"Ah yes, Mr Ian Keatan, a military man, if I'm correct?"

Her jobsworth tones really started to shine through, with the final statement.

"Yes that's him, he might have been military personnel once upon a time, but at the time of death, he was a vagrant. I will need you to confirm, in writing, his basic funeral, date and time, complete with declaration of his coffin and ambulance costs. He is to have no frills.

"The crematorium will need to be a simple service, one reading and the Lord's Prayer. That is it. It will not be open to the public."

Professionalism went straight out of the window, as I transformed into a one-woman ranting monologue.

"A vagrant? I sincerely hope I heard your comments on ex-military personnel wrongly?

"Ian Keatan was 46 years old, I believe, therefore Gemima, dear, I have no doubt in my mind that he was a war veteran. Furthermore, you are to refer to such funerals as 'public health funerals', which in itself is a degrading term, yet you chose the outdated Victorian term of 'pauper's funeral', which in our modern age is inaccurate, and derogatory.

"Do you treat every case with this little respect, insisting on 'no frills'? NO FRILLS, he is a military man! I tell you what, send me the paper work, I'll declare that I take full responsibility for him!

"He fought for our country, and you want NO FRILLS, the man deserves full honours, you cannot anonymise a brotherhood with no obituary and no public access to the ceremony.

"And the Lord's Prayer... what if he isn't religious, or is an alternative faith? Just because he is a British man, it does not mean he has assumed the Christian faith.

"You, Gemima dear; are insensitive, totally unsuited to your job, and furthermore, narrow-minded; I'd go as far as to say a bigot!"

I slammed the phone down, and was greeted by a round of applause. Jacob was leant against the doorway. Toby, George, and Joanna stood looking a little surprised at my spontaneous crusade against the council.

"You've met Gemima then?" Jacob quipped.

"Hmm..." All I could do was raise an eyebrow about such a vile specimen of humanity.

I went over to Jacob for a hug; a hug I felt like I hadn't had in weeks. I needed reassurance, and to know my partner loved me. I wanted him to hug away the immense trauma that I had in my life.

"Hello darling." He kissed my forehead, wrapped his arms around me, and held me tight. "Have you walked? Your car isn't in the yard."

"I thought I'd walk, Ray was having a visit from the…" I looked over at the three of them loitering in the office.

"Hop it you three, go have a coffee break, in the café, my treat, and thanks for keeping this all together. Give us an hour." Jacob fumbled in his pocket, producing a twenty pound note to Joanna. Joanna handed Hope over to Jacob in exchange, he started rocking her and cooing. It made my ovaries skip a beat, the prospect of him being the father to my babies one day, made me fall in love with him a little bit more.

"Hello Hope, how are you?"

Seeing him interact with her, made me incredibly broody, he would be a fantastic father, and I was desperate to share that with him, when the time was right for us.

"I walked, you're right; I thought I'd give Ray the space, while the doctor visited. I wanted him to open up, I didn't think he'd do that if Hope was there, making him feel guilty, if he said he wasn't coping and was having trouble bonding with her, which he is."

"I'll head over later, and do the man thing; did you enjoy your walk?"

"Enjoy my walk? NO, I had a barney in the middle of the village, with these four **horrible**ladies!"

"I know you did, we were driving out to Merriweather, and George saw you shouting at them. I couldn't stop, I didn't recognise you, or even expect to see you, with a pushchair, but it suits you."

"They were vile, really degrading to Ray as a father, and Hope too. They even asked if we'd adopt Hope, as Ray would always look at her and blame her for Helen's death. Hence my wrath. They even kept saying blood poisoning and sepsis were the same. Morons!"

"So, your solution was to shout at four nosey old ladies. Yep, that fiery, reactionary personality is you all over."

"Anyway, it's done with." I said, changing the subject. "Can you head over tonight, after work, he'll open up to you more, I'm sure. I think we should give him a couple more days' space, and then he's going to have to get it together, for Hope's sake. So, tonight and tomorrow, Hope will come to Keeper's Cottage for a sleepover. I've missed my bed, and I've missed you."

Jacob went over as planned, and Ray opened up as we'd hoped. He was scared; scared he wouldn't be good enough for Hope, that he couldn't fill Helen's shoes, and that Hope wouldn't get enough love. He promised Jacob he'd get himself together, and be a daddy to Hope, he'd find his way on his own, but could we promise to be there? He had no one, he felt so lonely and isolated. My heart shattered at his desperate honesty.

Of course we'd be there for him, I wasn't going to abandon him and Hope, I owed that much to Helen. Helen and Ray had entrusted us to be Hope's guardians, like God Parents but non-religious. I was honoured at such a question, now I felt my duty was far more important after Helen's passing, I would do anything for her, so in turn, I'd do anything for Ray and Hope.

Baby Bramwell stayed with us for two nights. On Wednesday, it was market day in Wimpleton, I was going to take Hope home before teatime, so I thought I'd head in to town and get us some delicious homecoming treats. It would give Ray the day to finish anything he needed to complete, and a chance to relax before bedtime. He and Hope needed to reacquaint themselves, before being left alone for the night.

I went into Wimpleton with mother, I told her all about my challenging the council, and how I'd taken responsibility for Ian Keatan; she looked in disbelief at my shouting fit to the delightful Gemima.

We were at the cheese stall; I thought one of our ploughman's suppers would be a good way to celebrate my homecoming, that evening.

"Hello Judy." A lady greeted my mother, who had hold of the pram, while I was served.

"Hello Brenda." I turned round, and managed to deduce, from anecdotal evidence from mother, that this was Brenda from Ladies Circle.

"Brenda, this is my daughter, Sophia."

"I didn't know you had a grandchild Judy, congratulations Sophia. What's her name?"

"No no no, she isn't mine, she's a friends; I'm just watching her."

I felt very sensitive about the whole scenario, I didn't want to tell a complete stranger chapter and verse, what had happened was a private matter. I couldn't go into the whys and wherefores; that my best friend was currently on ice, waiting for a cremation any day soon.

"Well, she's a bonny girl. Are you at circle on Tuesday?" Brenda inquired.

Mother said "Yes", and they both went about their own day. For what it was worth, Brenda seemed totally uninvasive, unlike some of the Ladies Circle, who had made such activities more like a coven meeting.

We went on to the meat stall; I wanted ham, specifically honey-roasted ham, and mother wanted, surprise, surprise: chops. It was mundane, but so very enjoyable.

"It suits you, you know? The pushchair. When are you and Jacob going to settle down?"

"Come on mum, it's hardly like Jacob and I are young and reckless. The most socialising I do is a one way narrative; we work hard, it's a lifestyle. We're in a happy place right now; we'll have children, one day, when the time is right."

Maybe it was a total copout, and the party line, I was well into my twenties and Jacob was knocking the door of fifty sooner rather than later, what were we truly hiding from? Marriage and children seemed to be the ultimate commitment, yet, we weren't trying to put these roots down any time in the immediate future; we lived with excuses, mainly our jobs.

The reality was though; by the time we got to that "right time" would Jacob feel he was too old? Was parenthood truly looking like it was going to pass me by? Was I content at this harsh prospect?

Hope was all packed up, and ready to go home. We'd made some ready meals for Ray; he needed to look after himself, life also needed to be as simple as possible for him. Looking after Hope, going solo for two days, was like a baptism of fire, I knew he'd need the little things, like food, taken care of; he just didn't need the added pressure.

Jacob made it home unusually early; he was making the effort for our first night together in, what felt like, weeks. His punctuality was noted as very much a positive act considering his normal approach, of playing silly beggars, he hated his time being dictated, it was an odd foible considering our profession.

The car was loaded; I was ready to make the trip in twilight, to reunite Ray and Hope. I had spoken to him earlier in the day, and he was ready to face the journey, just the two of them. I admired his strength and courage. He had come to terms that this was his lot in life, and now he had to raise Hope alone, the best he could, not only for Hope, but to honour his beautiful Helen. He knew the funeral would be the last hurdle to face, before they could fully focus on rebuilding their life.

Jacob was about to get in the car, our landline rang, mobile signal could be hit or miss here, more miss than anything. He dashed in, he was gone for less than two minutes, I was dreading his arrival back at the car, was he going to abandon us, and head out for a pick up?

"It was Joanna, the crem' have confirmed Ian Keatan's funeral."

"OK, let's get Hope home, we can address Ian's funeral tomorrow, tonight we need to be a couple, no talk of work... Have you put George and Toby on call?"

"Did I bring the ambulance home? No, I didn't, tonight is about us!"

The drive to Merton Major left me feeling anxious, I wanted to help Ray, but knew he had to find his own way. Hope was not my child, and I couldn't be there for him at the drop of a hat, my career was suffering enough, and I was living on a wage, for little to no work, the last couple of weeks. No other employer would stick for such behaviour, so why should I take advantage, just because it was my boyfriend's family? Although, after the sale of Pom's house, Dad insisted I take care of my future, he was adamant I sought professional advice. One of my investments was into Saunders and Son. I was more willing to take advantage than previously, I had a voice in exactly what went on, that included my working hours, I had the flexibility, and I had used it appropriately, it was a genuine need for Ray and Hope. I was Jacob's equal, nothing more, nothing less. Equal.

Ray was at the window, waiting, as we pulled up. He came to the door; he stood on the top step, not moving. I was willing him to move, to come and greet Hope. I went bounding over with Hope, in the car seat; he moved over to let me through. What was he playing at? He should have taken Hope off me. Already he seemed disengaged, like he was just talking the talk.

Wow! That momentary doubt was for nothing, he had done us proud. Ray had made a home for him and Hope, walking into the living room, his efforts shone through. Her Moses basket had a place by his armchair, so he could nurse her, he'd put the nest of tables the other side. You could see he had taken the time to think about it. On his window seat, he had lined up three baskets, totally blowing me away with his dedication to being a successful parent: one for nappies and spare clothes, so he never had to leave Hope alone, one for blankets, and one for toys. He'd even set the baby gym up on the floor for play time.

He explained this all to me, as he gave me an orientation of his living room, he was buzzing. I hadn't even had the chance to get Hope out of her car seat. Ray had taken on a positive tone, I was encouraged by this, all I could do was wish him every success, and be there if he needed me.

"Well, we'd better see if Hope approves of your efforts…"

I bent down to unbuckle Hope, when Jacob piped up, "Sophia, I need your help."

He placed his hand on my shoulder to indicate I should stop what I was doing; it was his subtle way of saying, "DO NOT take over".

"Well Hope, your Daddy has been working incredibly hard for you, and I think it's about time he showed you what he's been up to."

I turned to Ray as I stood up and backed away from the car seat.

"She's all yours, Daddy."

I walked into the kitchen, and mouthed, "Thank you." at Jacob.

Ray picked Hope out of her car seat, cradling her in his arms; you could see how scared he was, as his arms occasionally shook. He walked her over to his chair, lowering himself down cautiously. He held her like she was the only person in the world that existed. He lowered his lips to her head, softly placing a kiss on her forehead, took a deep breath in, and the weight of the world momentarily dissipated, as Hope's return started to heal his wounds.

I was a wreck. I cried in relief, I knew he was going to love her. I could barely make her formula, trying to level the scoops as I wiped my tears. I got to see this beautiful moment between father and daughter, and Helen didn't, it was bittersweet in the extreme.

"Well daddy, you have a good night with Hope. I've made her bottles for you, and left your dinner on the side. Call us if you need anything."

I didn't go down the whole gushing route, with the, "We are so proud of you." speech, it would have felt condescending. I left Ray in the chair, with his baby daughter in his arms. I left them to be a family. While it wasn't the ideal family they expected of mum, dad and child, they still looked beautiful.

Chapter Eight

Sophia and Jacob

Jacob and I headed back to Keeper's Cottage, where I had supper prepared. It was long overdue to spend the night together, uninterrupted. I wanted to sit in front of the fire, relax, and just watch the flames roar. Television didn't really have a place in our life; we never completed a series, as someone else always had better plans for us. We lay the coffee table with food to pick at, along with the teapot and two cups, I always used the same cup, Jacob could never find his so it was whatever was spare; it was a habit of his I found irritating at best. Tonight however, it was a well-deserved rest.

I nuzzled into Jacob; and he ran his fingertips along my right side. I closed my eyes as I slipped my hand up his jumper and was rubbing his hairy, grey-flecked chest. I looked up at him; his eyes always looked magnificent with the reflection of the fire. I yearned for him, I desired him. It felt like the first night we ever slept together, all over again, only now I was in love with him, it was certainly more intense, especially as we looked to enhance our life together.

Feeling his skin against mine, gave me butterflies. His hands wandered inside my top, the flats of his hands gliding under my bra, he cupped my breasts, lightly squeezing them, in a massaging way, while moving up to my nipples. He placed them between his thumb and index finger, rubbing his fingertips back and forth. My nipples immediately became pert with the stimulation.

I could feel Jacob had grown hard in his pants; I lifted myself off him, his hands falling from under my bra, with a playfully disappointed look on his face. I got off the sofa and knelt between his legs, removing my bra by unclasping it and pulling it through the v-neck on my dress. My nipples showing their outline through the fabric, he rubbed his palms over the red jersey, I positively shuddered with the tingle he created.

I spread his knees wide, resting my arms on his upper thighs; I leant forward, pulled his leather belt tight, and loosened off the buckle. His chinos had three antique-gold coloured buttons, I popped them open. Top... middle... bottom. He lifted himself, so I could slip his trousers under his bottom and thighs, down to his ankles, the belt buckle made a clink on the stone floor. Gliding them over his sizeable feet, I tossed them to the side, with a crumpling sound on the rug, and a few gentle thuds of whatever was in his pockets that night. I crossed my arms, pinching my dress fabric at the waist, and I pulled it clear over my head, dropping it to the side of me; the excited glint in his eyes telling me that he wanted me, every bit as much as I wanted him.

I leant into Jacob, his balls fitting neatly into my cleavage. My hands ran down his torso, from his shoulders to his pubic line, I repeated this several times, up and down. Up and down. I started to kiss his belly, pecking all the way down his inner thigh, slowly, tantalisingly, round to his balls, licking his scrotum with the tip of my tongue, flicking it.

I placed teasing kisses on his stomach and thighs, working every inch of him, before my lips grazed the tip of his hard throbbing dick. I licked the whole length of him, back and forth, back and forth. I maintained eye contact, so he knew I was all in it for him. I wrapped my right hand around his shaft, moving it up and down in time with my mouth.

I always knew when Jacob was excited, as he would grab a handful of my hair, thrusting back into my mouth hard. I didn't want him to come yet, I wanted him to be gagging for me. I pulled away and decided I'd give him a little floor show...

Jacob sat erect on the sofa. I got up, turned, and worked my bottom towards his face, as I walked to the opposite end of the sofa, sitting myself down. I raised my knee up and rested it against the back cushions; I kept my other foot on the floor, splaying my legs open, so he got a glimpse. I was adamant he was going to get maximum pleasure through voyeurism, it wasn't very often we got time to play. Sexual relations between us were normally were quite mechanical, quick and straight to the point. I knew I loved Jacob, that we had a future together, we had years ahead of us, and changing up the routine could only benefit the relationship, heightening excitement.

I started to rub myself, from my thighs right up to my stomach, running my palms over my nipples and caressing my breasts. I worked my body for a couple of minutes to heighten sensitivity; I looked at Jacob, gave him a wink and moved one hand down to my crotch. Rubbing my clit through the grey lace of my French cut panties, it was very much, you can look but you can't touch. I wanted to be that forbidden fruit Jacob was hankering for. I softly slipped the tip of my finger into my pants, finding the opening of my pussy, stroking upwards towards my clitoris. After every stroke, removing my finger and returning it to the start; when I wanted to add a level of intensity I'd introduce another finger. I was starting to feel truly moist. I took my ring finger, and using my natural lubrication, I pressed the tip into myself, covering it in my juices. More and more, I slid my fingers in deeper, faster, fuller, deeper still. I ran my fingers along my vaginal walls, exploring where gave me the most pleasure. The addition of my final finger was most welcome, as I pulled my fingers in and out, in and out. I arched them into a curled, hook-like position, ready to probe my g-spot. I began to make a beckoning motion with my inserted fingers, their tips grazing over my spot. I varied the pressure to heighten my stimulation.

I was teetering on the edge; I hoped Jacob desperately wanted to plough his hard throbbing cock right into me.

I assumed he'd finish the "job" and bring me to a piquing scream, so we could reaffirm those chemical and emotional bonds.

I pulled my dripping fingers out of my pussy; and Jake leant over and wrapped his lips around them, working them to the back of his throat, tonguing them all the way, tasting my intimate flavour as he cleaned them of every drop. Popping my fingers out of Jacob's mouth, I pulled him in tight so I could kiss his mouth. Tasting myself on his lips, it was the closest I'd ever got to a lesbian kiss; it was an undeniable turn on. While our tongues played with each other, I cupped his balls, giving intermittent squeezes, just to remind him...

With no hesitation, Jake stripped me of my knickers, ripping them off me like a cave man, flinging them across the room. Jacob worked his way down my body; he placed my left nipple in his mouth, stimulating it with sucks, varying the intensity, while he complimented these actions with his fingers tugging at my right nipple.

Leaving my nipples, he placed the tip of his tongue deep into my wet pussy, he moved in an upwards motion, lapping up all my wetness, paying particular attention to my bulging, throbbing clit, before pulling away, and repeating. He continued until he had me at the knife's edge.

I clenched a handful of his hair, pulling him roughly away. He had that look, smug, playful, and knowing.

I just wanted to remind Jacob how much I was gagging for him once more. I licked my lips. On my knees, in a cow-like position, on our sofa, I accentuated the arch in my back, and lowered my upper half down towards his hard erection, my nipples now tantalised by the texture of the fabric on the cushions. I opened my mouth wide, placing the tip of his penis just inside, barely covered. I rocked my body, bobbing my head closer to his pubic bone in a shallow motion, I did this one, two, three, four, five, six, seven times, on the eighth motion I went full deep throat.

The next cycle, I shallowly sucked, one, two, three, four, five, six, deep throat, one, two. I tried to maintain eye contact. Shallowly, one, two, three, four, deep throat, one, two, three, four. Then finally, deep throat, one, two, three, four, five, six, seven, eight. Jacob was ready to blow his load, he had that subtle taste, indicating he was imminent; he pulled out of my mouth rapidly.

He flipped me over, onto my stomach; so I was now face-down. He placed his hands under my hips, his palms pulling me towards him, as he drew my hips up, he edged himself inside me. Starting the tempo slowly, he held me tight, his fingertips over my hipbones and his thumbs on my buttock cheeks. He was in total control. I loved the feeling of his bodyweight against mine, all six foot three and 18 stone, 4 pounds of him, thrusting against me. His balls slapping against me, Jacob bent over, whispering in my ear.

"I want to fuck you hard."

I was flexible enough in this position to turn round to see his face. We kissed, long and intensely.

"I love you sweetheart."

"I love you too Jacob."

The momentum was increasing; Jacob had leant right over me, grabbing my shoulders, pulling them back, he was growing in intensity as he entered me bareback and throbbing. The tempo was soaring, the thrusting became harder, the frequency more, more, more.

I was panting into a cushion.

"Huh, Huh, HUH."

I was so, so close, I only hoped Jacob was too. I had to suppress the screams of enjoyment; our elderly ghillie knocking at the door would be far from ideal.

I'd peaked; I had that giveaway tone and phrase.

"Oh, oh, oh, ohhh." as I exhaled with euphoria.

Jacob grabbed my hair by the fistful; he slowed the pace right down, with three long, hard thrusts.

"Urgh, urgh, URGH."

He gasped with sheer relief, panting himself.

"Oh wow, oh my, Sophia, what a floor show."

He kissed me, lovingly, adoringly, like I was the only woman in existence.

"Gosh, I love you."

I was at heightened sensitivity, we wrapped up in the throw, and we spent the night in each other's arms. We'd needed a session of good, honest hard fucking, to be one again. We both knew we'd neglected each other. Now we sat, attuned to each other, in jubilation. Life had been so on top of us, but we had fully relaxed now, calm seemed to swamp my body.

Jacob woke me up; it was ten to one in the morning. We'd fallen asleep on the sofa. I savoured the moments that lead to our slumber. Reluctantly, I climbed up the staircase, wrapped in just the throw, it was cold; the wind whistled in the bottom corner of the stairwell window where it had started to rot; the harsh cold wind swirling around my body reminded me, I needed a carpenter to quote for the repair.

Getting into my own bed, naked, next to Jacob, was perfect. The alarm would go off in four and a half hours. They would be four and a half hours of endorphin-induced contentment.

Chapter Nine

Helen Elizabeth Bramwell

Helen had always been a prepared person; I had no hesitation in guessing this was due to her parents' death, and her having to survive as independently as possible. She was one for provisions. Ray had mused over the facts, that as soon as they were married, Helen had them take out wills, where there were clear instructions on what Ray was to do in the event of her death. In true Helen style, no detail would be left out; she would have her instructions, in the finest of details.

Helen's prepared nature was one to be admired, she was pragmatic, she didn't want anyone to know of her funeral, unless they were of significance in her life, she wanted her funeral to be exclusive. It was typical Helen to want an "A list" funeral; I loved that, even in death, she was still running the show. Helen was not one to tolerate fakery, or the gossip. She was down to earth, humble. There was no one like Helen. I couldn't imagine life without her, she was like the older sister I'd missed most of my life.

The pomp and ceremony was undesired, no readings, no hymns, no songs. She wanted a small window of contemplation, and then for her nearest and dearest to move on with life.

Helen had left her wishes in the hands of Jimmy Powell, it was long before we had become friends, I hadn't taken offence, neither of us had. In some ways, after the debacle with Pom, which had left me feeling drained, and the wedge that it created between Jacob and me, it was a blessed relief that I could mourn Helen as my best friend, not a client who had personal ties, with the world looking on. I knew though, the whole process would leave me conflicted.

I found it hard not to interfere, I couldn't detach myself from the fact it was another company taking the lead. Jimmy and I differed in our approach, there was no denying that, Ray had requested that I had an input, he was scared to be doing this alone. Jacob had reservations when I worked towards the funeral at Powell's, he thought I'd end up having a ruckus with Jim, over something trivial, and then I'd bring Helen home to Saunders.

I knew and loved Helen, but these were her wishes, they were plain and clear from the outset. I would be disloyal to her if I waded in and changed her vision; she had made deep-rooted plans, influenced by experience I couldn't possibly identify with. As much as it galled me at times, I let Jimmy fulfil his duty, without prejudice.

Helen had requested that no one view her body, I admired her decision, she wanted Ray to remember her as living person, and not in a box. Helen, saw both her parents bodies at 17 years old, and it haunted her. I knew she had some form of post-traumatic stress disorder, and she had touched on therapy a couple of times in her life.

She found it hard to understand how I was not a wreck, dealing with this every day of my working life, how I could come home and switch my feelings off for the evening. The truth was, I didn't switch off, I learnt to deal with them, and used every day as a reminder, we only had one life.

The morning of Helen's funeral, I put on the same clothing as I wore to Pom's funeral. I needed differentiation that Helen was my friend, and I was allowed to grieve her loss freely today. I looked at myself in the mirror, I had to change. Pom's funeral was a million miles away from Helen's, if I didn't make the effort she'd only come back and haunt me. With that, the forest green, retro dress it was. Helen adored my pink trainers, so I paired them up with the dress, she would be totally forgiving and 100% supportive of my eclectic attire. As I left the bedroom, I met Jacob on the landing.

"Not your usual funeral attire, Sophia, however, it's beautifully in keeping with you and Helly; She'd love it." Jake softly lay a kiss upon my cheek.

I was anxious, I think it was the not being in control that made me sick to my stomach, but it wasn't how it felt with Pom. Jacob had to go over to Powell's, to deliver the hand tied flowers, to dress Helen's coffin. He'd be about half an hour, there and back; if he had enough time, he'd pop in the office. I knew Jacob wouldn't let me down, but I did have the momentary, "What if he gets distracted?"

I decided to sit on the toilet, while I cradled my tummy, hoping the feeling would subside. Knowing my luck, today of all days, my period would happen; I leant into the bathroom drawer to grab supplies whilst I thought of it, ready for my handbag. I couldn't recall the last time I had a period.

I knew there was a test in the drawer too, the second one after the last scare a few months before hand. With Pom's death, I had forgotten to renew my prescription for the pill, when Jacob had returned from his trip to Italy, the first night back at Keeper's cottage, was makeup sex, that then lead to a possible pregnancy. Jacob was livid I had been so irresponsible, but was forgiving as to my faux pas in the circumstances. No doubt, this lack of period was due to the amount of current stress, it would screw anyone's body up.

Three minutes later, and there they were, two lines, glaring back at me.

Jacob had arrived home, punctual, for once. I was dumbfounded; it was a great juxtaposition for life, AGAIN.

"Look in the bathroom." I said, dazed.

He came back out, holding the test, studying it intently.

"You're pregnant! That's fantastic news darling and exactly where we want to be in life. I can't wait to share this with you."

"Yep, I'm not talking about it today!" I was adamant today was not about me.

We left it at that.

Jacob and I met Ray and Hope at his house; we travelled together, to the crematorium in Wilton Bishop. Silently, there were no words, how could there be? The backdrop of the journey, rolling on past, as if it were a silent movie.

We entered the chapel. There she waited for us, her tiny willow coffin, draped in the flowers I hand-tied the night before, I looked down at my hands, scratched and bloodied by the thorns that dug my hands as I wrapped the raffia around the stems.

Ray couldn't keep it together, Jacob stood back and held Hope, I kept glancing at him, knowing he'd be a wonderful father; I inwardly cursed myself as my attention flitted to our positive future. How could I be so cold today of all days? Whilst I comforted Ray, all he could say, over and over again, was "Why Helen, why did you leave me? I love you."

After about 15 minutes, Ray was ready to leave; I made a final promise to Helen that I'd look after them both. She didn't want a wake, and there was no provision left for one, her argument was, the money was best off in Ray's pocket, rather than spending it unnecessarily. Her instructions were to go home, be together as friends around a pot of tea, and of course, the obligatory packet of biscuits; if we really wanted to give her a final toast, there was a bottle of port stashed in the pantry.

That's what we did; we went to the Bramwell's and did what we always did best, put the world to rights over a good brew and a biscuit. It was the most original funeral I as an undertaker had ever been too, and as always Helen brought her own unique perspective. Cuddling Hope, she was the life we must all focus on now...

Chapter Ten

Ian Henry Keatan

Jacob had become quiet over the last 10 days; we had been manic, with Helen's funeral and Ian Keatan's. I think, on reflection, being able to support Ray and Hope in their needs had actually done us both the world of good. Being detached, participating as friends, rather than directors, had given us the focus we needed for Ian Keatan's funeral.

Ian's funeral had give Saunders and Son some serious press coverage, which we hadn't foreseen. Some of the old boys, soldiers from his old regiment, who we were fortunate enough to have made contact with, which wouldn't have been possible if it wasn't for Dougie Moreton down at the local Legion. From the photo of Ian's tattoo, on his lower right forearm; Dougie managed to trace his regiment, they had very few details, no next of kin on his records. I had pinned all my hopes on his military records letting him be reunited with family, but nothing. No one had heard of Ian Keatan, in the locality of Fremmington Ayshe.

The old boys, had tipped off the local press, about the injustice and prejudice Ian had received, when he had served Queen and Country. It even reached regional news; how some of the national papers ran with it, I had no idea.

The day before his funeral, Jacob was met at the office by police officers. I had done the final preparations for Ian, I felt responsible for him, Jacob was not entirely impressed at my desire to entangle myself with Ian, he refused to go near the body, this was my quarrel, not his allegedly, and as he wasn't consulted, he wanted to absolve himself of all responsibility now and in the future, where this case was concerned.

I felt guilty, I hadn't traced his loved ones, and no one had the chance to kiss him goodbye, one last time. Feeling deflated I had tightened the final brass screw, and he was ready for his final parade.

I couldn't help but ponder over the tattoo on his upper left arm; had I seriously missed a crucial clue as to who should be by his side tomorrow? But it was just initials, for all I knew it could have been an old girlfriend, or it could be a parent. With no hard evidence, who could it be using the initials "R.H.G"?

The lettering was hard to decipher, with the amount of scaring around it. There was the lasting marks of war, not only here, where his records confirmed a bullet wound, but all up his abdomen, small clusters of tissue scars thanks to shrapnel, a long vertical wound on his leg, it wasn't documented what happened in that instance. Every mark told a story, but nothing would let me write his final chapter.

There was no trace of anyone in his military records. They were as anonymous as Ian. I knew, in years to come, I could be answering questions as to what had happened; my meticulous note keeping was more crucial than ever, it felt.

I had locked the chapel door, and I was greeted by the three musketeers: Joanna, George, and Toby; they looked a little sheepish.

"You need to go to the office, immediately, no questions asked." George had been nominated spokesperson.

"Is this some sort of joke, I have old boys to ring, for tomorrow's funeral, I have no time for playing silly beggars!"

"We've been banished, a couple of blokes in black suits, you know, the thug sort of look, demanded Jacob get you in the office and everyone else was to, 'Do one'. Don't shoot me, I'm only the messenger!" George put his hands up, in mock surrender.

I rummaged in a pocket and pulled out some cash, "Here's a twenty, and I expect a slice of carrot cake brought back from the café."

I was furious, how dare unknown parties come into my office and command my staff about, and for Jacob to be compliant, what was he playing at?

I marched the 50 yards to the office, my blood bubbling, simmering. I strode in, and there they were, sat in the family chairs. An older, balding chap, with pale skin, slim, but in some way slightly menacing, and a younger, tanned, stockier man, with short-cropped dark hair, they wore almost identical suits, creased in a way that suggested they spent a lot of time sat down. Together they looked rather heavy in demeanour. I actually screwed my head on momentarily, they could be clients, unlikely, but they could be...

"Good afternoon, gentlemen. Jacob. How may we help you in your time of need?"

"No Miss, it's not arrangements we need to talk to you about..." The older man started, before I cut him off, eager to get to the point.

"OK Sir, my mistake, I'm sorry."

I looked Jacob straight in the eye; he looked wary as to my next move. He knew how worked up Ian's funeral had made me.

"Then what the BLOODY HELL is going on Jacob? Who dares to boss our staff around in such a bullying manner?"

"Darling, sit down, listen to me..."

"Sit down? Not on this earth! Not until I know exactly who these men are!" I proclaimed.

"SIT DOWN SOPHIA; or I will sit you down. God damn it, for once in your life, will you not be so reactionary. SIT DOWN!"

I sat down, feeling suitably chastised, I'd never seen Jacob so forceful.

"They warned us about you." The balding bloke chuckled.

"I'm sorry, who warned you about me?"

"Special Branch; we heard the council recording. You know the one, where you, hmm tell her, the girl, in no uncertain terms, to 'stick it' over the pauper's funeral."

"Am I hearing this correctly, Special Branch? Really? Pull the other one. Why would Special Branch be interested in the funeral of an ex-soldier?"

"He spent a lot of time in Ireland, need I say more? You have four new pallbearers, that's the only deviation you need be concerned with. We'll take care of the rest. My men will be here tomorrow morning, eight o'clock sharp."

He upped and walked out, with his younger colleague close on his heels. I was stupefied, dumbfounded. This was a soldier who died on the streets of Wimpleton, not a man who... I wasn't really sure what they were alluding to, I didn't think I even wanted to know.

On the day of Ian's funeral, I was greeted by old boys from his regiment, who had graciously provided regimental flags, and flowers in matching colours. I was incredibly thankful for them, reaching out and providing such honours to their fallen brother. The whole funeral had made me feel so very alone. Their gestures made the momentary isolation, feel worth every second, to be part of the brotherhood in a fleeting part of life.

Hope of Ray

I was trying not to be jumpy, but every man on the periphery of the service had me wondering; was he one of them? As the pigeons stirred in the trees, I was instantly looking over my shoulder. Getting into the hearse, the dread came rushing to the fore, my overreaction this time, towards the council, was, potentially, career suicide, if not it was my own.

Jacob decided at the twelfth hour to bottle it. I went alone, none of my normal team around me. Jacob had refused to let any staff attend on the grounds of safety.

I thanked my lucky stars that we finished the day without a hitch. How we came out of Ian's funeral with our reputation still fully intact was questionable, after the previous day's revelations, I was eternally grateful that the papers didn't get wind of the conversation in our office the previous day. Tomorrow would be a new start.

The following morning, Jacob and I had travelled to work separately; I still had a sour taste in my mouth over his actions, and his lack of moral support. It was Wednesday, so I would go into Wimpleton for market day, and Jacob would expect the indulgent ploughman's supper we liked so much. Maybe we'd even get chance to discuss our future, our baby and celebrate the news finally.

He was going to meet an estate agent, and look at acquiring a small plot of land out towards Beckley Heath, maybe another building project, two cottages if possible. If it was right for us, we'd add to our portfolio, for our family's future. We'd finally be a family, just the three of us, maybe one day a brother or sister to our heir or heiress. I had no doubt Jacob would negotiate a dog into the deal.

It was always refreshing when we did our separate things; we could still be our own people. I bought a book from a market stall, on this occasion, its cover caught my eye; I'd never heard of the author, but I was intrigued nonetheless.

I arrived home early, but just like every other day, I put my keys on the console table in the hall; the picture from Amy's christening was missing. I assumed Jacob must have knocked it off, maybe breaking the glass. It was there this morning, when we left for work, maybe he had been home during the day.

I headed into the kitchen, with my basket of goodies; he'd definitely been home, there was a note on the table.

Dear Sophia,

I love you. I loved you from the moment you walked into the office at 18 years old. I loved the way you'd sneak books in your bag, hoping no one would notice, I was always blown away by the titles you'd read to extend your knowledge. I was in awe of you.

The day we spent at Miltonbury Cathedral, I remembered the book you had read on it a few months previously. Its cover faded, the sleeve bent and ripped. I was curious where you found that book, once I knew the real you, it was easy to work out you got it from the church jumble, when you spent precious time with your dear Pom (I had never experienced love like you showed your grandfather, I wished I had such a constant in my life, maybe I'd have been a better person with such an example.)

As our time together became greater, I was saddened, that maybe I had expected too much from you, and now I never saw you with a book in your hand. Maybe I have stifled your growth?

Your drive and passion for a family to have a final rite of passage for their loved one was faultless, I often wished I could be like you, where you fight for your beliefs, no matter what the consequences. You certainly brought turbulence into my life in so many forms; Ian being a prime example. That's a story for the grandchildren.

Your raw passionate attitude for people you don't love or know blows me away, but it also makes me realise just how lucky the people you do love are, to have you in their lives. Helen couldn't have asked for a better best friend. Seeing you with Hope, I have no doubt what an amazing mother you will be, no one will mess with the innocence of a child of yours. That's honourable, but I can't live up to those expectations.

Your reactionary behaviour is lioness, things haven't been good between us in recent weeks; I thought the baby would bring us closer together again, but it hasn't.

I'm filled with fear, there isn't enough love in your heart for the both of us, and the lioness in you clearly demonstrates, there's no room in the pack for an alpha male by your side. I couldn't bring our child up, with the lack of respect and fear of recrimination.

For the sake of our child, we cannot be parents together, so I'll walk away now, before I bond and wait for my world to crumble, be that in a year or ten years.

Before you get self-righteous, I know I am destroying my own family without ever giving it a chance.

Drawing a line in the sand now, can only be in the best interests of our child.

Don't call the police, I am not going to do anything stupid, I am walking away with my honour intact.

I love you Sophia, and I will to the end of my days, but love isn't enough for our child. I can't be the father you desire. I'm sorry, I wanted it all with you and now reality has hit. I can't do it.

In time, please forgive me.

Jacob x

He'd taken his battered old satchel, a few clothes, and the photo from the hall table. My life had gone from wholesome to destroyed in one letter.

I couldn't be reading this, was life really that cruel, to gut-punch me, and then, while already winded, slam my face down into the gutter. I couldn't face the truth. I didn't want to face life without Jacob; he was my life, my everything. It was like an instant bereavement.

I rationalised that he was just spooked about the baby; that life had gone speeding on faster than we had planned. Maybe we should have spoken about it the day of Helen's funeral, but as usual, life had taken over and we had a different focus, words were left unspoken.

I made his excuses, for the immediate future, he had gone away on secondment, helping out a colleague we knew up country. It was a ridiculous tale, but one that, hopefully, bought him enough time to return home, and keep his dignity intact.

Jacob's words were harsh, they hurt, I didn't want to tell anyone of his letter, it wasn't the Jacob I loved and respected writing that, I was sure he was deliberately being vile, trying to push me away. All he had to do was come home, we could work it out; it was a tiny bump in our relationship, we'd had plenty of them and survived.

I spent the evenings rattling round Keeper's Cottage; I'd hide away in our bed, wrapped in the safety of our duvet, the duvet I refused to wash, as his smell slowly faded away. I read book after book, to keep me company, to stop my thoughts imploding.

My own company gave me time to grieve the loss of Jacob, it was no different to Pom, or Helen, the pain I felt. As I cried myself to sleep, I rubbed my belly, apologising for everything I had created, that my baby wouldn't have a daddy, and I couldn't stop it. I let it all out, bawling in the privacy of our home.

He'd never let me down in my hour of need, and I was certain he'd never let our child down. I left him text messages, and voice mails, telling him all this, pleading with him to come home, reasoning with him, declaring my undying love for him... NOTHING!

Chapter Eleven

Ray

I headed over to Ray's. He needed help shopping for Hope, I don't think he realised, until now, how much Helen did, and that he, like most men I guess, didn't have a handle on the domestic front with children. He had no idea just how quickly Hope had grown.

Jacob had been gone for weeks; he'd made no contact at all. I'd come to be ashamed of my desperate attempts to reason with him, still calling every day, until the day it all came pouring out to Ray. I hated Jacob, he was the bastard that said he wanted the world with me, and as soon as the dream became reality, he ran. Yet here I was still lying for him, protecting him so no one thought ill of him, maybe I hoped he'd get it together and come home.

I was still making the excuse he was on secondment, out of area, working with a friend. He'd been gone so long now the story was becoming weak.

I made a silent vow to myself, that day, not to call again. I was better than that. I was strong, independent, I was Sophia Hardy. Life had crushed me, but I picked myself up and carried on.

I was feeling the daily effects of pregnancy, I wanted to crumble, blurt it all out, but I wouldn't, in case he came home, or so I made myself believe. Reality was, I was too ashamed to admit that I was knocked up and fatherless. I wished, even prayed he'd come home, his absence clearly demonstrated he couldn't give a monkey's.

I was now having an up close and personal relationship with the toilet, several times a day, he wasn't there to support me, hold my hair back, or pass me a flannel to wipe my mouth. He had never reminded me to take my folic acid. The days of just muddling through, living off my nerves were dwindling, I felt incredulous about Jacob's actions.

I went into Ray's house, like I normally did, I opened the door with a, "Morning shoppers."

Ray and Hope were nearly ready; he was just packing up the baby bag. It still baffled Ray how much to put in the baby bag, he was one for extremes; I guess he would improve with practice.

I felt nauseous; I was trying to play it down, as I still wasn't ready to talk about it. No one knew about the baby, it was still early days, I wanted to protect my baby, and bond with them, without the increasing level of questioning that would follow.

"Sorry, just got to go to the loo, should have gone before I left home." I tried to deliver as casually as possible, while I dashed through the house, with a dive and skid into the bathroom, popping my head into the loo, delightfully trying to yak up quietly. All I could think was, "Please, don't let Ray hear me!" his house had paper-thin walls.

I was retching, but my stomach was empty, I hadn't entertained breakfast that morning, my body was doing the motions, yet nothing was materialising, my stomach ached. I hadn't had time to lock the door, Ray silently swung it open, he must have watched for a few seconds, I turned for the loo roll, to dab my mouth, and with that I heard Hope babble, I craned my neck round to see him. He had that look in his eye, just like the first day we met; it was that silent apology, an acknowledgement of empathy to my plight.

"Are you OK?" Ray enquired.

I took his asking as acceptance, like he understood.

"I'm pregnant, and the bastard's left me!"

I sobbed; it was like a floodgate had opened. I trusted Ray and he'd have no judgement. The tsunami of tears followed.

"He's what? He's left you!"

Ray offered his hand out, to help me up; I pulled myself up off the floor, and composed myself. Ray, like the kind soul he was, gave me a side cuddle and offered up some empathy, in his stilted manly way.

"Come downstairs, this involves tea, by the bucket load; I'll pop the kettle on. Here, hold Hope, you'll need the practice now."

He gave me that glint, and a jovial tone.

Now I had opened the floodgate, I knew we weren't going to leave, until detective Ray was satisfied with his questioning.

"Did I hear you right, he's left you? He's actually left you, pregnant and alone? WOW!" He scoffed.

"He has done some pretty wayward shit in his life, and gone off the rails, but hands down this has to be the lowest I've seen him sink. What a bastard!"

Ray was brewing up. He'd gone to the fridge for milk, it was pretty empty, and he was trying to block my view. I walked up behind him and pulled him away with my hand on his shoulder, pulling him back as I went from my tiptoes back to flat feet.

"Your fridge is empty, what's going on Ray?"

"I need to get some shopping; I've just been a bit lapse, with the sleepless nights."

"OK, we can pop into the supermarket on the way home, or better still, we can cut the shopping down and get Hope's clothes there too. How does that sound?"

Ray never acknowledged my suggestion; he just flipped the spotlight straight back onto me.

"When did he leave? He's not on secondment, is he? Why did you lie to me? You know you could have told me, I'd have been there for you."

"I realised I was pregnant the day of Helen's funeral. I wasn't going to say anything; I'd played it down as emotions of the day. When I was here, helping you out with Hope, I hadn't taken my pill, it didn't even occur to me with everything else going on.

"The night I returned Hope home to you, and you had it all together, I was so happy, I felt content. Jake and I went home and one thing lead to another. He got the floorshow of his life, it was the first sex we'd had in weeks, with all the drama of work, and bam! I got caught."

Ray was cringing at my candidness.

"For Christ sakes Sophia; it's not Helen you are talking to, she gave me no formal training on how to handle conversations like this." Ray replied, in good spirits.

"Yep, and all I want is her here, to tell me it's going to be OK. That he's a total knob, and doesn't deserve me. That it'll hurt like hell, pushing a tiny human out my lady garden, and instead I get you, the rookie to all things female."

"I can offer a hug, I am proficient in those."

"I'll take one of those. Only Helen could leave me the departing gift of a lone novice parent, like you; and you her knocked up best friend. Do you think she is laughing at our expense somehow?"

We both tutted and nodded, realising what an immense gap she had left in our lives, that we loved her, and now we had a bond growing on so many levels, mainly abandonment.

We headed into the living room, to watch Hope sleep; there was nothing more peaceful and pure than a baby fast asleep, with not a care in the world. I helped bag up Hope's old clothes, and we attempted a list of what she needed, the baby handbook was referenced more than once, it was a minefield.

Ray headed towards the bathroom, so I decided to pop the kettle on once more, before we headed out. Back in the kitchen, something pricked my conscience; I had that gut feeling all wasn't right. I opened the empty fridge for milk, and moved on to execute a raid on all his cupboards, while he was detained in the toilet, they too were empty, bar a packet of cereal, a jar of jam, with barely a scraping left in it, and the two crusts of a stale loaf of bread, in a plastic bag. I crouched down to his freezer, prizing the door open, there was nothing in it, just two ice blocks rattling round.

I heard the top stair creak; I got up and acted like I hadn't stumbled across his secret. I carried on making the tea, nonchalantly.

"Shall we skip today? You've had an emotional day, and Hope is sleeping well, I don't want to disturb her."

Ray had half-heartedly made his excuses. I knew at this point he was avoiding going out, not for the sake of Hope or me; that was just convenient to avoid admitting he actually needed help.

"But Ray, you need food for dinner, I have all day. We can go when Hope is ready, I can do some laundry for you if you'd like, or whatever you need help with."

My intention was not to quiz Ray, like I had been snooping. He needed to tell me what on Earth had been going on, in his own time, I had to look after them, support them as best possible. Tact wasn't my strongest point; we were both adults, wading through our own buckets of excrement, surely if we could help each other, then why wouldn't we?

"Your cupboards are bare, Ray. Why, what's going on?"

Ray rested his head in his palms and started to bawl. He was vulnerable, it broke my heart; he dropped to a heap on the kitchen floor. I joined him, my arm around his shoulders, as I comforted this broken man.

"I'm broke. I'm on the bones of my arse. I haven't been able to work since having Hope. Helen's funeral took what little savings we had. Now I have a choice, buy formula for Hope or feed myself. She comes first, every time."

We sat there, together, I cried for him, I was his friend, and I couldn't believe I hadn't noticed what a mess he was in. Through my blocked up face, I snuffled.

"Come home with me. You and Hope can come and stay, just for a few days. We can work out what to do. Instead of us both rattling around in empty houses, desperate for company, as we are consumed with our own self-pity, drowning in our thoughts, we can sound it out together.

"It'll be like the old days, when you and Helen would stay over, do you remember the time we made a den in the living room and slept in it all night?"

Ray nodded instantly; it was like someone had rescued him.

"Right, for a start, I'm going to need some shopping, so we'll stop off on the way back to Keeper's Cottage. I'll buy Hope the new clothes she needs and a couple of week's formula, nappies and wipes."

"Sophia, you can't support us like that, it's so very kind of you, but NO." Ray was a proud man.

"Ray, I'm not buying it for you out of pity, I'm going to need baby clothes myself, so why not just buy them off you, instead of money changing hands we just swap."

"You play a good game, Hardy."

We headed back to Fremmington Ayshe, via the supermarket, in Beckley Heath. While in the baby section, Ray looked totally out of his depth, it was awash with baby vests, short sleeve, long sleeve, sleeveless; pastels, floral, ditsy, cute animals. He had no idea on colour or patterns; he just wanted it to function.

"Wow, this really is a minefield, I have no idea, you choose, then it's your fault if Helen disapproves, she can haunt you instead of me." Ray joked.

"Well, if we get plain body suit thingies, they will go with anything, under clothes, and it won't matter. I guess then, for sleep, plain again, and then this pack of five pretty ones for jaunts out, that'll be ok won't it?"

It was the weirdest experience to date, shopping for my dead best friend's baby, with her widow. A silvery-haired old lady was in the aisle, she had on large button earrings, and a freshly blow-waved hair do. Her lipstick had bled out slightly; she had a scarf knotted to the side, with a nautical theme, and her handbag rested in the crook of her arm.

She made a comment about Hope, who was fast asleep in the trolley seat.

"What a bonny baby? What's her name?"

I looked at Ray, and reluctantly answered.

"Umm, she's called Hope."

I was cringing, I could anticipate how the conversation was moving, and I just wanted to hide in the blankets until the moment had passed.

"Well she's a beautiful baby; you must both be so proud, look after each other."

She departed, tapping Ray on the wrist as she said, "Look after each other."

We just smiled sweetly, it was awkward, but having to go into the ins and outs would have been far more uncomfortable, she really hadn't meant any malice by her comments.

This was hideous, we were friends, yet one innocent and well-intended comment had left me feeling dirty, like I was betraying Helen, I wanted to leave as quickly as possible. We threw Hope's new clothes into the trolley, and dashed around the aisles as if it were life threatening. Idiotically, we thought the self-service checkouts would be quicker than queuing; but every single item of clothing threw a customer service error, and required a staff key code. We'd have been better waiting for a regular checkout; I left the shop feeling increasingly tetchy.

Back at Keeper's Cottage, we were unloading. Opposite, lived Walter Mackey, the retired ghillie, he'd worked on the estate since he was a young lad, right up until his retirement. He'd taken Jacob out on several occasions, fly fishing, pheasant shooting, and hunting. We had gone to the Hunt Ball, in the early days of our dating. It was the November, with the theme of Alpine colour; I wore an emerald green halter neck dress with a black lace bolero. I accessorised with a dainty set of pearl earrings and pearl necklace from the 1920's which had been my grandmother's.

Walter attended to his Lordship and his guests. He was a knowledgeable man, who knew the land, he saw himself as a servant to Mother Nature, and devoted his life to serve the estate and its wild patrons. He'd never had a wife, or children, his answer was, "Lassies cause too much drama, just look at my sister."

If we happened to be home, you'd often see him roaming the estate, to pass his time. Walter was a good neighbour. He was empathetic to our jobs and unsociable hours; Walter was a man who, in the deer season, would be out in the dead of night, doing a deer census. He understood, this was our vocation; never did he moan about our comings and goings.

Walter had a sister, Maribel, a spinster, who rode her bike around the town; she couldn't drive. She visited Walter on a regular basis. Maribel liked to inject herself into other people's business, without any forethought. I'd come across her at Church, while taking Pom, she was in Ladies Circle with mum too, she liked to spout her bile and judgement, it was always hearsay, rumours, or misinformed opinion.

I knew she was at Walter's when I pulled into the drive; her bike was distinctive, with its woven, semicircular basket, black panniers, and the bell! The bell that, as soon as you heard it, would fill your body with dread, as you knew Maribel was in the vicinity. I dreaded the sight of that blasted bike, and had ever since our paths crossed in the office years previously.

Jacob and I had just started dating, it was early in our relationship, and I'd been a regular visitor to Keeper's Cottage, met Walter and formed a positive opinion of him. Maribel had come waltzing into the office one day, demanding to speak with Jacob; his comings and goings from the cottage were "antisocial", and he "needed to be more considerate of her brother". He, apparently, also needed to address the vehicle situation, as he was becoming a "nuisance". She referred then to the previous Sunday afternoon.

I turned to her in my rage, and it was rage. This was the worst weekend I had experienced, so far, with my career. I was still reeling from the call out to Bracknell Farm; it was a farm in the middle of nowhere, with dairy cows, and a famous apple orchard, they were renowned for their pressed cider.

We had been rung by the Coroner's Office. The police were at the scene, and had the body of a teenage boy. Marcus was seventeen years old, he wanted to join the forces, but his father was adamant that he was going to take over the family farm, carrying on from generations before him. Marcus wanted to be in the infantry; his father wouldn't sign his papers, and had forbidden his mother from doing so.

Marcus and his father's relationship had reached irretrievable breakdown, and Marcus saw his only escape to be suicide, he'd left a note at the foot of the tree. His mother had found Marcus' body; she was weak and downtrodden, as she endeavoured to save her only child, to no avail.

I'd never heard such a harrowing scream, as I took away a mother's child. She knelt on the floor, her hands clasped as if she were praying; she was alone, with no one to comfort her, the remnants of his noose above her head. Marcus was the last call out of the day.

Back in the office, I politely told Maribel, to stick her opinion.

"Mrs Mackey, isn't it?"

"It's Miss, actually." she barked at me.

"Miss Mackey, we have a job to do, and it involves unsociable hours; I am afraid people do not die between the hours of 9 a.m. and 5 p.m., Monday to Friday. If we have upset Walter, in any way, I can only apologise on mine and Jacob's behalf. But what we do with our work, and how we live our lives, is, quite frankly, none of your business."

"Aren't you the girl that comes to Church every Sunday, and brings that old man with you?"

"If, by 'old man', you mean Mr Walker, then yes, he's my grandfather."

"Walker aye, by any chance are you Judy Walker's daughter? She married that Hardy chap."

"YES, Mrs Mackey, they are my parents."

"It's MISS!" she snarled.

"Apart from reprimanding Jacob and me for our atrocious and inconsiderate behaviour, why are you here Mrs Mackey?"

"Jacob and me? You speak for the both of you... So you're the young bit of skirt that has his attention. Say, how do your parents feel about that one? He must be old enough to be your father. Still, his sort always want a fine young filly.

"What was so desperate that you left in such a hurry, in that van of yours, yesterday? It must have been what, the fourth time that you left in the wretched thing."

"If you think I am going to break client confidentiality for you Mrs Mackey, then I'm afraid you are sorely mistaken. PLEASE, remove yourself from my office immediately."

I made it perfectly clear; I was not going to tolerate her behaviour.

I had no time for the old witch, and refused to get entangled in her sort of behaviour, ever. When I saw her outside the cottage that evening, with Ray and Hope, I knew she wouldn't be able to resist some of sniping comment. She had her leg ready to cock it over the seat; she always pushed off with her other foot on the pedal.

"Lovely evening for it." And off she went.

'For it.' What did that mean? It wasn't that simple, as Maribel said it, Walter always went red, he couldn't stand the tension.

"Good evening Maribel." I yelled down the drive to her, as she disappeared into the sun. I always tried to be decorous, I refused to brawl with her, it was what she tried to provoke, but I refused to let her be a victim.

Chapter Twelve

Judy

"Hello?"

"Darling, what's all this I hear? You've moved Ray into Keeper's Cottage, and Jacob has left? There I was at Ladies Circle; Sarah Finney came over, I thought she was going to compliment me on my lemon meringue pie for light refreshment time, or mention my new two-piece from Marks', but oh no, she started to grill me on your, and I quote, 'nocturnal activities'.

"Well, I was flabbergasted. I mean... It's not what I expect to hear. I thought Jacob was on secondment? You were seen, you know? Unloading Ray and his offspring."

"Mother, really! I expected more of you than to buy into this type of gossiping, shame on you. Ah yes, Sarah Finney, that's right, she spends a lot of time with Maribel Mackey, they do the flowers in Church together, thick as thieves they are.

"There's a surprise, Maribel spouting her toxicity again. She is stirring, and you bought into it. More fool you mum."

"Darling, don't be like that, please? She caught me on the hop; I couldn't pour the teas after that, poor Brenda had to take over. I had to stay for the duration, knowing they were judging you, and I didn't know what to believe."

"Mum, I know their form, Maribel and I had words years ago, she likes to taint my reputation. Come over to Keeper's Cottage, you and dad; Ray is here with Hope, she'd love a cuddle. Then we can explain to you what is going on. Rest assured I am not having an affair with Ray; Helen is barely cold."

Mum and dad came over to the cottage pretty quickly. No doubt, dad would have preferred to stay home, in front of the news, rather than having to deal with charades, courtesy of Ladies Circle.

I greeted them at the door; mother had brought a 'Red Cross' parcel, she'd even mustered up a tea loaf, and a hand-knitted cardigan for Hope. She was all flustered as she gave me a peck on the cheek; she started her questioning on the doorstep, but dad was behind her, ooshing her over the threshold.

"Come on Judy, let me in, I'm out here braving all the elements woman."

My dad was a good man, he always looked as if he wasn't paying attention; he did, however, observe everything, without being obvious. He was a traditional man, he went out to work, and mother was in charge of the homestead; she had housekeeping money every week. Dad would always behave with the utmost propriety.

That evening, he walked into my living room without any bias, he greeted Ray with a handshake and a, "How you doing lad? Good to see you again."

Ray was awkward, he shouldn't have been, there was nothing to our situation other than friendship, and yet we were made to feel wrong. Mother had calmed down the rapidity of her thoughts, and was now ready to enter into a rational conversation. Dad parked himself in the wingback chair nearest the fire, it would mean he was furthest from the conversation, and could distance himself as he so desired.

Hope was in her bassinette, she was chuntering, and mum went over for a peek. "Well, can I? She is beautiful Ray. How are you both doing?"

Ray picked up Hope, and passed her over to mum for a cuddle. It broke the ice without doubt. Mum cautiously walked Hope over to the chair next to dad, sat herself down, and cuddled Hope; she treated her like the most precious and fragile object she had ever handled, I knew she'd be the most doting grandmother.

"Right then, I suppose we can't beat about the bush, we're all adults here." I slapped my hands down on my knees with my opening statement.

Mother glared at me with a stern, "SSHhhh, the baby is peaceful."

"Well mother, and this isn't a personal attack on you," I clarified, "your misinformed, bile-spewing, Ladies Circle are correct, Ray has moved into Keeper's Cottage, on a temporary basis."

Ray could already feel my loathing towards Sarah Finney, and by association Maribel. I bounced my right leg up and down, when I was wound up, he could see this out of his peripheral vision, as he sat next to me, and he took the conversation over.

"Sophia has been a true friend, oh my..."

He started to well up, and choke on his tears. He exhaled deeply, and tried to regain his composure.

"When Helen died, I thought I'd lost everything; never through all of this did I think I'd find a new best friend in Sophia. If Sophia hadn't been there for me, Hope, and by extension Helen, Hope and I wouldn't have a bond. I blamed my baby, my innocent baby girl, for her mother's death. It wasn't her fault, but I abhorred her, for ripping my wife away from me. Sophia, the kind heart that she is, gave me the chance to grieve, to come to terms with the immediate new life, which I had to tackle. In that time, I didn't realise that I was going to struggle beyond belief in every other aspect of my life. I had taken for granted every provision

Helen had made, and again Sophia has now rescued Hope and me from financial deprivation at this moment in time."

Dad said nothing, he just nodded his head, while Mother started to blub like it were a Hollywood romance.

Once that moment had passed, dad cleared his throat, and asked a question. "Hmm, and Jacob?"

"He's left me."

I thought tonight was not the right way to reveal that I was pregnant; I didn't want to make Jacob out to be totally heartless and irresponsible. I decided to be as vague as possible. I'd let them know after my dating scan. I elaborated on my statement, to satisfy my parents, and no more. In truth, I still didn't know what had caused him to leave.

"He's not on secondment; I have hidden under that story to allow him to come home without losing face. He left the day after Ian Keatan's funeral. He has indicated he won't be returning. This isn't the life for him, apparently. I haven't spoken to Christopher, but I doubt even he knows what the fool is playing at."

"Oh darling..." Mum was mortified; she beckoned me over for a hug. Hope started to stir in the moment, so I picked her up from mum's arms, and took her back to the sofa. I faced her to Ray, and he began to rub her feet.

"There's Dadda, Hope."

"Peeka."

"Can you say, 'Dadda'?"

I knew, at weeks old, she wasn't able to speak, but even as a 'baby dummie' I wanted her to feel secure.

While we were playing with Hope, dad looked over, deadpan, and he piped up, "The solution seems to be simple. You have a spare room, Ray and Hope could come and lodge with you, it's not like you have a mortgage to pay on this place. Ray, until he decides his future, could rent his place out, to cover the monthly repayments."

Dad had put forward a simple, yet plausible solution. Ray and I looked at each other, I think we were both on board; we just didn't want to commit.

"Yeah, definitely a discussion point for this evening." We both managed to entwine the words and form a sentence.

"Oh Roo! What a wonderful idea." Mother was engulfed with emotion. It was a lot for her to take on in one go. It was real life, and not Ladies Circle.

"Crikey lad, if you need to store your belongings, you can have Sophia's old room at our house. You seem an able kind of chap; you could do some maintenance work in the area, and fit it around the buba. If you need help with childcare, Judy will be more than happy to help out. Won't you, Judy love?"

"Oh, of course." Mother jumped at the chance.

"Right, that's settled then. Let us know if you need help with moving. Sophia, take advice from Chaineys and Daulton about Jacob." Dad was up and ready to leave, he pulled his jerkin down to cover his paunch.

"Darling, you take care of each other." Mother pointed and waved her finger between Ray and me.

I nodded, replying, "We will."

On the way out of the door, she turned, "Ooh, I've a casserole in the slow cooker, there's enough for four, I'll freeze you a dinner. Better still, I'll pop it by the office tomorrow for you. Pear and rhubarb crumble for afters, I'm sure I have a tin of custard I can muster up."

"Yum, thanks Judy." Ray's face lit up, it must have been months since he'd had proper motherly cooking. Helen could cook like pro, until it came to desserts, she always fouled them up, and he was lumbered with my pitiful attempts.

It must have been about 5:45 p.m. when they left. We had not prepared dinner. We opted for mum's tea loaf and cereal for supper. We decided to talk about dad's idea once we could give it our full attention. Hope was settled down by 7 p.m. most evenings, and generally wouldn't stir until 11 p.m. for another feed.

I wasn't on call; George and Toby had been on the rota for a prolonged period. We had come to an arrangement to suit us all while Jacob was 'on secondment'. For every evening/early morning callout, they would start later, at 10 a.m., and finish at 4 p.m. instead. It was not ideal, but it was working out reasonably well. They were paid for all callouts at weekend rates, I was haemorrhaging money. I took the upper hand and still paid Jacob his weekly wage, into his account. I refused to say anything about my intentions in his absence, other than they were honourable. Most people would probably argue they were stupid intentions, but I wasn't most people.

I wasn't ready to address my work team, and admit my domestic situation had crumbled. They now had two bosses who had gone from a committed relationship, to split apart and one absent. That instability could ruin a business like ours; and I was not going to lose the shares I had invested through mismanagement.

I pottered about the house, laundry needed folding. Ray was bathing Hope, I could hear her little cooing giggle, and it was such a heart-melting moment that I got to experience.

Luckily, she wasn't settling down to sleep. I had forgotten to turn the phone volume down, and when it rang out, it made me drop towels all over the floor.

I pressed the answer button.

"He's not on secondment, is he? Why didn't you tell me? He's gone and left you." Chris was never one for hellos, straight to the point.

"Hi Chris, have my parents rung you?"

"No girl, I haven't spoken to Roo, or Judy for that matter, since that day at yours. Maybe in town, I saw Roo in the Iron Mongers. That aside, I had a letter from Chaineys and Daulton. He has signed his shares over, which now makes me the minority shareholder. He wishes to make a new life for himself, and will not correspond, unless through them."

"Chris, I don't know what to say. You seem to know more than me. I have no letter, so I guess when my new partner turns up in the office, courtesy of Jacob, all will be revealed. Oh, Christ, who has he sold his shares to? If it's Harry Gilbert, over at Larkham and Sons, I will throttle him, he needn't worry about returning. That man's breath could wake the dead. He also has no perception of personal space."

"Well girl, I suggest, if you don't get a letter by the end of the week, you ring Chaineys and Daulton. My letter has informed me that he has signed his shares over to you. You now own the majority of Saunders and Son Funeral Directors. Congratulations."

With that, Christopher put the phone down. I felt awful. The man who had built up his business, and worked his entire life, forging a glowing reputation, that was countrywide, had just been completely and utterly shafted over, by his own son.

I couldn't leave the conversation like this; I grabbed my keys and went to head out the door. Hope's crescendoing giggles vibrated around the house. I poked my head around the bathroom door.

"There's a work drama, I'll be home later, I'll explain then."

I headed over to Christopher's house. I didn't have a clue how to play this. He was, in many respects, my father-in-law, and had been for several years, he was also a partner with me. I had a lot to owe Chris for, investing in me, in the early years, and for allowing me to have a career.

His latest girlfriend, Emily, was at the house. She informed me that he had left the house, after opening a brown envelope from Chaineys and Daulton. Emily, who was just scraping 40, at a push, was pretty, she was always made-up and had her hair perfectly blow-dried, her nails were natural, yet immaculately manicured. She liked to be a kept woman – my nails were broken and chipped. She had informed me, as she tossed her luscious brunette hair over her shoulder, they had a wonderful day at the gold club, and now he had walked out with no explanation.

I reassured Emily that it wasn't anything she has done, and it was a work related issue, hence my turning up unannounced. If Chris wasn't at home, I knew exactly where he'd be.

I drove back to Fremmington Ayshe, past Keeper's Cottage, and down the hill into the town centre. I drove over the bridge, where the River Dyer ran below, pulling up into the yard, Chris had his sports car parked up. It was typical Saunders, navy blue, with private number plate. I walked down the cobbled path from behind the Chapel to the office. The door was off the latch, and there he was, sat at his desk. His desk lamp was to his left, lighting up the brown envelope he had put on the desk in front of him.

I walked in, I felt crushed for Chris, and angry at the absent arsehole, for laying this all at my door.

"I thought you might be here." I gave a weak smile.

"Ah, come sit yourself down." He gestured with his hand, to offer a seat, his tone was comforting and warm; it was inviting an honest and open conversation.

"I'm sorry Chris, it's all my fault." I offered up apologetically.

"I'll make the tea." He went to push himself up, as if he were about to head towards the kettle, and then sat himself back down. I had my back to Chris when he asked, "Fancy anything stronger?"

"Bottom right drawer." I instructed.

Chris hunched over the bottom right drawer, where I stashed a bottle of brandy and a couple of glasses, I never knew when it was going to come in handy. He placed the two glasses on the desk and poured himself a very large helping. He went to pour me a glass, but I hovered my hand over the top and declined, making my excuses, 'I'm driving'. I hadn't decided yet whether to tell Chris I was carrying his grandchild, and that's why Jacob had run. I had a moral dilemma, I wanted my parents to know first, but telling Chris would offer up part of an explanation as to why Jacob had acted as he did.

"So where's he gone?" Chris asked, in that indignant manner towards his son.

"I'd love to know myself; I came home to a note on the kitchen table. Telling me not to worry, he wouldn't do anything stupid, so I needn't be alarmist. He couldn't make the commitments I desired from him, and he couldn't fulfil his duties by becoming a family man.

"He took his bag, you know the scabby one he travels everywhere with, and our suitcase, some clothes, and the picture of us from Amy's Christening, the one on the hall console table."

"A family man?" his father questioned.

"A few months ago, we decided to make plans towards starting a family, and maybe even marriage in the shorter, but longer term."

"Had his mood changed? Maybe not dramatically, but on the odd occasion, he's reacted differently to how you'd expect?"

Chris asked this question, and I had the harsh realisation that I had been so caught up in work, Pom, Helen, and Ian Keatan, that I hadn't been attuned to Jacob. I couldn't answer Chris, because I didn't know.

"Honestly, I don't know Chris, I've been too self-involved."

"There's one thing I need to know Sophia, has he been taking his medication?"

"What medication?"

All the worst possible thoughts started to run through my head. Had he got some terminal disease, and now he was now alone in a hospice, that's why he didn't take much clothing, and all he had was our picture by his side. I was bewildered at his father's question. Was I going to get the call to pick his body up, would I be doing the funeral for my long-term partner?

"Oh dear God, please tell me he's told you. He hasn't told you, has he?"

I was losing my composure, and hysteria was creeping in rapidly.

"Can you tell me what the hell is going on? WHAT MEDICATION? Chris, you need to be honest with me!" I demanded.

"You're telling me, you have been together all this time, and you have no idea he was on permanent medication? Well, I'll give him his dues; he's played that one well."

"WHAT MEDICATION?" I screamed.

Chris was now backed into a corner; he was reluctant to tell me, but really had no choice. After a heavy sigh, he resignedly whispered, "Lithium, he takes lithium carbonate. Jacob is bipolar."

What could I say with such a revelation? I'd been lied to, made a fool of all these years. Strangely, I wasn't angry. I felt immune to Jacob's stunts, in that instant, it confirmed to me, with the enormity of such a lie, that he must have another woman in Italy, and maybe I was worth a little more than all this deception.

I departed from the office with no more than a...

"I have to go!"

The journey home, I mulled over every plausible reason he would lie, but there was no excuse, we were meant to be in this together, for the long haul. I decided I didn't want to discuss it with Ray, hoped he would assume it was just funeral related, and not ask any questions. I started to feel anger as I pulled up on the driveway, bloody-minded and adamant he wasn't going to have a platform, or thrive off of his own drama, I decided, I take this secret to the grave with me.

Chapter Thirteen

Lucy

My dating scan had been booked into a private clinic. After all the unwanted attention from the town's busybodies, over Ray's temporary stay, and with the revelation that my baby's father was a fruit loop, I wanted to cocoon us both into a bubble, away from everything and everyone. I decided that sitting in St Cuthbert's was not going to be a good idea, for those reasons alone.

My appointment was at 4 p.m., and I had told mother a white lie so that she'd look after Hope. Ray had kindly offered to go with me, so we told mother we were off to see a financial advisor for him. Mother was more than willing, but I couldn't help feeling guilty that I had embroiled Ray into the web of deceit that was my life. He was still so fragile and reeling from Helen's death, but he put all that aside and came with me, even though, the last time he'd have been at a scan, it would have been Helen's. He hid his anxiety to support me; I could never repay him for such loyalty.

We arrived at Mayben's Private Hospital, with a generous 15 minutes to spare. I booked in and waited. I people watched, I wondered what stories they had, how had they ended up here?

Ray wasn't Helen, but he was coming in a very close second. Our relationship had strengthened through hardship; I was feeling particularly reflective as I waited to meet my baby. I was so excited, but riddled with 'what ifs'. I was angry with Jacob, he'd quit out on our child, never giving them the chance to meet or bond whilst I grew them. Maybe we were better off, him leaving now; at least the baby would never have to experience the heartache of abandonment.

I was concerned for Ray, his beautifully noble act of chaperoning me was courageous, but I didn't want it to evoke memories he'd rather not revisit.

The sonographer came out; her nametag said 'Joyce'. "Sophia Hardy, please."

I looked at Ray, he nodded, holding out his hand to take my bag, he was incredibly chivalrous. He let me lead off and followed behind. When I handed him my bag, I noticed he was wearing the same clothes as the first day we met, and those boots, I'd never forget those boots.

"Come in Sophia, make yourself comfy on the bed, bring your trousers down to your knicker-line and pull your top up. Dad, make yourself comfy next to her."

It was one of those moments again; having a male-female friendship had lead to an innocent, but incorrect, assumption. I was getting nervous, exhaling lots of short breaths. Ray sat crouched over, ready to see the screen. He tapped my left elbow; I turned my head from looking at the blank screen. He held his hand out, and I took him up on his offer; naturally, our fingers laced together.

"Are you ready? The gel will be cold."

Joyce squeezed the gel onto me, and then she started to manoeuvre her wand about my abdomen. I held my breath in anticipation, waiting for her to say it was all 'OK'. My baby magically appeared on the screen, they were having a little wiggle. I looked at Ray with sheer relief and elation; he was beaming, and we clutched each other's hands tight.

"You can hear the heartbeat." Joyce turned the sound up. I melted. How could something so small make me fall in love so easily? I made them, they were part of me.

"I'd like to call my colleague in a moment please; it's nothing to worry about."

Joyce left the room. I started to panic, worst case, what? Why had she left? Why did she need a colleague? I looked at Ray in desperation.

"Oh my God Ray, my baby, what's wrong with my baby?"

I was breaking up internally; I could feel the shakes creeping in. Joyce returned with her female colleague, Doctor Parker. I kept it together; how, I don't know. I regained my composure, ready to hear what they had to say. Ray rubbed my shoulder as reassurance. In the last few minutes, he had become my rock.

Doctor Parker began, "Joyce has voiced a concern, NO! Concern isn't the right word. Joyce has a slight issue with audio of the heartbeat. I'm going to listen in; it's nothing to worry about."

They played the heartbeat again. I listened intently. It sounded to my untrained ear to be a regular, albeit fast, heartbeat.

"Do you hear that? There, faintly in the background" Joyce pointed it out to Doctor Parker.

"Yes I do. I'll watch you complete the scan."

It was a horrific feeling of no clarity as to what was going on, whilst they talked cryptically.

"I'm going to scan you quite tight to your pubic bone, if it creates discomfort let me know, we might have to consider an internal ultrasound."

I nodded. Joyce pressed the wand down hard as she manipulated it across me. My bladder was now feeling abused. She worked left to right, in linear motions.

"There, that's it." Dr Parker pointed to the screen with her pen tip. "As Joyce thought; well done Joyce."

I looked puzzled; Joyce turned the screen back towards me.

"Congratulations, Mrs Hardy, I thought I could hear a second heart beat, hence my inviting Dr Parker in. There they are: your fraternal twins!"

"Tw what? Twins, NO, it's my first pregnancy, are you sure?" I blabbered.

I looked at Ray; he kissed my hand, still wrapped in his. He let it go to put his arms around me, and he hugged me tight. I got pictures of my babies, and I was high on love.

We left the hospital arm in arm, neither of us noticed; it just assumed a natural part of our behaviour. I was over the moon, on an adrenaline rush like no other I'd ever experienced. Twins though...

I had left the hospital having been made fully aware of all the risks. I was now considered a high-risk pregnancy; I'd be offered more antenatal appointments than a singleton pregnancy.

Ray drove us home. We got nearly all the way home in silence; I guess Ray was waiting for me to comment. About two miles from Knowling Hill there was a lay-by lining the side of the road, it was backed with evergreen trees, and had a 'mind out for deer' sign at the end, as you pulled out, back onto the main road.

"Can we pull over?"

Ray obligingly did as I asked, and then he looked into my eyes.

"I want an honest answer Hardy, are you OK?"

I burst into tears, hysterical, not quite sure why. I currently had two healthy babies, who were going to get the best care possible.

"I'm alone, no; I'm abandoned, by Jacob. It was bad enough he'd left one child, and now I have to face two babies, one day having to tell them, their father didn't love them or their mum enough to stay around, in fact, their dad cut and run before knowing if they were safe, well, and viable."

"Sophia, quite frankly, it's his loss. You'll be better off without him. Him doing this now, will, in the long term, be better than him walking out when they are new born, or even worse children. At least now, you have time to come to terms with it, before they arrive."

I sniffed back my tears, dabbing my eyes with my thumbs. Ray fumbled in his pockets, producing a handkerchief with an 'R' embroidered in the corner.

"Do you always carry one of these?" I enquired.

"Yep, always have done. They make great baby puke moppy cloths. Don't worry... that one's clean." Ray looked at me mischievously.

"Wow, twins, I mean, I know I like a good bargain, like the next person, BUT fertilize one, get one free, I wasn't expecting that.

"My mother, oh my mother. No, let's not. Not today. I'm not ready; she'll go over the top. I don't want Ladies Circle, and everyone else she comes into contact with, knowing; certainly not that it's twins.

"We'll just tell her that you received good financial advice, and it's manageable, is that ok? I'm sorry asking you to lie for me, the induced stress the truth will cause, I don't want it. I just want to grow my humans a little more and bond with them first, with no one's input or advice." I rambled at him.

"You know I'll do anything for you, so it's our secret. Can I tell Hope? She won't tell a soul, I promise."

At home, getting rid of mother was easy, we fobbed her off with the story about Ray, she had to leave "sharpish" as she put it, as tonight was the Garden Association AGM.

Mother had lovingly left us a meal, minted lamb casserole, with chocolate fudge cake; she even left us a tin of scones. Her kind gestures like this made life a little easier at points. It was her way to illustrate I was still her little girl. We sat in the kitchen, tucking in, Ray loved mother's cooking; it was streets ahead of mine.

"How long do you want to leave it, before you tell your parents?"

"As long as possible, I don't want to cause any stress, I'm really going to have to reconsider my life now. Maybe even sell my share, I'm not sure yet. Raising two children, and undertaking, as a lone parent, really aren't compatible.

"Anyway, how are you doing, I know today can't have been easy for you, I'm so grateful you came though, you were my rock. Thank you."

"What happened to Helen was rare, I'm battle scared by events, but life can't pass me by, I'm in my early forties. Helen wouldn't want me to take a vow of celibacy.

"Besides, Helen is having a good laugh at us both, ending up as roommates, who'd of thought it? On that note, once you are ready to tell people, Hope and I will head back to Merton Major; you'll need the space."

"Oh no Ray, please don't feel you have to go. I recon we have a good 12 months before we even need to consider change, well, unless you get a lady friend, I'm not playing gooseberry! 12 months should have you back on your feet, and me dead on mine. By then you'll be ready to go back on the market, the women will swoon after you, a single daddy; you're prime fodder." I jokingly remarked.

We agreed to let it play out as it was, until such time as we needed to address it.

In the following days, I had the results of my screening tests from the hospital, the babies were doing well and there were no concerns. Knowing my future was double trouble, I all but knew my life balance of being a single parent and having a full time career was over.

After consulting Chaineys and Daulton, I offered my share for sale, with first refusal to Christopher. It felt immoral to offer them to anyone else before him. I knew Powell's and Co. would easily snap them up if Christopher didn't want them. I left it in the hands of Chaineys and Daulton to negotiate. Putting it in the hands of a third party took away all possible unpleasant scenarios; it was managed by the professionals. I kept the sale a secret from everyone; it was my life and my choice. I wanted the deal signed and complete before a soul knew.

The last funeral I did at Saunders and Son was for Lucy Ridley; she was an elderly lady, who lived on her own, with her cat, Rufus. She had dropped down dead in the garden, whilst pottering around; she was found a couple of days later, when her cleaner came in. There was always trauma or heartache when someone had lost their life far too young, or in horrific circumstances. Ending my career with Lucy was poetic; I knew the day I prepared her body for viewing, whilst setting her hair, like I had done all those years previously for Mrs Maureen Brown, that was the way I wanted to finish this chapter of my life.

As I stood in front of the coffin, and genuflected in my official capacity one last time, it confirmed to me, this was the right thing to do. That night, I passed the reins back to Christopher. The last hymn I sung was

'Abide with Me'. Lucy's funeral was 11.30am, and by mid-afternoon, I had the chapel and the cars back in order, ready to serve once more. I couldn't leave anything outstanding. Lucy was the last burial of the week, so the timing was perfect.

For the final time, I called a staff meeting, my parents and Ray had also been invited. Four p.m. struck, they all knew there was going to be some announcement. Chris had made it, by the skin of his teeth, fully clad in golfing attire; I wondered how he'd fare back in charge after retirement had allowed him so much freedom. I presumed they all thought it might be about Jacob.

"Right everyone, thank you for another great day, honouring Lucy Ridley; you did me proud, with top levels of professionalism as always. Mum, Dad, Ray and of course Hope, thank you for joining us.

"Joanna, Toby and George, I need to inform you all of mine and Jacob's domestic situation, we have, in fact, parted company. He has however, left me his shares in the company. That aside, along with recent happenings, it has made me re-evaluate my life, I have other ambitions I want to fulfil, and experience I want to gain. Today was the last funeral I will direct, finishing with Lucy Ridley feels so perfectly apt."

No one spoke a word, they gawped at me as if I was some Victorian circus freak, I continued, "Joanna, I have arranged, under the terms of sale, that you are able to progress into a fully qualified undertaker; if you so wish. You are suited to the job without doubt; you're wasted in the office."

"'Terms of sale?' Sophia, you're selling up?" My dad asked for clarification.

"I've been in negotiations with Chaineys and Daulton as my agents, they've taken care of it, and both parties are happy with the conclusion."

"Please don't say you've sold to Harry Gilbert, you know, 'im over at Larkham and Sons." George gesticulated to Toby. "The one with no sense of personal space, he'd sit on Sophia's lap if he could. Powell's would surely be a better solution?"

"Yes, thank you lads; luckily for you both, you will not have to suffer Harry Gilbert, and you're right, he has a terrible sense of personal space. Stay upwind of his armpits too.

"I've sold it back to Christopher, he trusted in me, and I have no doubt he will do the same for you all. I have enjoyed my time here; I'd never change a thing, not even meeting Jacob; I've been heartbroken so many times, but I have also been moved by the love and unity families have in times of grief.

"I have left everything in order, so tomorrow morning, when you come into work, just like every other day, do it to the best of your ability. You have incredible futures, don't let me down.

"Always look forward." I placed my keys down on the table. "Look after Christopher for me." I walked out, not looking back on the place.

When I sat in my car on the other hand, I shed a tear. My entire working life was here, it was all I knew, and now, at my most vulnerable, I thrust myself into the unknown.

Chapter Fourteen

Maribel

At Keeper's Cottage, Ray and I had committed to at least six months living together. I'd given up my career and was more than content with my choice. Ray had Hope to focus on; I'd look after her two days a week, while Ray built up his business again.

Through the sale of Pom's house and the shares, I was financially viable, if I was sensible. I'd saved my wages, as I'd had minimal outgoings for years; that was a tidy sum, as a nest egg. Part of the pay out, I'd invest into the twin's future, I guess Jacob leaving his shares was to provide for his child in his absence. I was now becoming increasingly grateful he'd left before bonding with my bump.

Once Hope settled of an evening, we'd fallen into a very boring routine, supper at 7 p.m. and bed by 10.30 p.m. at the latest. I'd cook, and he'd do the dishes, bringing in a cuppa afterwards. Our relationship as housemates was harmonious, we didn't think anything about the situation, it was our normality. Ray had been at Keeper's Cottage for a few months, it wasn't something we broadcast, and it was really no one's business but ours.

The door knocked as I was putting Hope to bed, after her bath. She'd had an explosive nappy, and Ray also needed to clean up. He was in his dressing gown, about to bath, as he answered the door, I heard it unlatch.

"Oh, it's you." Ray was greeted by the indignant tones of Maribel Mackey "I need to speak to Sophia. Are you staying the night?"

"Sophia is busy, and my activities are none of your business." He flung the door in Maribel's face. I was at the bottom of the stairs.

Hope of Ray

"Nice look, did Maribel cop an eye full?"

"I didn't give the old bat chance." Ray said casually, as he went off for his bath.

The cottage had such picturesque landscapes from every window, and being relatively secluded, we had normal glass in the bathroom window. Lying down to soak, while watching Mother Nature, was indescribable, your worries just faded away.

In our previous commitments, we'd both gotten into the habit of not locking the door to the bathroom, but this had made us self-conscious with our new living arrangements. Ray had left the hall and strode straight back to his hot drawn bath; he hadn't asked me if I needed the toilet, and the urgency of needing the loo crept up on me fast these days.

"Ray, how long are you going to be?" I bellowed through the door. I couldn't hear his reply, it sounded muffled, "How long?" I pleaded.

"Open the bloody door Sophia!" he bellowed.

I opened the door, and stood back, I didn't want to be inappropriate.

"How long are you going to be? Pregnant lady jiggling here!"

"Just come in and pee."

"What?" I exclaimed.

"Just come in and pee. I'll put the shower curtain around the bath, and you can then pee in private."

"OK then, no peeking." I joked.

Reluctantly, I went in. I was so desperate, I couldn't have hung on much longer. Once I started, it was like white water rapids gushing. Ray was behind the curtain offering social commentary on the functions my bladder.

"Have you thought about getting a second bathroom? I mean, I must have lodger's rights. Or are you simulating white noise, maybe a waterfall cascading?"

"I'll have you know, Mr Bramwell, it is extenuating circumstances, I'm cooking twins in here."

"Are you staying in here for the duration, shall I get you to scrub my back?"

I was about to walk back into the kitchen, when Maribel at my door started to play on my mind. My thoughts started racing, I paused at the sink, looking out over the fields behind our house.

"Ray, what are we doing? I mean, what happens when the whole town finds out, courtesy of Maribel and her misinformation, that we are 'an item', and you answered the door scantily clad, in just a dressing gown? And finally, when it comes out I'm pregnant; they'll all think we've been having it away, while Helen was dying."

"SO!"

"Doesn't it bother you?" I whined.

"Can I open this curtain yet? So we can have a rational conversation, while I'm in the bath, where all rational conversations are held, of course. I promise the bubbles are in the right place."

He opened up the curtain, and I pulled up the stool.

"Make yourself comfy there. Ignore what people say, I know, easier said than done. We know the truth, and that's all that matters, so what if we live together. Maribel has a very empty life. If she needs to fill the void with our sad, pathetic, I'd go as far as to say 'living arrangements', then let her. At least it gives someone else a break while she pesters us.

"You've got to feel sorry for poor old Walter, having her as a sister."

I sat rubbing my belly. I knew he was right, and I shouldn't give a damn, I was resilient and thick-skinned, but now the idle gossip didn't just affect me, it affected my babies, and Hope too. One day, Maribel would curl up her toes, she wouldn't plague me forever.

"You're a wise man Mr Bramwell." I got up to leave, taking my finger, and hooking up some bubbles, placing them on his nose as I passed.

Of late, I had been reactionary. Life in Fremmington Ayshe now seemed so negative, I wanted to exist in my bubble only. I didn't want to be part of this community, or bring my children up in such a place. I had never foreseen a time where I'd consider leaving, I'd loved living here, my family had been here for generations, and they'd walked the same cobbles I had.

If Pom was alive, I don't think I'd have ever considered moving, not even out of the town. Now, I was contemplating a fresh start... anywhere. I wanted my babies to be raised without the prejudice. They were innocent, and I didn't want them to experience nasty people like Maribel. Staying here would mean they were exposed.

Again, I decided, like the sale of the business, not to mention my plans until I was certain it was what I wanted. I had to draw a conclusion to my thought process before I could thrash it out with anyone else. I wanted to be fully informed of my choices.

I waited until Ray was back over in Merton Major; he was doing some maintenance work for a few elderly clients, gutter clearances, and roof slate replacing.

I had been online, looking at property. I didn't know where to start. Where did I want to live? I had no idea. I chose to start looking over the border, in Wales. We had several holidays there when I was a child, around the Brecon Beacons, and in North Wales. I was just looking, it was a harmless exercise. The first house to catch my eye was a three-bedroom, detached cottage. It had a drive, and generous gardens; I could imagine a swing set for the twins, it had great potential. But I could easily see I would be replicating Keeper's Cottage.

I looked over to Hope, who had exhausted herself on the play mat; she had crashed about an hour before. I couldn't leave her; she would leave such a massive void in my life. I was feeling guilty at even considering leaving her. I knew one day though, as Ray moved on, with a new relationship, I'd have to be a smaller part in her life, it would be idiotic to think otherwise.

I continued to look, there were some great properties, maybe four or five, within village settings, which would suit my needs. The idea of moving left me feeling deflated. It wasn't what was on offer that was the problem; I could buy any of them outright, and not worry about having a mortgage. Essentially, what bothered me was that I was moving my problems from one town to another. Nowhere was dissimilar to Fremmington Ayshe, so therefore it was going to have the same type of characters. It would only be a 'honeymoon period', before we got embroiled into that type of life again, before we met another 'Maribel'.

I knew that what I wanted was to be independent from any type of community, interacting on my own terms only. I couldn't even envisage my children going to the village school, maybe I didn't have to, and that was another avenue worth exploring. I wanted to grow my own veg, go and collect my own eggs for breakfast. I'd created a dream so many have; my position did give me the opportunity to make this utopia reality.

Hope of Ray

I didn't need to be looking for a three bedroom house; I should be looking for a smallholding. I'd lived on the outskirts of Fremmington Ayshe, making the leap to greater isolation didn't seem that drastic, more 'progressive'. The good life could easily be more than a dream.

The search threw up a bungalow; it was a bit dated, a fixer-upper. It had a pink bathroom and retro tiles, the kitchen cupboards were hanging off. It had a sizeable garden; I could definitely have a vegetable patch, swing set and room for a few chickens. The house was a wreck, it bizarrely piqued my interest, but my biggest reservation was how close it was to civilisation.

At the bottom of the web page, were suggestions of other properties that may be of interest. There was a cottage belonging to a farm, it was away from the main farmhouse, being sold as a separate concern, again I'd have a reasonable amount of land, but I'd still have neighbours, it was no different to how it was now, with Walter opposite.

Both of these places interested me, I'd made some judgements, maybe unfairly; but I decided I needed to go and view them. Hopefully, that would confirm to me if these were real feelings, or was I just romancing about the grass being greener. I rang the agents, and arranged for viewings in a couple of days time.

Now I had to lie to Ray about my whereabouts, the idea of not sharing this with him felt heartbreaking. I didn't want to cause him another period of unsettlement, he'd come so far since Helen had died. He'd given up his house, and been faced with the twins arrival, I didn't want him to feel pushed out of his home here at Keeper's Cottage too.

I made my excuses to Ray, that I needed a couple days away, to unwind, and I thought, upon my return, I'd tell people about the babies. Ray was, as always, supportive and understood my needs; he would drop me off, and pick me up, at the train station.

The morning came to drop me off. I had packed a holdall for a couple of days. I wanted to come clean to Ray about my trip; I felt I was betraying him. I kept running it through my head, right up until the moment I had to leave the car.

"Have a RELAXING time, please. I'll be here to pick you up."

Ray got out of the car, and brought my holdall around to me. He opened the back door, getting Hope out of her car seat to say "Goodbye". I gave Hope one last cuddle, and told her to, "Be good for Daddy".

Ray gave me and Hope a cuddle, then put his arm around my neck, his stubbled cheek met mine with a kiss. "Look after yourself."

I picked up my bag; walking into the station, I was looking over my shoulder to see Hope's hand waving at me with Ray's help. I sat on the bench, on platform two, with tears streaming down my face. I couldn't do this to Ray, he deserved better.

Boarding the train, a young man, in a brown suit, with pink tie, offered to take my bag for me. His seat was next to mine. "How far along are you?" he enquired.

I was taken aback; I didn't think I was showing yet, but a stranger had noticed. He didn't give me time to answer before continuing. "I saw your fella and your little girl wave you off, it was sweet, how old is she?"

It was that dreaded assumption again, I answered like every other time, I didn't want to air my private life in public.

"She's nearly six months." I answered, pleading silently that he wouldn't do the maths.

"We're trying for a baby, me and my Laura. I've just had a job interview. We want to relocate somewhere nice, anywhere; we don't care, so long as it's not where we are now. I'm going to another interview now, in Wales."

"Where was your last interview?"

"Chaineys and Daulton, have you heard of them?"

"Yes, they're local to me."

"What are you heading to Wales for?"

"I'm looking at a property to buy, maybe move into, I'm honestly not sure."

"What's the prices like around your area? We'd be looking to rent, if I got the job. We rent in a god-awful street at the moment, you've probably heard of it, was on the news last week, it's rife with crime and rioting. Corbumn Street."

"I don't know about rental prices, I own my home, sorry."

"Well, if you ever want to rent it out, you know, if you move, let me know."

He got off at his station, parting our conversation by leaving me his business card. The next train station was another six miles away. I was being met by Neil, he'd take me back to his office and go over any other interests with me, and then he'd take me to viewings. It was drizzling when I got off the train; but I knew exactly who Neil was, as he sheltered under a red and green golfing umbrella, with 'Beaumont's Estates' written on it.

"Hi, Sophia, welcome to Wales" he put his hand out to shake mine. "My wife has one of those cooking too."

"Ah, the bump, you don't need your ear chewed of about that." I said, politely trying to cut off that particular avenue of idle conversation.

At the office, Neil and his staff were very accommodating. They knew exactly what my budget was, and what I was willing to stretch to. They set about searching listings, so I could maximise my trip.

"We have a smallholding, with business potential, it's quite an undertaking, but judging at what you already want to view, that won't deter you."

Neil turned his screen to me, and that was it. All my previous ideas dissolved. "Stop looking, that's it! I know that's the one, my gut's doing that thing, you know, when you have that instinct. I want to view this one. That's my home."

"Well, if you insist, I'll grab the listings particulars, and the others you previously wanted to see, just in case. You can leave your stuff here. We'll head over to Lovett's Farm now."

We drove to the village of Aileni, and then a further four miles into the rugged valleys. At the top of a hill was a gateway, Neil pulled into it, winding down the windows. "You see that, that's Lovett's Farm. It's remote at best, is that what you want?"

"After what life has thrown at me recently, Neil, outer space isn't remote enough, this'll be just perfect. I want my children to grow up carefree; village life will never allow such freedom."

We pulled into the private track, taking us down to Lovett's Farm. Just before the farm gate was a ford, it was plenty shallow enough, with a crumbling footbridge of sorts; it was quaint. The stream meandered along the edge of the fields. The iron latch on the wooden gate was rusty and aged, stiff from the weather and infrequent use, the matching strike plate was fixed into the dry stone wall.

Hope of Ray

At my request, we parked by the ford. I wanted to explore the rest on foot. Once through the gate, we stood on dusty, rubble earth from the farm yard; on a raised level, up four steps, stood the farm house, constructed of granite stone. The porch, with white wooden door and carriage lamp, placed in the centre, stood proud. Either side of the porch were sash windows, flaking, in need of some T.L.C. It illustrated that winters battered the house, they were rough. It was my first clue that I'd need to fix a few things.

The condition of the house really was a minor problem, when I walked up those four shallow steps, framed with dry stone wall; I turned to look out over the green luscious fields, nestled in the valley bowl. The mountains flecked with faint purple tones as the heather crept in. In the distance, as I strained my eyes, I could see the ruins of history and devastation, lying dormant in the slag heaps, as a constant reminder of the past.

In the field beyond the yard was a barn, it was falling in on itself. I had already imagined Ray coming for extended holidays to fix it up. Neil pointed out some more of my barns and out buildings; he was certain I could apply for planning, and be accepted, to use the farm as a campsite, I'd be adding to the local economy. It was beautiful, why wouldn't you want to stay here? I could imagine the summers here with my children, playing, picking wild flowers, putting them in a vase on the kitchen windowsill.

"Shall we go inside, take a peak...?" Asked Neil, in that friendly, leading, but slightly patronising tone, which seems reserved exclusively for estate agents and primary school teachers.

"Hmm, yeah." I was awash with contentment.

Opposite the front door was a staircase, it was large and traditional, either side were heavy oak doors, the right lead into the kitchen. The

Aga was worn and filthy, I knew already I'd need a new one; this one was beyond an engineer's help. I was besotted with the house, with the whole set up the farm had to offer. I hadn't seen upstairs, but I was ready to put in an offer though. It was idyllic. I may have been running away from all I knew, but I was certain, I was meant to have this as my forever home.

"I want it Neil. What's the crux of the situation, how much is the lowest you think they'll take?"

"It was an elderly farmer, the kids don't want it, so when he died, it went up for sale."

He inhaled through his teeth. "I'd say you can go in fifty thou' under the asking. I'm certain they'd take it."

"I'd like to make an offer, a very cheeky offer, stupid you might say. Seventy thousand under the asking. We can move ASAP, I have no chain."

Neil was stunned, excitable; reading between the lines, it had been on their books for too long, the remoteness had been a sticking point. He went in with the hard deal.

Twenty minutes, back in the office, three phone calls, and sixty two thousand under the asking price, I was now the new owner of Lovett's Farm.

No doubt, I would be accused of being impulsive. I'd gone on a fact finding mission, but the house felt right. Now it was mine and the babies', independent from the absent father. Our life was on our terms.

I decided not to stay over, as intended, for two days of house hunting. I left Beaumont's Estates, and Neil dropped me back at the station. I waited until the next available train came. I didn't care how long I had to wait, or what time I'd get home, I wanted to be with the people who matter in my life: Ray, Hope, Mum and Dad. I arrived back at my home station in darkness. Hope would be fast asleep. I hailed a taxi to drive me home. The driver and car had that acrid, musty, sweaty, stale cigarette, smell about them, which wafted through the entire vehicle. I distracted myself from gagging by thinking about what I was going to tell Ray. I didn't know, I couldn't lie, he was too kind and deserved far more than to be treated like that. I imagined the tongue lashing Helen would give me.

The taxi pulled up at the drive gates; I walked from there, so as not to disturb Walter, and in turn, Ray and Hope. I walked up the gravel, crunching as I went, it echoed in the silence of the night. The song of the owls floated on the wind, the sky was clear, not a cloud in sight, and the stars guided me to the door, my fingers stiffening in the chilly night air.

Peeking in the window, I saw Ray slumped on the sofa, with Hope's toy bunny in his hand. At a guess, he'd momentarily sat down, and the exhaustion of parenthood had taken over.

My keys clunked as I took them out of the door, and I heard Ray wake with at startle.

"It's me Ray." I whispered loudly.

"What's wrong, are you OK?" Ray rushed up to meet me in the hall.

"I'm fine, I've got some news; it's pretty huge."

He coaxed me into the living room. I looked at him, white as a sheet.

Before I could start with my preamble, "You're getting back with Jacob, aren't you?"

"No silly. Crikey, I stopped loving him the day he abandoned me; well, it took a few weeks to come to that realisation, granted."

"Sorry, go ahead, I'm all ears."

"Well, I bought a house." Ray's face drained of all expression. "I don't want to bring my babies up being told stories of who they are, and where they come from, by toxic characters like Maribel. I'm the only one who has the right to tell my children such things, but living here will mean it's not my choice, and I expose my children to unfair judgement."

Ray leapt up, he started pacing, rubbing his hands on the back of his shaven head. I'd never heard him shout, I knew he was fiery, I'd seen him play rugby many times. He was a redhead; his temper on the pitch always conveyed this, as he would often have a ruckus with the ref.

"That's great, THAT'S REALLY GREAT SOPHIA! I've given up my home, and now I'll be homeless until I can get the tenants out.

"Why have you done this to me? I thought we were friends, you promised me we'd have twelve months, at least."

"Ray, RAY!" I snapped.

Ray wouldn't look at me, he'd turned his back.

"Look at me Ray, please. You don't have to leave, you can stay here. You think this is easy for me? Do you know how guilty I felt doing this behind your back? How much of a void you and Hope will leave in my life? When I said, 'goodbye' to you both, this morning, at the station.

"Ultimately though, one day you'll move on, so maybe this is a good thing."

"Sophia, don't."

Ray left the living room; he headed upstairs to his room. The commotion must have woken up Hope. I could hear her little whine. Ray came back down the stairs, straight into the kitchen, I heard him flip the kettle switch. I followed him in.

"All the lies and deceit, you're just like Jacob, no wonder you got on so well." Ray was angry.

"Ray, please say you don't mean that. Ray that hurts!" I begged him to retract his statement.

"I can't look at you right now." He left the kitchen to tend to Hope.

I was mortified, heartbroken we'd fallen out. I didn't want to go to bed with such ill-feeling, disrupting Hope was not an option either. I sat on the sofa, staring at my new home. I was desperate for Ray to reappear after he'd fed Hope. He didn't.

Twenty minutes or so later, I heard cries coming from his room. It was Ray. The last time I heard him cry like that was in the days after Helen's death, when he'd cry himself to sleep. I'd caused his suffering this time. Me. I was a despicable woman. I had to make this right.

I lightly walked up the stairs to his room, the landing always creaked and groaned, pushed the door open, it was slightly ajar. He was laid on his side, facing Hope's cot, his back to the door. I didn't know what to say or do, I had caused his pain. My instinct took over, I went over to his bed, knelt on, climbing on, so I lay next to him. My growing bump tucked up tight to him. I kissed his shoulder. He briefly glimpsed at me, turning away instantly.

"I'm sorry, what else can I say Ray? I'm sorry. Sorry I lied to you. I don't want our relationship to end this way." I started to cry, we had been through so much, and I didn't want it to end this way.

"Mr Bramwell, I appreciate everything you have done for me. Coming with me to meet my babies, being so calm, when inside I knew you were bricking it too. I know that day must have left a bad taste, knowing Helen was the last person you experienced this with. You are my best friend; life without you in it is unimaginable."

I kissed him and removed myself from his bed. I headed to my room, wrapping myself in the duvet to console myself. I'd alienated the one person I'd truly allowed into my life. I left my door open every night, so I could hear Hope, and in case Ray needed moral support.

I sat up, in my cushion, pillow, and duvet fort, the glimmer of light shone through my window. I never shut my blind; waking up to nature's alarm clock was a habit I had come to enjoy, becoming accustomed to seeing first light. Waking up to untouched countryside gave me faith in humanity.

I was staring out of the window, watching the silhouettes of trees moving was like seeing them dance in the darkness.

Ray latched his bedroom door; I guessed he was shutting me out, excluding me, as a defence barrier.

Then he appeared at my bedroom door. "I don't want to lose you. I can't imagine life without you."

"But one day you'll move on."

"I don't want to move on. Hope deserves the best in her life, and I don't see anyone coming close to Aunty Soph."

I put my arms out, he was still at the door, inviting him in with, "Come and give me a hug."

He honourably perched on the edge of my bed. He had his dressing gown over his t-shirt and boxers, completed by his socks. I had to bring humour in, just like I normally would to our life.

"You're never going to pull if you wear socks like that."

"You don't complain. How long have we lived together now?" he asked

I rubbed my lips together, "Months, although it feels like years."

"You know, the minute Jacob laid eyes on you, he was fixated with you. He wouldn't stop going on about this hotty at work. How natural she was. He wouldn't shut up about you. The lads always told him to do something about it, if he felt she was so perfect. He was scared of being rejected. He was ribbed relentlessly about his crush.

"The day I met you, I knew exactly what he'd been trying to articulate. I saw you and, wow! I was mortified at how rude he was. You had this wit and charm that gave him a run for his money. Your hair was the untameable mop it is now, look at it, flopping all over the place." He tossed my curls with the back of his hand. "I told him, if he liked you, he had to treat you right, any man would snap you up and love you."

"Ah, so you're the reason I got lumbered with the arse." I jested.

"I'd met Helen a couple years before. She had a natural beauty; I wouldn't have left Helen for anything. She came into my life when I was really ready to settle down. But you, you left a mark on my life back all those years ago. Being your friend meant so much to me. I'd never have jeopardised that. Watching you and Helen become inseparable, to me, was a prize like no other. We always knew you'd be a good Godmother to Hope.

"You're astonishingly headstrong; I don't know how you do what you do, or did, without becoming full of hostility to life. You picked up the pieces of my crumbling life, and now I'm scared you'll leave me, and no one will ever make me feel this way again."

"And now... you hate what I've done?"

"No, No! I hate the idea of you leaving here, and not sharing my days with you.

"I buried my wife; I shouldn't feel like this, it's wrong, oh so wrong. I shouldn't feel like this, but I do, I can't stop the feelings."

He leapt up, started pacing again. I wrestled my way out of the covers, and I caught him mid-stride.

"Look at me. Look at me, Ray. Look at me. You're human. What would Helen honestly say to you? You knew her best."

"She'd tell me..." Ray broke down into tears.

"She'd tell me there was no one better to have in my life than you. Hope and I would be lucky to have you. And, if I peed you off, she'd come back and haunt me."

"Yup, that's our Helen, right there."

I faced him, placed my hands either side of his face, over his ears, both my thumbs gently placed into the corners of his eyes, to wipe away his tears.

The feelings I'd been experiencing, of disloyalty, while house hunting, it was guilt. Guilt I couldn't admit, I was more emotionally involved with Ray Bramwell than I should be, a barrier had been crossed, I couldn't return. The idea of leaving Ray behind made me hollow. I felt I was betraying Helen though. I'd never have had a relationship with Ray if she were living; surely I should honour this in death?

Hope of Ray

That day in the bathroom, as I placed bubbles on his nose, I knew we were crossing into dangerous territory. Maribel's potential gossiping about us evoked such a reaction that, in hindsight now, the initial desires for a fresh start were because I wanted Hope and my babies brought up with no prejudice. Why would that matter if Ray and I were just friends? Even then, subconsciously, it was for us all. Who was "us", I had to ask myself for clarity.

I questioned myself, with my internal monologue, was this out of convenience for both of us? If we crossed that boundary, we couldn't ever repair it, should it break down.

"Lay with me." My hands still on his face.

"Are you sure?"

I nodded; I took his hand and led him onto my bed. I was so nervous I met him with my usual sarcasm, he had become accustomed to it, "Take your socks off, I'll warm your feet."

We lay on the bed, looking at each other. We lay, not touching. Both content, we had finally admitted there was more to it all.

Nature was stirring outside; I could hear the birds getting fractious, as dawn slowly edged upon us. I could hear Hope, she wanted her bottle. I made my way downstairs to make her another feed. In all the furore of last night, I hadn't turned the lamp off. Coming back up the stairs, Ray was at the top, ready to greet me, with Hope.

How were we going to handle this? Were emotions so high last night, that today we would regret it?

"Good morning, how are you Hope? Do you want this bubba?" I offered up her bottle. "I'll be in here." I pointed to my room.

Ray put his arm out to stop me, it was a soft, gentle touch, opening and warm. "Come and join us."

"Can I feed her?" Feeding Hope was such a peaceful experience. She was beautiful; her little duck feathers on her head had a little red shading in the sunrise.

"You'll make a mighty fine mother, you know."

"I hope so. They deserve everything possible in life, they didn't ask for this."

"The house..." Ray started.

"Not now, don't ruin the moment." I pleaded.

"The house looks out of this world; you'd be stupid not to move. The only question is... can we come too? In whatever capacity you want, even if that's as your lodgers, we'll pay our way. Why wouldn't you want to raise children there?"

"We can take it one day at a time. When did you see the house, anyway?"

"Late last night, I came down once you were asleep. The particulars were on the sofa. I rang Beaumont's, left a message, asking to go and view it with you this week."

We headed back to Aileni, and Lovett's Farm, to view the property. Ray thought it prudent to calculate the journey time by car. We arranged to meet Neil at the farm. The journey wasn't too troublesome, I'd only requested a toilet break twice, Hope had slept most of the time, we stopped a third time to feed and change her.

"Well, I suppose a bigger vehicle is going to be needed. Three children under one, that's a lot of car seats." Always practical was our Ray.

Hope of Ray

Driving along the track, Ray's face was beaming, "Only in my wildest dreams could I imagine such a beauty. You picked well." He gushed, with enthusiasm.

We stopped at the ford, just like I had with Neil; the rest was discovered on foot. I let Neil show Ray the majority of the land, while I walked Hope around the yard. She had her purée al fresco.

Ray and Neil made their way back to me. I could see Ray had life and purpose in his stride; it was a moment I'd savour forever.

Neil handed me the key, "Go see your new home."

I chewed Ray's ears off about how I envisaged the house. Upstairs I showed him the master bedroom; it looked out over the front of the house. There were two rooms put aside for the twins, when they were ready, the forth room was for Hope. I knew, deep down, from the outset, that I wanted Ray to come with me. I knew one day we'd share a bed, and have a life together; maybe out of convenience, maybe out of love, only time could tell.

"This is Hope's room."

"But you bought this before I made a fool of myself."

"I left that day, knowing I wasn't going to eradicate you from my life. If you didn't come with me, I imagined you visiting, helping me repair the barns."

Ray held Hope, while cuddling me. "You're beautiful, I'm falling for you."

He pulled me closer, leaning in to kiss me. I closed my eyes, his lips were soft, his kiss tender.

"A da da da!"

"That's right Hope, dadda."

I took Hope from Ray, she was all excitable.

"I honestly couldn't wish for more! Sophia, you are massive. You're going to have to tell your parents. Maybe you could tell them everything at once?"

I must have thrown him a look.

"WE, we can tell them." He corrected quickly.

Leaving Lovett's Farm, knowing the next time we arrived here was to start our life as a family, I was filled with happiness. Maybe fairytales did happen? We were caught up in the moment; I didn't want to acknowledge my trepidation.

We drove through the mountain roads for a little under an hour. The lakes reflected the sun. We both had the look of contentment. I decided to drive, until we got over the Severn. When we stopped, we'd swap. Ray would then drive the rest of the way. We kept glancing at each other; words weren't needed to express our feelings.

However this relationship was developing, we would always be part of each other's lives. We were happy and relaxed in Wales, before we got anywhere close to Fremmington Ayshe, maybe we should have an honest and frank conversation, about what we were about to embark on, there were three lives here who had to be protected.

I kept repeating the opening line to the conversation in my head. Over and over. It felt so clumsy, even cutthroat, mercenary. I wanted a neutral place, where we didn't need to worry about censorship. The next car park I saw, I'd pull into, taking it one step at a time.

"Are you OK, why have you stopped, are the babies alright?"

"Calm down, we're fine. We just need to talk. I thought, while we had the chance to experience such spectacular surroundings, we'd be foolish not to.

"We have been so caught up in the moment since the other night; by the way, I wouldn't change that. We do however, need to be responsible adults and bring ourselves back down to reality."

'Phew, that was easier than I expected.' I thought to myself, I'd opened up the conversation, without screwing up what I wanted to say.

"You're so beautifully well-intentioned, what a relief!" Ray smiled, "I was absolutely bricking it, knowing we had to address all these issues, I didn't know how to, I didn't want to crush the feeling. I knew leaving Lovett's Farm we were caught in the moment, and the idyllic lifestyle it entices you with."

"If I'm going to rip my parent's lives apart, I need them to have solace in the fact that every detail has been thought out. I have great amounts of internal conflicts. I have to move, I know that is the right thing to do. I still don't want to hurt them; I have no idea what to say."

"Sophia, when the time is right, I will be there with you, if you want. Try not to over-think it. Just let it come naturally, it'll be more heartfelt. Are you going to tell them about the twins too?"

"No, I'm not telling them it's twins, just that I'm pregnant, by Jacob. BUT, I don't want the Saunders to know, I want no input from the family."

"And us?"

"I'm going to tell them we want to develop our relationship further, but I'm not thinking about it now, it'll be too rehearsed, you're right."

"Sophia, you're certainly different. How many other people do you know, who decide to move hundreds of miles away from what they know, while cooking twins, as a lone parent, may I point out. And then, you decide to embark on a new relationship, with your best friend's widower, taking on his daughter. Making a grand total of three children under one. You're barking mad Hardy!"

"Yep! Joking aside, how is my pregnancy truly making you feel, is it not all still a bit too raw? I don't want you regretting all this, that we haven't give you enough time to grieve, and spread your wings."

"I know Helen isn't coming back. Some days her death is still hard to comprehend. It was tragic; it is rare though, as I've said before. Yes, it is soon to be moving on, but it's not with a stranger. It's with you. The woman I have seen evolve over seven years, who I've grown with in friendship, it's an organic progression we've experienced.

"If I'm having a hard day, or struggling, you will understand me, because you knew and loved Helen. You will embrace that hardship, not tell me to 'get over it'. You've seen me at my lowest, beaten and in the gutter. You, Sophia Hardy, picked me up and gave me purpose once more. You gave me a chance. Why wouldn't I want to share my life with you? To have you as a role model for Hope, it's not about replacing Helen, with a mother for Hope, it's about a partnership, knowing how we got to this point.

"I know Jacob will always be the twins' father, I hope one day we reach the point where I can be that role model for them too. These three children will never know any different than what we create for their childhoods, they should have a proper family unit, and if we can give them that...

"We have a chance of a life together; we shouldn't pass that up because of time. We both have raw wounds, let's heal them together."

I disintegrated into tears at his tender sentiments.

"Ray, never in my life, did I envisage this is how it would be. I couldn't, in my wildest dreams, imagine being on this adventure with you of all people. Now we're here, at this point, I don't ever want anyone else by my side but you, and the courage you have."

Chapter Fifteen

Roo

We took a couple of days before we decided to tell my parents. I wanted to tell them about our plans and rationalise our behaviours. I knew, in order to do so, we needed to present my parents with a cohesive plan, which provided us with an income and safety net. Dad had been a planning officer, for one of the local factories; he did development into longer-term company futures. By asking him for his input, I knew he'd get on board a lot quicker.

We made outline plans to convert the barns into camping facilities, a shower and toilet block. Measured thirty camping pitches on the largest, flattest field, and in the meadow we could possibly entertain a few 'glamping' pods. We even considered a honeymoon pod, that could compliment a 'wedding barn', if we converted the one nearest the yard. It was a very basic vision, but one with a long-term future and diversity.

Ray offered to sell his house in Merton Major. It would make us financially more viable to complete the works quickly, but I didn't need him to do this, I knew he wanted to show he wasn't "sponging" off me, but he was going to be doing most of the work, so it really wasn't the easy option. Ray had to sell his and Helen's home when it was right for him, not just rushing into it as gesture for me. Besides, keeping a safety net here for us in the interim didn't seem unreasonable. It would provide some pocket money for us.

Keeper's Cottage was going to be rented, I left it in the capable hands of Chaineys and Daulton; they could act on Jacob's behalf. I suggested they get in touch with Josh, the young chap I met on the train, offering him first refusal on the tenancy.

Hope of Ray

I decided we'd go to mum and dad's; it was easier for us to leave then, if things did get ugly. Mum and dad were waiting for us in the living room. Dad had turned the telly off, and mum was propped on the arm of his chair when we walked in. Her apron was all to pot, she was fluffing her hair, and dad was wiping his mouth.

I walked in with my cardigan wrapped around my maternity dress; it contoured my bump, my bump that I wasn't ashamed of.

"Darling, what's all this about? You sounded flustered on the phone." Mother went straight in for the gossip.

"How are you doing lad? Baby's grown I see." Dad put his hand out to shake Ray's.

"I'm good mum, I, well we, have some news." I beamed as I smiled at Ray.

I stood up, showing my parents my side profile, and pulled back my cardi, revealing my bump.

"You're, you're..." Mum pointed, while stumbling over her words.

"I'm pregnant. With Jacob's baby." I hastily clarified.

"You'll be grandparents in a few months."

"D'ya see that Roo? Sophia's pregnant!" Mum asked my dad, as if he was incapable.

Dad composed himself, and then said, "I assume that's why he left you, damn fool. It's come as a bit of a shock, I can't deny. But, it's most welcome. I thought you'd gone and got one of those wretched tattoos, I can't abide the things."

"I'll get my knitting patterns." Mum went into overdrive.

"Before you do mum, there's more I need to tell you." I beckoned her to sit back down.

"I've been doing quite a bit of soul searching recently. I don't want the baby growing up knowing it was abandoned by its father, or for the Saunders family to be involved. I want the child to grow up with an enchanted childhood, where they are carefree, and not exposed to toxicity. Just like my childhood was, and I may have rose tinted glasses but, I can't do that here, my baby deserves to not have its innocence jaded by gossip of their heritage, especially from third parties.

"I've known for some time that this is how I felt. I went to view a house, and fell in love with it. Using the money from Pom's house sale, I can buy the house outright. There is business potential there too."

I gave my dad the listing particulars; he took his specs off the side table and started to investigate.

"Are you sure darling? All alone, in a new village, and with a baby. I know you're capable, but still, you'll need help in those early days."

"Mum, I have more news; I've entered into a new relationship. He knows I am pregnant, and understands my desires to raise my child in the way I want…"

Mum cut me up. "What about poor Ray? He's let his house out. Does this new chap know you live with another man, what did he have to say about it? I hope he's understanding of the dynamic."

Before I could reply, my dad nudged my mother. "Oh Judy, for goodness sake, use your common sense. Sophia, I suggest you spell it out for your mother." He tutted.

"It is Ray mum. Things came to head the other evening, when I told him I was leaving Fremmington Ayshe. We had both experienced 'feelings', shall we say, but didn't want to admit it. We felt wrong; society would take a dim view.

"After trying to deny what was happening, I put it all down to grief and being in such close quarters, loneliness, the hormones, I assumed it was unrequited. It all came spilling out, after a few hours of heartache we knew it was worth a try, and so here we are."

Before mother got a chance to fuss, asking irrelevant questions, Dad jumped straight in. "In all honesty, your living arrangements are somewhat unique. I could see this evolving one day, granted I wasn't prepared for it to be this soon, nevertheless…

"Sophia, seeing you with Hope, I've known from day one you loved her, and I always feared, if Ray moved on, it would rip you apart. She is a lucky little girl to have you in her life.

"Ray, seeing you raise yourself from the depths of tragedy, becoming a brilliant father, now showing strength and support to our daughter, and taking on our grandchild; I couldn't ask for a better man."

Ray was completely taken aback by how pragmatic my dad was. There was still, at every meeting, a level of formality with them. Ray wanted to assure them he'd look after me, in no uncertain terms.

"Mr Hardy…" he addressed my dad.

"Now come on lad, less of that, it's 'Roo'."

"Roo, I want assure you, I'm not going to take advantage of Sophia, I don't see her as an easy option, so that Hope is raised in a family unit. Gosh, she has the most fiery temper, and is passionate, sometimes to her own detriment.

"I've offered to sell my house in Merton Major, she is insistent we keep it as security."

"And she'd be right. You're a good man, for crying out loud lad; I've seen you at your lowest. You've shone through.

"You'll make a good team. Good luck to you both. You'll need it, she is a fiery little number, always has been. I think we spoilt her, rather a lot actually."

We all made a scoffing noise at dad's suggestion.

"When do you leave?" Dad cautiously asked.

"As soon as possible, I want to be in the house before the baby is due.

"If we set about work, weather permitting, we should be ready for the next camping season; though I'm doubtful as to our chances for the wedding barn conversion."

"I tell you what Sophia; you fill your mother in on the details; Ray and I are popping to the shed."

Dad winked at me, I knew exactly what he meant. All the anxiety melted away.

Dad beckoned Ray to follow him. As he left, he ran his hand up my arm and clenched my shoulder. "Are you OK with Hope?"

Once they had left, mother flapped her arms in the air, landing her palms on her knees. It was a terrible habit; I had inherited it from her as well. She started to cry.

"Oh it's silly really, I'm relieved, happy, excited, a mix of emotions for you. I'm sad that our family's roots stop here now. Though you do deserve every happiness."

"Mum, I'm sorry, I truly am. I'm sorry I kept all of this from you. I had to be sure I wasn't causing unnecessary heartache; I've had an absolute gutful of it this year.

"It all came to a head when Maribel knocked the door, AGAIN. Well, Ray answered in his dressing gown, I was putting Hope to bed. Afterwards, Ray and I ended up in the bathroom together. Nothing like that! He had to talk me down over that old witch. I knew I was developing feelings for him after I hooked some bubbles from his bath and placed them on his nose."

"Darling, I know all about this. After her last attack, I chose to ignore Sarah Finney, and not bother asking you. I trust your judgement.

"When it came to tea time at Ladies Circle, I had to hear it chapter and verse. How Ray answered the door scantily clad, only to slam the door in poor Maribel's face. She plays the victim well! Sarah proceeded to tell me how you two intimately shared a moment in the bathroom, describing EXACTLY what you did with the bubbles.

"They're like a pack of dogs where you're concerned."

"Do you see why I had to make the choice, not just for me, but for the baby? Can you imagine the bile they'd spout at an innocent child, what they'd say about Jacob and Helen? The little ones deserve better than that."

"Darling, truth be told, I came home ready to sell up myself. Be who you want, and be the mother you desire, without fear of recrimination from trolls like them. We will support you, no matter what; you are my little girl darling, you always will be."

I assumed from mother's statement, she'd had another encounter at Ladies Circle.

Mother and I continued to make plans: when they would come and visit, and how she would look after Hope when I delivered. The reality was, she was going from no grandchildren to many, and she was very excited at the prospect. From her undertones, I think secretly, she desired more children of her own, but it wasn't meant to be.

Dad and Ray returned from the shed. I could tell by the flushing in Ray's cheeks that I would be driving home. Dad and he were both full of chatter; they had worked out a basic plan. They already had a work schedule, to ensure we were in before the babies arrived. Dad and Ray were off to appraise the farm as soon as practicable. I loved my dad more than ever that day; his actions were selfless.

Pulling away from the house, I knew exactly what my dad had done to Ray. "He got the whisky out, didn't he? Does he still keep it in the red toolbox? And you had to drink out of old honey jars, the jars he tells my mother are for washers, nuts, bolts, that sort of thing."

"You know your father well! He also wrote a cheque for five thousand pounds, towards a new vehicle. He offered up the rest of your wedding fund, apparently you won't need it now we're shacking up." Ray had that tipsy, cheekiness about his statement.

In the weeks that followed, we decided to isolate ourselves from Fremmington Ayshe; it would make disappearing less troublesome. Rightly or wrongly so, I wanted to leave without a soul knowing I was pregnant. The actions of a few, had led me to withdraw, until such time as I felt safe to be me again.

I felt violated in my own home, knowing Maribel had watched us in the bathroom, and then decided to let the whole town know. I was angry and bitter towards these people who saw fit to inflict themselves on my life, and be nothing but poison. They left me feeling dirty and used.

Hope of Ray

My dad and Ray formed a good rapport; they took it upon themselves to head up to Lovett's Farm, and prepare the house for new arrivals. Finishing the house in a short space of time was not achievable with only the two of them, so it was agreed that we'd get some local tradesmen to come in and complete the necessary work. I trusted Ray to make that decision, we wanted it simple and functional, neither of us would have time to be swamped in chores, especially with our three little helpers. 'Wipeable' and 'neutral' were both high up the list of criteria.

From the comfort of Keeper's Cottage, Mum and I ordered the home furnishings, the pieces that made a house a home. Although we were leaving, I'm sure that letting my parents have an input into the planning gave them a greater sense of involvement. I didn't want to raise suspicion with all the deliveries to the Cottage, so I sent everything directly to the farm.

Ray and Dad spent a month at the farm; they'd come home on a Friday, and head back early on a Monday, at the crack of dawn. Our farm was four miles from the nearest village, Dad and Ray had been frequenting the local public house, where they'd managed to rally the troops to assist in the house completion. I have no doubt it was instigated by dad, he was like an unleashed beast when mother was out of sight.

To the locals in The Miner's Lamp public house, Aileni, we were just 'The Bramwell's' and expecting another baby. Our life, to the new locals, would be so normal as to be boring. It was a breath of fresh air for us not to care about opinions. Fortunately, being so far out of the village would mean little contact, after the initial work.

We were expecting the house preparations to creep on for a couple more weeks, and at this point, I had weeks left, we were now racing towards single digits. As usual, we anticipated Dad and Ray home on the Friday evening. Mum had spent the Thursday with me, as I'd had an atrocious night with Hope teething; her cheeks were burning up, and the teething gel gave her little to no comfort. I spent most of the night cuddling her, she was clingy, wanting reassurance, and she was so helpless I couldn't be cross with her.

Dad's car pulled onto the drive at about 4 p.m. There was no Ray, I really hoped he'd be putting in an appearance, Hope needed her daddy. I needed Ray to hold me tight. As much as I wanted to go and enquire as to Ray's whereabouts, I thought better of it, I could see that blasted bike, propped up against the fence. Dad let himself in, and once I knew the door was latched I could ask what was going on.

"Where's Ray, why are you here, what's wrong? Is he OK? It's only Thursday."

"Sophia, calm down girl. Ray is fine, he's collecting something, and he'll be home shortly. Yes, I do know it's Thursday, we have some wonderful news, the house is complete."

Mum and I leapt up and down; my dad was swamped in hugs. He took Hope from my arms.

"I don't know what all the fuss is about, do you?" he asked her.

I heard gravel grinding under tyres. Ray had been to collect our new, second-hand 4x4, in silver. It was practical, seven seats, and a decent boot. He parked it up, and made his way into the house like it was nothing different. He too had noticed Maribel's bike.

I was worried that, by employing locals to help with the house, we'd not be able to start works on the barn for next season, but both Dad and Ray pointed out it was a necessity, and there was still plenty in the kitty, through buying only the bare minimum for the house by way of interiors. We'd bought from cheap stores, I'd seen it so many times in my career, a house chock-full of materialism, and they couldn't take it with them, this always resonated with me, rich or poor, in death we were equal.

Both Ray and I had very few belongings to take with us, none of the furniture in the cottage was mine, except the wingbacks; they were a double-edged sword. I didn't want to take them with me, they were part of Keeper's Cottage and I wanted a fresh start, with nothing of Jacob's, apart from the obvious... our children. However, these chairs were bought for Pom, and I couldn't bear to part with the memory of him sat in them. Mum and Dad kindly offered to store them in my old room, with Ray's belongings, until we drew a conclusion on what to do with the stuff.

I'd been packing our stuff into boxes, and every week he'd take a little more to Lovett's Farm, meaning that when we were ready to do a moonlight flit, we had very little to move with.

We decided, with the help of Mum and Dad, we'd pack the cars once it had got dark. Ray would go on ahead in the morning, allowing him time to put up Hope's cot and air out the house before we got there.

We knew, by moving out under the cloak of darkness tonight, we'd be safe. It was Thursday night, and by 6 p.m. Maribel would be safely tucked up in the Church Hall for the weekly whist drive.

Hope spent the night in the travel cot, Ray and Dad had dismantled her proper cot, and they loaded it up, whilst I visited Walter. I wanted to say goodbye to him, without him knowing the truth. I went to thank him for being a good neighbour, under the guise of going on holiday and him keeping an eye out. It also bought us time, before the gossip started again.

We decided saying goodbye to my parents was best done in darkness, rather than tomorrow. I wasn't prepared for goodbyes; I was a wreck before we started. I would be seeing them in a few weeks, and I'd be ringing every week. We arranged Saturday nights at 5.30 p.m. as our phone call time, and we'd alternate weeks for who called whom. Ray vowed to my parents that he'd look after me.

Once my parents had gone, we sat in silence, on the floor, Ray propped against the sofa, with me in between his legs. He cradled my belly, the twins were always more active in the quite of the evening. We'd made a promise not to sleep together until after the babies had been delivered, there was a psychological boundary there I was willing not to cross, I had to respect my unborn children, and not violate them in utero. We also went as far as not sharing a bed, until it was in our home.

Tomorrow couldn't come fast enough, Keeper's Cottage had some wonderful memories, memories of my dear Pom, but they were memories, they weren't bricks and mortar, I could take them with me. I always imagined Jacob and me raising our two children and a dog at the cottage, even growing old together by the fireside. Life didn't have that mapped out for me; life had bought so much more. I couldn't wait to take one last journey out of Fremmington Ayshe, and I silently vowed to myself I'd never return.

"Tomorrow night Ray, it's our life, our home and our family. Our choices on how we live, I can't wait."

"Darling, bed. Then tomorrow will arrive here sooner, I can't wait to take you in my arms, in our bed."

For the final time, we kissed goodnight and retired to our separate quarters, knowing the next evening, I would get to lie in our bed, with Ray by my side.

Ray headed out early, dawn had barely snuck upon us, he wanted to maximise the day. He was buzzing with the get up and go attitude. He headed out as soon as he could, kissing both of us goodbye. I made the most of one last sunrise, sitting on the bed, I felt saddened yet excited, I guess indifferent. I made haste, stripping the beds down, I put the laundry in black bags; Monday was bin day so I put them in the dustbin ready; I refused to take sheets tainted by Jacob into my new life. It was Friday; I wanted to be away before ten. I had packed the kitchen into a suitcase, it lay bare, just Hope's breakfast and bottles waiting on the side. She hadn't stirred yet, time was ticking on, it was 8.30 a.m. but I couldn't wake her, it was the best sleep she'd had in days, granted it was Sod's law, but she deserved to rest. I packed the remainder in the car, knowing Walter wouldn't flinch at a couple of suitcases.

After Hope had finally eaten breakfast, we did one final sweep of the place, Hope held in my arms, propped up on my hip. Then, I closed the door to Keeper's Cottage for the final time, hearing the latch click on the blue door. I held Hope tight, biting my lip to hold the tears back. I poked the tarnished brass letterbox open, posting my key back through the door. I kissed her sweet little face. "Let's go home baby girl."

My life had already turned out the polar opposite to how I had envisaged it. I never had any ambition to be an undertaker, yet it had made me the woman I'd become, I'd learned compassion, patience, and most importantly, love. That love comes in all shapes and sizes, we find it in the most obvious of places, and we can also find it in the most obscure. I learned to love as if tomorrow may never arrive. We, Ray and I, found love in the most extreme and now we were free, to be each other's. Hope could have love, as a child should, from a mother or mother figure, and I would love Helen eternally, for the most amazing gift, her family.

It was five to ten, I'd just felt the rumble of the cattle grid for the final time. Regular as clockwork, there she was, on that blasted bike.

Siân Vidak

IT WAS OVER NOW!

Chapter Sixteen

Robson

Life at Lovett's Farm was one of firsts; our first night in our new home was nothing of grandeur, no house warming, a cup of tea whilst sitting on the wall, looking at the stars, as we toasted our future. Never had I seen such a pure glimmer, the clarity, with no light pollution, was magnificent. Ray had his arms wrapped around me as we shared the warmth, on the crisp clear night.

I was quiet, finally able to digest the enormity of what we had done. I had no regrets, no momentary doubts; I could envisage a wonderful future. Just the five of us. Before long, we'd be meeting our twins. My children would be Welsh, what had I done? Well, at least they had options come the Six Nations.

"Darling, let me take you to bed, let me cradle you in my arms, until you fall asleep. Lying with you by my side is all I need; it's all I have longed for. I want to feel your soft skin pressed up against mine. I can't wait to kiss you goodnight; and in the morning, wake to your smile."

"No sex until after the babies are delivered, you're OK with that? I'm sorry, it's another man's child, and for me it just feels morally wrong to sleep with a person who isn't biologically bound to them, whilst I carry them, does that make sense?"

"Sophia, we have all the time in the world, I don't think we exactly conform, do you? Our life, our choice, our bodies, it doesn't need justifying to anyone, if we are both happy with our decision. If I get a little hard, take it as a compliment, that I find you incredibly sexy, you turn me on and, in all honesty, I want to ravage your body. But I do understand"

"Well then Mr Bramwell, take me to bed."

Locking the door for the first time felt satisfying, it was ours, I could let in whomever I chose, and from now on, could shut the door to the rest of the world.

Getting into our bed, with fresh linen, I burst into tears; I was overcome by the day, by the last few weeks. The linen symbolised the fresh start for me. I was overcome with relief. We had become a "normal" family by taking a massive gamble. No one could hurt me anymore.

I had no nerves as Ray undressed himself, the amount of body hair he had didn't put me off, although it was all burning orange, I was concerned, in the middle of the night, I might think I had been captured by an orangutan. Ray's arm muscles always bulged, even an XL t-shirt, looked like it had shrunk in the wash, he was big and strong, and I wasn't disappointed to be with him. Ray, on the other hand, had to share his bed me, it wasn't exactly 'sexy' I was exuding at this stage of pregnancy.

"Squeeze up then, I know you're a wide load, but really the whole bed?"

"I was warming your side, honestly." I giggled.

Ray got into bed, lifting my side of the duvet, placing a kiss upon my belly.

"Goodnight you two."

I melted at his gentle gesture, and I drifted off in his arms, I was at ease. I hadn't slept so well in months, the pain and hurt had been worth it all.

Waking up at first light, as the autumnal sun shone through, I looked at Ray, fast asleep, lightly snoring as his face rubbed a wet patch on his pillow. I was appreciative for the gifts I had in Ray and Hope.

Hope of Ray

Walking down the staircase, watching the dawn light filter through the house, I was humbled by such a simple pleasure. Looking out of the kitchen window, across the farm, the morning dew glistened; I imagined how amazing a winter's frost must crunch under welly boots. I couldn't wait to explore, and meet each season as it came.

Taking us both up a cup of tea, I was in no doubt that our empire would be built on brews by the bucket load. I stood at the window, alternately looking at Ray, and then looking outside; neither showed any sign of stirring quite yet.

Hope had other ideas. Picking her up, knowing I was going to be her main carer, day in and day out, as Ray ran the farm, was a daunting prospect. At the moment, she had all my time and focus, how would I split my attentions three ways in a few weeks time? Helen played on my mind, would she approve of me, and how I reared her child? She must have had faith in my capabilities, to want me as Hope's guardian.

I took Hope into our room, I held her in my arms, and as we looked out over our farm, I made her a promise.

"Well baby girl, I love you, I have since the very first time I held you. I promise you, Hope Elizabeth Bramwell, I will be the best Mumma I can be to you."

"What beautiful sentiments to wake up to, from the woman I love, who holds our daughter in her arms."

"Our daughter?"

I sat on the foot of the bed, as I lay Hope next to Ray.

"Yes, our daughter, our twins, our family... I can't wait to spend the day exploring with you both, making plans for the future."

Ray pressed his lips against mine as we greeted the morning.

"Good morning, nice tits in that dressing gown, by the way."

He leapt out of bed, like a child, ready and raring to go, he'd have skipped breakfast given the chance. He was excited, and I didn't begrudge him that feeling, he just had to remember that he had a heavily pregnant woman and an infant in tow.

Ray had become the father of all lists, he'd started making plans, sketches, and he was wading through a collection of 'red tape' booklets from the local council; it was more than amazing to see him come back to life with such spirit.

In the first couple of weeks, we met our antenatal team, it was a great relief, and I now felt prepared to meet my babies. I would be left until 37 weeks, hoping for a spontaneous labour, but otherwise I'd be induced, not being allowed past 38 weeks.

We were incredibly vulnerable. Ray had ghosts, that would no doubt haunt him, and I was birthing multiple babies, on my first attempt. There was no reason I shouldn't birth naturally, this was preferred, but I was open to anything, providing my babies arrived safe and well. I didn't bother with a birth plan; I didn't want to be disappointed if it didn't happen how I had planned, so instead I opted to go with the flow.

Mum and Dad came to the farm for their first visit; they'd stay for up to a month. All three of us stood at the gate, waiting to meet them. Ray crossed the ford to greet them, and, like we did the first time we saw the farm together, we walked them in on foot; it was far more impressive that way.

The first thing my dad did was shake Ray's hand; he was always still so formal. Ray chivalrously helped mother across the bridge. The bridge was one of the first repairs we did on the farm. Ray widened it, allowing for a handrail on both sides.

Mum put her hands straight out for Hope, and she gave her an enormous cuddle, it was a moment to savour like no other, Hope was their grandchild.

"My, my, how you've grown little one, are you going to show me your new home?"

"Hello Mum, hi Dad, welcome to Lovett's Farm."

"My, look at that view; I don't get tired of that." My dad was romancing at the view he'd enjoyed so much while renovating.

We headed into the house, mum was super excited to look around, dad looked forward to seeing how we had turned the bare shell he left into a home. First on the agenda though, was putting the kettle on.

I had an island in the kitchen, it was my pride and joy, we had stools and three highchairs tucked away under the counter; I very much saw the kitchen as the hub of our home.

There was a bench seat, which we had reclaimed from the local Wesleyan Church; according to the locals, yuppies had bought the chapel and were doing it up; they were all up in arms about it. Crikey knows how they didn't feel that way about us, I had a sneaking suspicion that dad's 'customer relations' in the pub may have smoothed the way for us. We gave the locals employment, while the house was done up.

Our table was dressed with a jug in the centre; eventually I would fill it with seasonal flowers from our farm. The house was already baby proof; with gates on all doors and the staircase. Hope couldn't walk yet, she couldn't even crawl, but she could roll and pull herself along on her belly, she was a nippy number. I did foresee my mother having terrible trouble with the baby gates, and my dad referring to them as blasted things every time he struggled.

Mum gushed at how airy our kitchen was, and how homely and warm the living room looked. She loved the old horseshoes, which we'd found around the farm, being displayed on our oak fireplace lintel.

Upstairs, we showed my parents to their room first; we knew mum and dad would be regular visitors, I wanted to make them as comfortable and welcome as possible. They had grey curtains, complimented with soft pastels, greens and blues. Their room looked out over the wild flower meadow, at the back of the house.

Mum adored Hope's room, soft pinks and lilacs accessorised the magnolia walls; it was everything a little girl's room should be, according to her.

While in the nursery, mum questioned why we had two cots in there, if Hope had her own room. We had to come clean; I had a guilty smirk on my face as I announced to my parents that I was actually expecting twins. They didn't say a word, they just looked in disbelief.

I could only apologise for such selfish actions, rationalising that I'd not wanted to induce stress with anyone knowing, or that I didn't know how this pregnancy would pan out. They warmed to the idea quickly, or at least pretended to.

It was going to be a long month; I hadn't lived with my parents for years, and I was under no illusions that each other's foibles wouldn't drive us all scatty. I didn't want to hear about Fremmington Ayshe, it didn't have a place in our life any more; I'd left all that toxicity behind. Mum kept going on about this one and that one, I had to suck it up and pretend I was interested, it was mum's way of clinging on to the commonality we had.

Although, it appears I should be very grateful to Sarah Finney, for taking the limelight off us and our "moonlight flit", as it had been dubbed. According to mother, she was caught having a little extracurricular activity with Dean, the local gardener; who is about thirty years younger than her. He was paying particular attention to her petunias, if I knew what mother meant. I knew Dean; he was in my year at school. I did have a titter at mother's euphemism.

Dad had set about the paperwork that had daunted Ray; we wanted to submit planning to the local authority, I was relieved he had taken the task on, Ray and I didn't have the time or focus for it, yet we needed to address it, ready to maximise our opportunities for the next wedding season.

One evening, dad decided we'd all go for some, as he put it, "good old pub grub" at the local, called the Miner's Lamp. He was at the bar, ordering another Scotch for himself, when he bumped into a chap called Robson Gable, who'd done some of the work in our house. Robson worked in the local villages as a casual labourer or farm hand. Before the evening was over, dad had negotiated a price to hire Robson for three weeks work.

Ray and dad had decided to fix the barn roof, before winter truly set in. If they needed to, dad would apply for permission on the work, retrospectively. Mother was all of a flutter, according to her, she'd never seen dad this alive and commanding. I knew I'd be sleeping with a pillow over my head, to muffle any noises tonight.

Dad brought Robson over and introduced him to mum and me, when I got up from behind the table, to shake Robson's hand, the first words he ever uttered to me were, "Wow, that's some bump!"

Chapter Seventeen

Faith and David

I'd been doing the nesting thing for weeks, it was infuriating not being able to work the farm, and I was experiencing cabin fever with mum. Her desire to rearrange parts of my kitchen, and leaving the teapot out continually, with the sodding tea cosy she brought, was now causing my pregnant state to want to beat her senseless with the cosy. Ray said I was hiding my feelings very well. I had a feeling he was lying, as he feared for his own safety.

We'd fallen into a routine where the men would work and come in for a hearty lunch, Robson included. He had slipped into the dynamic well with Ray and my father. We'd vowed not to mix with the locals, and here we were, feeding one every lunch time.

I was feeling restless. A good walk, to the top fields, where the men were working, clearing the grounds ready for the new campsite, should blow away the cobwebs. It took me a fair while, as I puffed and panted, with my waddling body. Ray was not impressed at my straying so far away from the house, though he couldn't express that in front of my dad, and Robson, and the two extra labourers who had appeared. I don't know how he thought he'd explain all the wages being paid. We had a mutual, 'I beg your pardon' look at each other, and left it at that. Ray insisted on driving me home.

I'd made it to 36 weeks and three days. The walk had worked, I retired to my bed early, about an hour after I put Hope down, I was shattered, and maybe the fresh air would help me sleep. I'd been having shooting pains on my left side, I put it down to overdoing it during the day, but I wasn't going to tell Ray and get the 'I told you so' lecture.

I woke at 4:48 a.m. when turning over, I'd had some pain killers but they hadn't numbed the pain. I lay awake, I couldn't switch off, I went downstairs for a drink, and roamed the house, plumping the cushions, folding the laundry on the airer. I headed back to bed with the idea of maybe a couple of hours more sleep, if I were lucky. Lying back in bed, I started pawing the pillows like a dog would his bed, my head finally felt comfortable on the pillow, I closed my eyes.

I felt a trickle down my leg, I must have wet myself; I embarrassedly tapped Ray on the shoulder, I'd have to change the sheet.

"Ray, I've had an accident, I need to change the sheet."

I stood up, ready to get the fresh sheet out of the drawer, more liquid came running down my leg. I was sure that was my waters.

"Scrap that Ray, my waters have broken, I'm certain I haven't wet myself, I think."

Within 15 minutes we were on the road, the hospital ready and waiting for us. Twenty minutes into the journey, I started feeling pressure; it was causing me to arch my back and raise myself off the seat, the pain was intolerable.

"Do I need to stop?" Ray cautiously asked.

I was like a grizzly bear snapping at him, "Don't you dare stop!"

We were met by the maternity team; with a room already prepped, and an anaesthetist on standby, ready to administer the epidural, just in case. I didn't like the feeling of being restricted; luckily for us, I was able to move around quite easily, which made the experience less stressful. With our initial examination, I was already in established labour, at about five centimetres. The pains I had been having the previous evening must have been the start labour, unbeknown to me, baby novice.

We were good to progress naturally, with all adequate precautions in place, just in case. The pain started ramping up out of nowhere and caught me off guard. How could a woman do this at all, never mind going back for seconds?

Gas and air was the most fantastic invention I had ever come across, although it made my mouth feel dry, and my voice husky, I was not giving it up for anyone. I was told on several occasions I should breathe some normal air. Normal air made the reality of the pain come sharply into focus, gas and air, on the other hand, sent me to new worlds I hadn't ever explored before.

I lost all my inhibitions, I think Ray wanted the room to swallow him up, I felt like I was drunk. Drunk me was always more fun. I proposed to Ray; apparently, it was incredibly romantic, as I confessed my undying love for him, in between grunting in pain. He was, "My knight in glittering armour, who rescued me!" apparently.

The midwifery team, had switched shifts, and now a new girl was examining me; she was definitely eager, my eyes popped out of my head, as she felt like she was trying to locate my tonsils. She pulled her gloves off, and pressed the call button. Ray's face drained quickly, as she didn't communicate with us.

"Is she OK? What's happening? The babies?"

I could hear what was being said, but the gas and air made me feel like I was under water, the voices muffled and distorted.

"She's fully dilated; we're going to move her to theatre, just in case. Sophia, we're moving you to theatre, do you understand. Take some air

Sophia, natural breaths." She was very insistent, as she nudged the gas away from me.

I was desperate to dull the pain again, flee the untold agony. I had my gas and air replaced with a portable canister. The bed railings were snapped up, and I was ready to be transported.

I felt like royalty as I was about to be wheeled to theatre on my NHS sedan chair, my entourage poised to follow me.

A wave of heat came flushing through my body, as I felt this immense pressure, and an urge to poo.

"ARGH, I need a poo, I need to go to the toilet!"

"Sophia, we're going nowhere, you're pushing, go with your body, when you feel another contraction, take a deep breath, put your chin on your chest, and push."

It felt like there was no respite; I could barely catch a breath before I had to push again. I wasn't breathing anything but gas and air, I was not letting that bad boy go. I felt this stretching; my skin felt like it was being pulled apart, fibre by fibre, just like Blu Tac; I felt like I was burning, as if someone was giving me a Chinese burn.

"Blow Sophia, blow, blow..."

"Here she is, Twin A, a girl. The midwife took her away, giving her a vigorous rub, and she let out an almighty bleat. I was brought back down to earth with the most amazing endorphin-filled thud, I had a daughter. Looking at Ray, he let the tears freely flow.

"Come on then Dad, you can cut the cord."

He looked at me...

"Go on then!"

"Sophia, Twin B is in the right position to be delivered, take some gas, take the edge off, before you start contracting again, let your body guide you, let it do the work."

I felt like I was in a time warp, I'd just had all this pain, and here I was, repeating it all again. Not having to wait for my cervix to dilate again was a bonus; that had been boring and exhausting. I was feeling a little bit like a pro as I embarked on another round of pushing, it wasn't as much of a shock this time. Seven minutes after Twin A, Twin B was born.

"We have a boy, Sophia, a girl and a boy."

Ray cut the cords for both babies; life in that instant became wholesome.

"Do they have names yet?"

"Not yet, you'd think I'd had nine months to think about it?" I jested.

I was introduced to my babies as they were brought over and placed on to my chest, for skin-to-skin contact. Our daughter lay on my chest, while our son lay upon his daddy's. I would have to stay in hospital overnight, just for observations, and hopefully we'd be discharged tomorrow, then the real fun would begin.

Each bed on the postnatal ward had accompanying reclining chairs, for fathers to stay the night on, but we had such a long drive facing us tomorrow, after much persuasion, Ray agreed he'd stay in the local lodge, near the hospital, and be fully rested.

By 10am the following morning, I was discharged, complete with a box of iron tablets. We took the road home slow and steady; Ray was diligent, knowing he had such precious cargo on board, and that I was a smidge fragile too.

We were greeted at the door by my parents; seeing Hope's beautiful face, I realised how much I had missed her, I took her out of my mother's arms, bursting into tears. I was overwhelmed, and so thankful we'd been given a chance of a life together; our journey of the last 24 hours had really driven it home to me.

"Mum, Dad, and of course, our big girl Hope, I have two very special babies for you to meet. Hope, this is Twin A, your baby sister. Introducing: Faith Joyce Bramwell, six pounds, three ounces. And this is Twin B, your baby brother: David Parker Bramwell, five pounds nine ounces."

My parents just kept staring at the twins as they held them; they'd gone from no grandchildren to three, in the space of six months or so. It was hard to take in such enormity.

The initial couple of weeks, while my parents were there, were delightful; I could take plenty of naps, having moved on to formula, as breastfeeding was too demanding; having a second set of hands was most welcome. Ray had theoretically taken time off, but still managed to go out most days, and plot with my father. Mum made us proper home-cooked food; I couldn't have had better treatment, and was so thankful for her efforts. Ray was delighted with the cooking, as he knew, once they left, it would be more 'fend for yourself'.

My parents left when the twins were three weeks old, Ray took some time out, so we could now be a family of five, and not to throw me completely in at the deep end, it was more of a phased return to work for him.

I was so thankful we were our own bosses; Faith suffered terribly with colic, nothing would sooth her, it felt like hour after hour, we'd be walking around the house with her, tag teaming it when Hope or David needed attention.

David was a very settled baby, he was quiet, late at night you'd find him snuggled with Ray, as he attempted to plan more of the works for the farm. David was always content in Ray's company, they had a special bond. Ray had Faith in his arms, her screaming was relentless, he thought of singing to her; maybe that would help, if she could feel the vibrations in his chest. The only snag was, Ray could barely manage a rugby song or two. Faith didn't really like Swing Low Sweet Chariot, however, she did approve of Jerusalem; whenever she sought comfort as she fussed, this was our 'go to' song from here on in.

Chapter Eighteen

Noël

My parents decided that they would let us have Christmas as a family; the babies would be more aware and active next year, so they'd spend Christmas with us then. However, they'd be with us for Hope's first birthday.

We bought a Christmas tree from the village, and brought it home to decorate. We hadn't any baubles though; we hadn't factored in that crucial part of a Christmas tree. I knew, in a box somewhere, I had paints, so we set about printing the children's hands and feet, a task easier said than done. The squirming led to my arms looking like a paint colour chart. In our wisdom, we thought it was such a beautiful idea, that we'd make it our family tradition.

Christmas Day was an anticlimax, we had three children who were clueless as to what was happening, but they still had high demands and needs, it was a day like any other really. Hope had new presents, a dolly, a wooden cart with bricks, stacking things, we decided not to go overboard, and the babies had new clothes, not wrapped.

Ray came up trumps for my present, how he managed, with all the other chaos going on, to even think of such a heart-felt gift, I wasn't sure, he had set the bar high for all future Christmases. Helen was still alive when Ray heard me tell her about a paperweight I had gifted my grandparents; I was eight years old at the most, it was a snow globe with a piglet, dressed in his swimmers and a rubber ring, all around the outside of the globe, it looked like sand and shells, with a bucket and spade. It was gaudy. It got broken a couple of years later, and it was the only one, in the set of Pom's paperweights, that was missing. Ray had spent countless hours searching until he found one; I could place it on the bookshelf and complete the set once more.

My gift to Ray was pathetic on reflection, a gift voucher, so he could get some new work boots, it wasn't very original, but it was appreciated. I think the snuggling up on Christmas night, and the unexpected Christmas fumble, on the other hand, was much more to his taste.

We didn't bother with a roast, it was far too much faff and just increased the workload, so a bacon sandwich it was, and in the evening, a ploughman's. We did treat ourselves to a luxury tin of biscuits, and some fancy tea, for the occasion, it was perfect. Our Christmas, our traditions.

Christmas and New Year had been and gone, we had conquered the festivities. Now it was time for another first, Hope's first birthday. I was excited our daughter had reached one as a happy and healthy baby. It still amazed me how she grew every day.

The evening before her birthday was remarkably calm. Mum and dad were in the living room, putting out the birthday bunting, while I finished icing her cake; I couldn't stop reliving this time last year, remembering Helen, the last time I saw her. I put the pallet knife down, breaking out into tears.

"Sophia, my darling, what's wrong?" Ray lovingly asked, as he came to comfort me.

"It should be Helen, she should be the one here faffing around, worrying if the icing is smooth, not me, but Helen. I feel guilty, she was robbed of her dream and now I'm in her shoes living it."

"You and I both know Helen couldn't ice a cake if her life depended on it! Do you remember the cake she did for Tori Atherton? The horse looked more like a sheep."

"You're right, I just feel the gnaw of guilt."

"Well don't, Helen would be so thankful to you, loving Hope the way you do."

I licked the icing off my finger, and Ray set about cleaning the spatula, it was phallic at best.

"I can't wait for my turn." I suggestively whispered in Ray's ear.

"Do you know what a fucking tease you are? Whose ridiculous idea was it to abstain from sex until after we are married? Apparently, it would make our bond greater, and now you tell me you're gagging for it, you dirty bitch." Ray retorted, with equal playfulness.

I coyly turned my back; pulling my face as if to say, 'smart arse'.

"Ray, you'll spoil your dinner, I've been slaving over a hot stove all afternoon, it's lamb casserole, and crumble for afters." There was nothing like a parent to ruin the moment, as mother chastised Ray.

Hope's birthday, was wonderful, it indirectly symbolised new beginnings; we had survived all the trials that the first year of life brought, and waded through a little bit more than that too.

My parents bought Hope a gold ring, with her initials engraved in the heart, it made a beautiful keepsake. I was consistently blown away at how they treated Hope as one of their own, with no hesitation.

We had one last birthday tradition to finish with. The cake, no doubt she would make the room a disaster zone, as she decorated the floor with crumbs.

Before we commenced with the cake, I decided to give her my personal and heartfelt present. Ray sat on the floor, while she stood and rocked.

"Happy birthday, my darling girl, I love you." My voice cracked.

I gave Ray a wrapped package, so he could open it on Hope's behalf. He looked curious, as he knew nothing about it. Ray cautiously unwrapped the paper, peaking in at a white box, which gave nothing away. Opening the box, he pulled out a photo frame, which was hinged like a book, in mahogany wood.

To the right was a photo of Helen, it was my favourite picture of her, she was sat under a tree, in the park. The sunlight filtered through the trees and leaves, her hair laden in golden tones. To the left was a certificate. I decided to name a star in Helen's honour; she would always shine on us, guiding us through life.

Ray never articulated how he felt about the frame; he was never negative, nor positive. We never spoke of it again. Hope's birthday finished on a high, I'm sure of that.

Then we faced the anniversary of Helen's death. We both wanted a reminder of Helen, which we could look at, but was abstract enough the children wouldn't ask questions about it, at least until they were adults, and could comprehend the upbringing we tried to create for them.

We planted an apple tree, in the side garden; the fruit it would bare would always show us new beginnings, which is what we now had to do, a year on. Look forward not back. It was cathartic, freeing us of the guilt; we could share a final tear, as we had closure.

It was a late Easter that year, we had been in the house a little over six months, but we finally had something to celebrate. The council had approved the use of our barn as a wedding facility. It had been a long hard slog, throughout the winter, to ensure we had the barn fully functioning. Ray had done us proud, working in all winds and weathers; he battled the elements, with very welcome help from Robson Gable.

After completing his three weeks work, Robson disappeared off the farm that final day, and we didn't see him for maybe a month or so. Out of the blue, he knocked on our door, he wanted to appeal to our better nature, and see if we would employ him on a regular basis.

I admired his courage, putting faith in us, the two blow-ins, who completely removed themselves from village life. We were an unknown quantity. I was tired, the twins had broken me, and I couldn't spare any time to help Ray, even with the most mundane of tasks. Having spoken to my dad, he supported the employment of Robson, as of then he became a regular at the lunch table.

As the bulbs peeked through the earth, we decided it was time. What better way to launch our new venture than to have the first marriage at Lovett's Farm... our own.

We decided it wasn't about what we looked like, or what we spent, it was about the journey we had made to get here, and making one final commitment to complete us as a family.

I had bought the children tops, with fairies and dinosaurs, they encapsulated gender stereotypes perfectly. They were babies, and I was making the most of dressing them cutely; before I knew it, I'd have to relinquish control, as they waded through the levels of self-expression.

Ray wore the boots, shirt and trousers that he had on the first day we met. I'm not quite sure, after middle age hit, how he managed to shoehorn himself into those trousers. I found a dress in the charity shop; it was blue and red silk, depicting a meadow around the bottom. I fell in love with the dress, and I paid £4 for my wedding outfit, I couldn't have been happier with my find. I scooped my hair up on one side, popping a flower in its usual ragged mess. I didn't wear shoes; I'd rather have nature pressed against my soles.

Mum and dad were surprised at our impulsiveness, but they had become accustomed to our lifestyle, nothing really fazed them anymore, and they went with the flow where we were concerned. They saw it as a huge privilege to be our witnesses.

Ray and I had decided to write our own vows, we wanted simple and to the point, I was more than happy with our efforts.

"Forever, in our home, forever our family, forever I'll be yours."

The wedding photographs were more than I could have ever imagined. The five of us together.

After the official Registrar had been and gone, we put on our work clothes and headed out to the fields, just the two of us, as we got to work together for the day. I always enjoyed when mum and dad visited, as it gave me the chance to be Sophia again, creating part of the dream I had desired.

Our wedding breakfast was a packed lunch of cold pasta from the night before, caramel biscuits, and a flask of tea.

My parents were mortified that we'd just slipped right back into family life, no chance to be 'Mr and Mrs Bramwell' in the Honeymoon Suite. Mum had the gorgeous idea to put us up in our new glamping pods. She made the pod into a beautiful retreat for the night; she made us feel supported and loved.

Swept away since we had arrived at Lovett's Farm, being the parents to three infants, the night of freedom, to explore my husband, in full physical form, was finally here. The past few months, being in such close quarters, it had been excruciating to abstain at times. Having the twins, and letting my body recover from such brutality, was a blessing in disguise. So many times, I had wanted to break the no sex rule, but deep down I was glad we hadn't.

We had a friendship built on many, many years of good, bad and indifferent. We had a relationship built on mutual support, strength and courage. We had a marriage built on trust and love; now sex was a bonus.

My body had changed so dramatically in recent months I had lost some of my confidence, but I knew Ray loved me, his gentle touch demonstrated that, he took it slowly, letting me lead, as he explored my body.

The scene had been beautifully set, as we spent our wedding night in soft illuminations of fairy lights. Our favourite cups, set on a tray, tin with an enamel painting of the South Devon coastline, a place we held dear, it was our happy place. The sheepskin rug fibres danced between our toes as we toasted our future with a warm brew.

"The Bramwells, today, tomorrow, and forever, my darling Sophia."

I didn't have to say a word; I let out a small sigh of contentment, as the smile beamed across my face. I hid my head in Ray's arms, as he stroked my forehead, kissing it. I knew it that instant, I was his everything.

In the months before we got to this day, the touching of one another, but never fully exploring, it had lead me to feeling ready to explode.

Although the anticipation was standing at the fore, in the back of mind, apprehension crept in. Breaking the biscuit seal, I bought a moment to compile my thoughts. Would I be good enough?

Would my post partum body be a letdown? The last person he slept with, was Helen. I found it hard to commit to the moment, as I wrestled my demons.

Ray had started to kiss my neck; his hands met my shoulders as he started to massage away the tension. I pulled away. Scared our wedding night was going to be an anti climax

"Can you give me a second darling? I'm sorry."

"Sophia, we have all the time in the world, I'd wait an eternity for you. We can take it as slowly as you want... or, alternatively, we can just go to sleep for an entire night, uninterrupted too. I love you Sweetheart"

"Aren't you just a bit worried it's all too much pressure? That we'll be disappointed?"

"I'll let you into a little secret, wonderful wife of mine. I'm more than bricking it myself; I want to be your everything, leaving you wanting more, I hope to God I live up to your expectations.

"You blew my mind, the last time we slept together, I can still smell your perfume, taste your lips.

"It feels like barely a second of time has lapsed, yet here we are two different people, and most definitely in love. It was like a chemical explosion between us then, I have no doubt, it will be now. This time though, it's forever"

Ray didn't have to say another word. He was right, we'd been here before; he'd left me once upon a time questioning everything, he left me infatuated. It didn't take long for those feelings, to resurrect themselves. The only boundaries I had to respect now though, were ours.

Our clothes were rapidly heaped on the floor, we tried so hard to pace ourselves, attempting to explore one another sensually, it was so clumsy, and the notion was quickly abandoned. Ray may have been relatively short, but he was brutish. The dynamic of hard and fast was easily established. Feeling like I was being pounded into the middle of next week, hadn't left me disappointed, he left me screaming, wanting more.

Hard and fast was to become the story of our lives. His mighty thrust, as he pinned my arms to the bed, may have been routine, it was how we enjoyed it, it was failsafe sex, an easy way to reunite us and re-affirm those important emotional and physical bonds we had as man and wife.

Birthdays, anniversaries, Christmas, the times that were significant; we'd make the effort to spice up our sex life, keeping it fresh, even that was met with routine. I'd get the little silk number out of the drawer; it only saw the light of day a handful of times each year. I'd spray the good perfume, hoping to mask the smell of baby vomit, and even go really all out and brush my hair, to try and remove the yoghurt from it. It didn't matter how much effort we made, the extra foreplay, more nipple stimulation and considerably more cock sucking, until he was nearly cumming in my mouth. The fun and diversity always had the same conclusion; I'd ride him, all the while dangling my tits in his mouth.

From an outsiders view, we no doubt lacked spontaneity, but when you're up at 5 a.m. every day to the screaming of a child, and the demands for food start instantly, where you have to schedule in a crap three months in advance, and ask permission to speak from your tiny captors. Anything you can get is a bonus, the passion never dwindled though; you got to appreciate the small acts, the little gropes here and there, a stolen kiss. Just the look of burning desire between the two of you over the battle field. That, despite the fact neither of you has showered in two days, you're tired, and in such a rush to stop the screaming first thing, you put yesterday's pants on inside-out. Given the chance, right now, you'd still do each other. The internal monologue, when he walked in the room, all manly and ready for work, of "Fuck I want to do you, you're buff, please ravage me now."

The way we shared our days, being in each other's pockets, that's what made us; happiness and contentment was a huge part of our sex life. Having so many interruptions, made us appreciate intimacy, never taking it for granted.

The twins first birthday was another momentous occasion to mark in our life. We'd survived another year of firsts. They were incomparable to Hope's first year. Faith and David's first years were polar opposites. Faith had spent most nights crying and screaming, as she battled colic, and she let us know as she painfully cut every tooth. She was very highly strung, most definitely her mother's daughter. David was a dream, in comparison, he slept well and you barely noticed when he cut his teeth, he was a much more contented child.

As of yet, as a twosome, they weren't showing the dynamic their father and I had; I hoped Ray's influence, and nurture versus nature, was to have a play in their development.

I was adamant the twins had to be individuals, they were different personalities. NO joint presents, two cakes, it was a precedent I was certain had to be fulfilled. My parents were with us for another milestone, I really hoped, by the end of their visit, they might have the chance to see Faith take her first steps. David was too relaxed to even bother attempting such a feat; he could get around perfectly well shuffling on his bottom. Faith wasn't satisfied being restricted like this; she was all over the place, pulling herself up cruising.

I admired how my parents treated the twins exactly like Hope for their birthdays, there was no division of my children, Ray's children, they were ours, and I was eternally grateful for such warm tones they showed. Faith was gifted a gold ring with her initials in the heart, and David a signet ring, not dissimilar to my father's, gold with a Victorian-esque pattern, and his initials in the centre. Just as Hope had a star named for her as a special present from us, alongside her new toys, I did the same for the twins. Two stars, 'David' after my dear Pom, and 'Jacob'. I couldn't rationalise my decision, my gut told me it was the right thing to do.

I may have been broken by them, physically and emotionally, but I was far from whole before I fell pregnant. Jacob had spent years systematically chipping away at my being, the twins however made me into a woman, a mother. The day I held them for the first time, my life had new meaning. I was scared, intimidated by these tiny beings, their fragility, they depended on me. I was empowered. Lost, yet found. I would die in an instant for them. I was defined for my lifetime as their Mumma.

Over the last 12 months, I had fallen in love, finding something organic. I'd had a lot of time to re-evaluate the relationship with Jacob, we had more unhappy times than I cared to admit, battling our egos, our politics, and getting the upper hand. It wasn't what I wanted the twins to turn into, if they did, we were in for a rough ride in teenage years.

As we sang happy birthday to them, we had the final chapter of closure needed. I did it, we did it, Jacob was finally thought of for the last time, and I didn't need to feel guilt. I felt admiration, to the man stepping up to the plate, changing their nappies, comforting them and providing a life for them. Ray was their daddy.

Chapter Nineteen

Reuben-Ray

We had been so busy with life on the farm, and the business, that the house had become overtaken with outgrown clothes and toys, and we'd never cleared out the children's drawers since we moved in. I was drowning in hand-me-downs.

The weather had set in; black clouds boasting heavy showers, and the wind was like ice. Ray couldn't work outside for the day, so I was going to tackle the increasing mountain of child paraphernalia, in my head I'd end up with a streamlined house. Ray was under strict instructions not to let the children interrupt.

I pulled out the clothing onto the floor; I would work through it, separating it into strategic piles. The charity box was filling up fast; it overflowed before long. Hope's floral baby grows, which Ray and I had bought together, that day in the supermarket, were now in my hand. I had a flutter in my gut as I placed them in the top of the box. As soon as I let go, I whipped them back out of the box, clutching them for all my life was worth.

I headed downstairs; the baby grows still firmly in my grip. Ray was about to start prepping the children's lunch. I stood in the doorway, crying, watching him be a wonderful father; I could hear the babbles of the children in the next room. I wanted this all again, with him, with our child, made from our love.

"Ray, I want another baby."

"OK."

"Did you hear me Ray? I want another baby."

"Yeah, I heard you; I thought you'd never cave-in and ask."

"You want more Mr B?"

"Darling, I'd have an army with you, I want a large family; I love you, why wouldn't I want your babies. Just tell me when, and I'll give you one for the team. Why the change of heart?"

"Putting the baby clothes in the charity box, it made me realise, I'd never have those firsts again, or the smell of a new born, and I realised I wanted it all, with you, from start to finish."

Reuben-Ray was conceived within three months. After I had the positive test, I was elated, nothing felt jaded this time, just pure. We went through the usual motions of booking in with the midwife and going for dating scans. It was no different this time than it was the first; it still felt as daunting, waiting for the confirmation of their heartbeat. Feeling them kick was just as exciting, their rhythms were totally different to the twins, giving me a gentle reminder that they'd have a completely different personality.

At every antenatal appointment, Ray clenched my hand tight; reminding me of the first time we shared the experience.

Ray had been out on the farm, he was fencing the top field, Robson, as always, was by Ray's side. Considering we had never wanted to employ anyone, or be part of the village, Robson had fitted in to our family perfectly. He knew, only too well, how village gossip could impact your day-to-day life, and affect you mentally, ambushing your thoughts.

We had started building a good reputation, as a family-friendly camping experience, being child-centric was a huge selling point, so new play equipment was being installed as well.

It was first light, as always, Ray would be up and out with the larks in the spring and summer months. He'd do a couple of hours work, and then head in for breakfast. The beauty of living in isolation was having no neighbours to worry about being antisocial with.

I was about 38 weeks pregnant, with our first child together; we knew I'd go to full term, unlike with the twins. The children were ready for their day on the farm, they had two types of footwear, mules for the garden, and wellies, nothing else, they were farmers, and quite insistent about such issues.

I loved hanging the washing out, watching it flap in the wind. David was a typical boy, he'd wield his wooden sword about, as he dodged through the sheets, commanding his teddy to "man the ship", and the naughty toy to "walk the plank", as his toy crocodile lurked in the water. The girls were always a lot more political in their play; they both had wonderful imaginations, filled with all the girly unicorns, fairies, and princesses.

If not, they were vets or mums. Hope and Faith always wanted what the other had, they had power struggles in every game, neither would compromise, and they would end up brawling over the tiny details. They couldn't play with each other, or without each other, and they were very needy. Poor David always ended up in the middle of those conflicts, as they'd both try to insert themselves into his game, causing him much distress. David was a lone ranger, and didn't want to tolerate his sisters' antics.

At breakfast, I was feeling rotten, and I was off my food. I'd put it down to lack of sleep and the discomfort, the general end of pregnancy feeling, of having a human rip my body apart from the inside out; plus, running after three children, that played a huge part in my depleting energy levels.

Hope of Ray

The girls had fallen out as soon as they woke up, I hadn't even considered ascertaining what the issue was, this was just a normal daily occurrence; micromanaging it was impossible, in the blink of an eye they changed their feelings towards each other. The feud had overflowed downstairs, and was now present at breakfast; it resulted in cereal and milk spilling across the table, both the girls, and sweet David, who ended up crying, as he sat drenched, in-between his sisters; he was inconsolable. The girls were allocating blame to each other, in their juvenile little way.

I lost my shit, marched over and removed them both from the table, timing them out. They very quickly burst into hysterics and wailed for the duration; all the while, I'm monologuing: how they are sisters, and should love each other, they are both to blame, 'six of one, half a dozen of another'. They didn't understand half of what I said. They just kept going with the noise, and getting louder. I felt hypersensitive, walked away from them, back to the kitchen, into Ray's arms, and started wailing myself; proclaiming how rotten I felt.

Poor Ray didn't get an easy time of it, with three females in the house, David being his only ally. He told the girls off that morning too, it was rare for him to be the bad guy; the girls wrapped him around their little fingers as soon as they said "love you", and threw their arms around him. The girls promised him they would behave for mummy. I promised Ray I'd try and take it easy. I knew exactly where he was on the farm, and that if he came back at lunchtime, to check on me, I'd be fine. He promised he'd work until noon, then call it a day, and take over the childcare.

The children were playing on the slide Granny and Pom had bought them for Christmas; the better weather was now allowing us to enjoy the outside once more. The girls had clearly learnt their lesson, and were now the best of friends; I, of course, was waiting for the tide to turn on their moods. Faith came down the slide at speed, flying off the end, with a thud to the floor. She was in a crumpled heap on the ground, sobbing incoherently, she was definitely going for best dramatic performance. Faith had become a rigid ball on the grass, picking her up caused a tight shooting pain, my back was hurting.

The children played outside as much as possible each day. They had disbanded from the slide, and there were now balls, ride-on toys, and skittles, all over the lawn. I tried to keep a handle on things by picking bits up. Another sharpening across my belly happened, but I carried on; maybe I just needed water. We headed in for drinks and snacks, the children sat at the table, and while filling David's bottle I dropped it, in pain again.

"Silly mamma!" I told them.

These were familiar pains, and I had no doubt where they would progress, I briefly wondered if they were, just maybe, possibly, Braxton-Hicks, and I'd jumped the gun. Nope, seven minutes later... Another! It was 10.30 a.m. and I already felt frazzled by the day. I had an hour and a half, before Ray would be in for the day, I could handle that, he'd be good to his word.

Unable to settle, I couldn't decide if I want to stand, sit, or squat, like a cat on a hot tin roof. I popped the children in front of the electronic babysitter; they didn't watch much telly, so this was a novel treat for them.

I started to time the pains; they had become regular. I could handle it, I'd done it before. This would result in our beautiful baby. I changed into suitable clothes, ready to leave as soon as Ray materialised. He would have to change first however; I'd chosen his clothes for him. I rang the hospital, they advised we come in as soon as possible. My parents weren't due for another week; when I told mother she was flummoxed, all flappy on the phone, but dad assured me they'd be here by the end of the day. I didn't have a clue who'd mind the children in the meantime.

The pain was intensifying, I kept pacing, I had half an hour before Ray would be home. Mind you, if he was late, I was tempted to rip his face off; the pain was flowing in unbearable bouts. My pelvis was excruciating, the contractions had gotten closer together, and they were lasting longer too.

I was at the window, waiting for Ray's return, I could hear the children laughing and singing to the television programme, they were oblivious to the unravelling in the kitchen. I waited. He wasn't appearing; knowing my luck, today he'd overrun and be late.

"I hate you poopy-head!"

David was crying, Hope comforting him. Faith had decided he was playing with them, regardless of David's feelings, she was adamant. David was being comforted in my arms, when Ray's body bobbed over the gate, as he climbed it, heading towards our yard. David was ushered back to the living room, while I edged to the door, stopping amid the pains.

"Ray!" I bellowed. "Ray... argh!"

I dropped to the floor, crouching in agony, as the pain consumed my body. Ray sprinted across the yard; even at his age, he left Robson on the starting blocks. I was writhing in pain; Ray scooped me off the floor, taking me to the kitchen, in the quiet.

"The baby, it's coming."

Robson came charging up, a little puzzled.

"Go sit with the children." Ray commanded Robson. Then, turning to me, "I'm ringing an ambulance, we'll never get you to hospital in time, I'm not having you on the roadside, making the car dirty, with my only assistance being a couple of Welsh hill sheep. No way."

Robson looked so spooked; he nodded, and made his hasty retreat to sit with the children. They loved him; he was great fun to be around; very often being a fairy, as per the girls' instructions.

"Ray, change out of your clothes, look in the pile there." I directed him to his pre-approved birthing outfit.

"I'm not leaving you, so it'll have to be a striptease act, right here; I see you've preselected how I should look."

"Shut up, and put your bloody boots on, you arse!"

Robson gingerly came to the door, he'd arranged for his mum to come and help him watch the children; she'd had seven herself, so Jenny was an old hand. We'd met her a few times, she was young, and didn't look old enough to have Robson; she had a tale or two, and her general opinion of men was low, she'd clearly been trodden on a few times, but she had a heart of gold.

"Ray, get the clean towels, they're in the laundry basket, put it on the Aga. We're going nowhere."

"He's going to be born at home?"

"No Ray, I thought I'd just nip into the village, see if there's room at the inn. Don't be ridiculous, of course at home!"

He was always so calm in the face of me panicking, he was old hat at my labours now; he'd seen me at my lowest, most vulnerable, and he still loved me.

Hope of Ray

"Call that ambulance again. It's coming; I've got that giant shit feeling."

I was on all fours, my skirt thrown up over my head. Ray, as relaxed as he was, lined the floor with clean linen, fresh off the line; he had towels to hand, out of the basket. He had to come to terms with a home birth very quickly, and that he was the only one here, he had improvised well.

"Sophia, darling, I need to take your knickers off."

He chuckled, I knew where his dirty mind was, he got the glare. My internal voice was saying, 'Make the most of it, you're never coming near me again!' The pains were barely allowing me to catch my breath, they were exhausting.

"I need to push Ray." I was scared, we had no help; what if the baby needed assistance, how would we cope? I was overcome with heat, my body had taken over, I couldn't rationalise with it. It was a natural process, I instinctively, and uncharacteristically, decided I should let my body do what it needed, and I went with it.

Reuben-Ray was delivered, by his father, in our home. By the time the paramedics arrived, he was wrapped up in a towel, nursing in my arms. They gave us the onceover, and a midwife visited. Reuben-Ray was our farm boy; he didn't have to leave the security of home to make his first appearance in the world. I adored his birthing experience.

Chapter Twenty

Leanna

Ray and I had been recklessly irresponsible since the arrival of Reuben-Ray. We had decided that, until I had stopped breastfeeding, an experience I strongly desired after such a wretched attempt with the twins, contraception wouldn't be critical, and we could play 'Russian roulette', maybe.

I fed Reuby for just over 18 months. After a ropey start, a midwife had come to the house, preaching how I must conform solely to his needs, to the exclusion of the other children. My temper and determination got the better of me, as I gave the wishy-washy, simpering-toned idiot, her marching orders. I had to balance the needs of them all; she left with a flea in her ear, never to darken my doorstep again.

I wasn't going to give up on the most natural experience I could ever encounter, I'd struggled before and was realistic, if he needed to go on a bottle, then that was OK too. Reuby had different ideas, he was a redhead, and determined, he finally decided to wean when he was ready, and on his terms.

The luxury of no periods was something I had taken advantage of; now they had returned, but they were erratic, sometimes on time, other times late, they had no established regularity. Ray and I didn't use condoms, we were lazy in that respect, and they killed the mood, I'd rather have not had sex than relied on them.

We went with the withdrawal method, we weren't ignorant to the chances of becoming pregnant again, but probably a little to blasé, if Mother Nature had better plans for us, who were we to argue.

By the time Reuby was two years old, I was staring back at two blue lines, and we were in the system yet again, going through the motions. The all too familiar signs were there, very early on. According to Ray, he only had to look at me a certain way and he'd knock me up. He was now a veteran to my pregnancy symptoms. In his words, I turned into a mamma-saurus, ready to rip anyone's face off. For him, it was a key indicator to my pregnancy.

My parents handled the news of Reuben's pregnancy pretty well. He would be the child that biologically connected all the children together. Rather than telling them over the phone, as I did with Reuby, this time I did it in person.

I was shitting a brick about telling them, it was like announcing, 'Hey, your daughter is a randy bitch, who doesn't use protection; she's just reckless, like some juvenile teen.'

Why I worried was beyond me, they had the usual dynamic and set response: mother started to flap, and dad was relaxed. I never understood how he remained composed in the face of my news; I had gone against everything he wanted for me in life.

Chapter Twenty-One

Augustine

It was a Tuesday morning, in early November; the twins had not long had their third birthday. A brown envelope had arrived in the morning mail, addressed:

Miss Hope E Bramwell

Lovett's Farm

Aileni

North Wales

I was curious who had written to Hope, she wasn't due any boosters, so who could possibly want our daughter's attention. I ripped the top of the envelope open, tearing the top of the letter in my rush.

I didn't recognise the crest in the top right hand corner. It was the local education department, inviting Hope and her parents to visit the local school, ahead of her application, ready for enrolment next September. I tossed the letter aside; I didn't care to enter into the school life culture. I'd made that decision subconsciously before I left Fremmington Ayshe, no child of mine would be exposed to school, and the host of issues it brought.

I'd lived so happily, in the private bubble of my toddlers and baby, that it hadn't occurred to me I would lose them in a few months time; for a large portion of the day, outside influences would care for my children, and have a bigger part in their life than I could.

Ray and I had never discussed the matter of schooling; we were ignorant to each other's wishes. I didn't see it as a smooth decision, Ray would definitely want to conform; I had such a traditional upbringing and schooling, yet bucked the trend on every ideology.

Ray and Robson, had made their way back in for lunch, I decided to let Ray know about the letter that had darkened our doormat. Then he'd have the afternoon to think about what he wanted.

"Over there." I pointed, with the knife in my hand. "On the side; a letter for Hope. Read it."

Ray studied the letter, flapping it back and forth, as he gave me his initial reaction.

"OK darling, phone and make an appointment, then we can sign her up."

"NO! She's not going Ray; our daughter is not entering the system. I don't want other people in her life."

"She has to go to school." Ray protested.

"She isn't going to the village school, which has no prospects. Robson, you went there, and your brothers are there now. What's it like?"

"Christ Ray, I know you said she was volatile, but really?" Robson quietly muttered.

"I bloody heard that Robson Gable, you forget who cooks your lunch!"

Robson looked sheepish.

"She's right Ray, it's shite; under-funded, falling down. It's not the nicest of environments to inspire children in, but the nearest school to that is

10 miles away, it's just not practical for most families, so they endure what is on offer."

"See, I told you!" I gleefully retorted.

"And what is your suggestion, oh wise one?" Ray asked, with sarcastic curiosity.

"Home education, we take full responsibility for our children's future, we'd have control over what they learn and the skills they acquire, and they can still get qualifications longer term.

"I'd made the decision long before we left Fremmington Ayshe, I didn't want the playground gossip, the pressure to conform, being dictated to by the school on where, what, and how our children should be. I feel no differently now, my feelings are stronger than ever before, having had so many years of freedom with the children, I don't want to let that go.

"You learn from life, Ray. Goodness, look at us, where we were, and how we arrived here. Conditioning the children to think a certain way doesn't create forward thinkers, the Einsteins or the Hawkings of this world."

I left Ray to digest my heartfelt plea. I said no more about it. We set time aside to thrash out our views. We had to draw a conclusion we were both happy with, after all we'd be here again in a year's time, with Faith and David.

We had a couple of days cooling-off period. Sitting across the table from Ray, he made his opening statement.

"Sophia, I'm going to make my position perfectly clear, so there is no misunderstanding."

I was dreading his next line, knowing full well this would end up escalating, and we'd lock horns. Maybe even the 'my child versus his child' divide.

"I've been to see the village school, yesterday. I also went and saw the school ten miles away. I'm sorry I went behind your back, but I wanted an informed opinion, one I could be objective with."

"Ray…"

"Let me finish Sophia. The schools are… falling down around themselves. Our barn, with the roof collapsed in on itself, is in better condition. I didn't like it. The ethos on children wasn't something I fully felt on board with either; in fact, as the head spoke at me, hearing her drone on made me realise, I would become very anti-school, before Hope was there even a month.

"Our lifestyle, our dream, and our children, lend themselves perfectly to home education."

"Really? You're serious? No school? No conformity? I have to say, Ray, I am hugely relieved; I thought we'd end up banging heads over this. I guess your wife's bad ways are rubbing off on you."

"I'd rather my wife was rubbing up against me." Ray beamed.

Ray and I declined Hope's school place, it was liberating. Telling mum and dad would be interesting. On our Saturday night phone call, I casually slipped in that we'd be home education the children. Mum didn't fully understand our choice, but was as supportive as she could be. Dad was positive, but didn't express an opinion, it was highly unusual for him to do that; I feared this time I may have tipped him over the edge with his tolerance to my lifestyle.

Dad rang me back the following day. He had spent the evening investigating home education, league tables in our area, and Ofsted findings; he was now fully informed to have an opinion on the matter. He was horrified by the local schools, and wholeheartedly supported our alternative choice.

Chapter Twenty-Two

Sophia and Ray

I hadn't heard Ray come in through the door.

"Can you help me get my boots off?"

When I heard, his voice I jumped, letting out a little yelp.

"Bloody ghost feet, Mr Bramwell!"

"Well, could you?"

"What've you done? With that attitude, and asking for help, it must be something quite serious."

"I had a minor accident. Well, more a falling out with some breeze blocks. I did it first thing; I think my foot's swollen. Can you GENTLY unlace it?"

I knelt down to Ray's foot, as he sat on the pew, cautiously undoing his laces. He winced as I loosened the tongue, to wiggle his boot off gently. His sock was damp with sweat; I rolled it off his foot, which looked angry, red and inflamed.

"Ray, it's more than swollen, you're lucky if you haven't blooming broken something. I'll get a pack of peas, reduce the swelling, you need to elevate it.

"I haven't any peas, will sweetcorn do?" I called from the freezer.

Ray was sat looking out over the farm, watching the clouds move on by. He was already away daydreaming.

"When did you do this? Where was Robson, I thought he was working today?"

"I did it before lunch; I knocked a block on my foot. As I tried to steady myself, I tripped, causing more to topple onto the back of my leg.

"I had to finish the foundations for the new toilet block; we have contractors in next week. We can't afford to delay."

"So Robson is AWOL again, that's just typical. He's been doing it a lot recently."

"GIVE HIM A BREAK Sophia! You don't know the half of it. Leave it be. Has he rung?"

"No, and I'm not your bloody receptionist, don't shout at me, it's not my fault." I threw the sweetcorn at him.

"Ah, the typical closet redhead is back. Don't have a temper tantrum with me, I'm doing my best."

"I know you are. But your solution to an injury was to carry on working, and then hobble home when it suited you. Cracking judgement there Raymond. I suggest you go take a bath, try and bring out the swelling. Maybe even consider resting up for a few days?"

I let him get on with it, he was stubborn, pig-headed, and I didn't want to have a ruckus with him. Some days I couldn't live with him, he had tunnel vision, to the exclusion of all else, even his health and wellbeing.

I'd gone back to preparing the children's dinner, cheesy pasta and trees (broccoli) and pink sparkles (ham), at Hope's request.

"I'll be fine, I'll strap it up, tomorrow I have to finish."

I slammed the knife down.

Hope of Ray

"NO Ray! You aren't just carrying on. You are having the week off. Sod the contractors, it can be deferred. OK? I have a wedding party arriving on Thursday, the last one before maternity leave; I'll get Robson in to help. It may have escaped your attention darling, but I am heavily pregnant with our fifth child."

I got the painkillers and threw them at him; I poured him a glass of water, leaving it on the windowsill. I was trying to show him that I loved him, and cared, while seething at his strong-willed nature. He made me so angry when he wouldn't look after himself. It was always made worst because his intentions were honourable; he was trying to better us as a family. I couldn't help but be in love with him for this.

He took to his bed for a couple of days; I knew by this action alone, that he must have done more damage than he was willing to admit. His foot was tender; he couldn't put any pressure on it, or weight bare. I think, this time, even Ray realised he wasn't superman. His calf was looking red, angry even. The red glowed among the Technicolor of bruises, blue, purple, black and green.

Ray thought he might have had a reaction to the cement mixture; he'd had shorts on while out in the fields. It was the height of summer, and the hedgerows were abundant with all sorts of foliage. He'd also taken an earlier tumble, before his accident. I only found out about this a couple of days later. Maybe the rash was caused by something botanical?

Ray had told me not to worry; he'd had a reaction on his legs before, well, on several occasions, over the years, normally at the rugby pitch. He recalled a story; when he was about 15 or 16, he and Jacob had been doing a bit of alternative training, primarily goofing around, which resulted in them wrestling into the hedge, and continuing until one was triumphant. He was pickled with a rash that took several days to clear.

Apart from the times where he was missing, with no explanation, (that is how it seemed to me, Ray was privy to more, but he was courteous enough not to repeat it and break Robson's confidence) Robson was a real asset to us. Ray still wasn't fit for proper business duties. Robson had come to my rescue, spending his weekend on the farm with us, being on-call for the wedding party, who had arrived on Thursday. Ray's leg was painstakingly slow recovering; it was driving him scatty. He was under my feet, and making child duties, along with all other chores, a nightmare. He was needy, and clingy, it had been years since he was confined to the house. I couldn't wait for him to get back to his days out of the house.

Becky and Nick, the bride and groom, had a quiet and intimate wedding; a second marriage. It was always an illuminating process, people watching, seeing a couple's wishes play out. The complexity, the simplicity, the firsts, the seconds. It always revived the memory of our wedding day. I wouldn't have changed how simplistic, non-existent you might say, it was. Ray and I had more than a wedding when we got married.

In the four years at Lovett's Farm, every wedding had offered such diversity. Turning the light off, late on the Saturday evening, I could smell the embers of the fire, laced with remains of hog roast; looking out into the field, I could see Becky and Nick dancing into the fading light. I smiled at the memory of the first time Ray and I danced. He wrapped his arms around my ever-expanding waist, our spare hands, locked together, his palms were clammy. I could feel his heart thudding against my chest, as we swayed around the living room. Ray paused, retrieving his handkerchief from his pocket, to mop the beads of sweat from his brow, we continued to what was playing on the radio; he even offered me a twirl. I hadn't laughed that much in a long time.

Hope of Ray

We had contractors in the following week, and had initially shut the farm down for the week, on health and safety grounds. I'd waved off the new Mr and Mrs Corby at 2 p.m. Robson had been home to check on his mum, poor Jenny had been having no end of problems with his younger sister, Lowri, bunking off school. If she wasn't doing that she was disappearing for one or two days at a time. Robson had missed parts of the week off work. He couldn't apologise enough for his absence on the day Ray hurt himself, he felt responsible.

It transpired that Robson's sister, Lowri, had been in with the wrong crowd for a while now, she was 14. On the Monday, Robson had been by his mother's side, as Lowri lay in a hospital bed, getting her stomach pumped for the third time. Robson had a lot on his shoulders, being the eldest of seven. Jenny was beside herself, facing the reality that the authorities would now be in her life. After Lowri, there were another two boys, younger again. Robson was born when his mum was sixteen, she'd had a life of hardship, his father had never been in his life, and he didn't even know where he was.

While in the barn, Robson told me about his life; he had nothing but admiration for his mother, as he spoke about her with endearing warmth. We'd never really had an in depth conversation, it had never had a place in our working relationship. I took it as a compliment that he was willing to spill his guts. I was more than happy to listen, though I was apprehensive of how the conversation would flow. When he asked questions on our past, I knew it would be hard to reciprocate with as much openness. I didn't want to reveal our previous life, potentially risking the village mentality we left behind in Fremmington Ayshe manifesting again here.

Robson gave the impression that he couldn't be bothered with village life. His family had seemingly had a rough deal one too many times.

"Where did you grow up, Sophia?"

I cleared my throat, just to buy a few seconds of time. "In a place called Fremmington Ayshe, it's in the South of England. It's a small town, near Wimpleton."

"No way; I know it. I travelled there when I was about eighteen, and then again when I was in my early twenties. It was the last known place my father lived. I didn't find him, he must have moved on.

"They have a market on a Wednesday, with livestock in the street. It was a bizarre experience."

"Yep, that's Wimpleton."

"So, when did you and Ray meet? I mean, I know I've worked for you for like four, nearly five, years, and been here the day Reuby was born, but how long have you been together?"

"Ray and I've known each other thirteen years, through friends."

Robson's innocent questions were making me uncomfortable; I changed the pace, by suggesting I send the walking wounded out, to hold the ladders, while the last parts of the wedding banners were removed.

Ray was more than happy to escape; Reuby was always a bit repetitive in his demands for milk. He'd mostly weaned off bottles, with only a morning and night milk, it didn't stop him trying to wear us down. Hope and Faith always struggled for power. They both wanted to be in charge, when they played nicely it didn't take long for them to strop with each other.

David, the poor child, just disappeared, they were too bossy for him, he was a lone ranger, wanting to play with his dinosaurs, or safari animals.

He tried his best to tolerate Reuby, who could contribute, "Tiger, Raa." I don't think Ray had really comprehended four children's constant needs.

I took my boots off at the door; there was nothing better than being barefoot and pregnant. My faithful maternity skirt was now holey, faded, and bobbling, through so much wear. The skirt had had its day; it was just about fit for the bin. Wearing it about the farm, it didn't bother me how battered, or well-loved, it was; it was special to me. Ray bought it as a gift when he moved into Keeper's Cottage; he referred to it as his first month's rent. It was the skirt I wore to the hospital when I had Faith and David; the skirt I pulled up around my ears as Ray caught Reuben-Ray's head. It was now the skirt I wore while our daughter rented my womb. Ray suggested, after this child, I should retire the skirt. He'd buy me a new one for our next pregnancy. Ray never shied away from the fact that he wanted lots of children, maybe six or seven; we were well on our way.

The children were in their playroom, at the back of the house, they'd made a den with old sheets and blankets, Ray had given them the peg basket. They wanted tea in their den, obligingly I started making rounds of cheese sandwiches, ham sandwiches and cut up banana, ready for a carpet picnic.

"HE'S COLLAPSED, RAY'S COLLAPSED!" Robson thundered through the front door.

I bolted out of the open door he left, chasing across the yard barefoot.

"Go call an ambulance, keep the children in their den." I hollered over my shoulder.

Ray was heaped on the floor, near the folding glass doors.

"Ray, can you hear me? Ray, it's Sophia, speak to me Ray!"

I lay him out, ready to perform CPR. He was unconscious and not breathing. I wasn't confident enough for rescue breaths, so did hands only CPR. I placed the heel of my hand on his breastbone, in the centre of his chest, I placed my other hand on top, interlocking my fingers, I used my body weight, not just my arms, placing my shoulders over my hands. I repeated the compressions.

I started tiring quite quickly, my baby girl kicking as adrenaline took over. I think I had that instinct just to keep going, I was sweating and panting, but Ray was unresponsive.

I knew his best chances were if I persisted, it felt like an eternity. I couldn't hear the noises around me. I pleaded with Ray to respond, through my broken breath.

"Come on Ray, talk to me!

"I know the kids are hard work, but this is no way to get a rest."

I was oblivious to the paramedics entering, "Miss, we'll take it from here."

I continued the compressions.

A middle-aged man gently pulled my hands off Ray. "My colleague will continue, how long have you... been doing this?"

"I don't know."

Stepping back, I watched my husband, unresponsive. They worked on him tirelessly. I begged him to wake up.

"Ray, wake up my darling, come on Ray." I pleaded with every ounce of strength I had left.

"Ray, I love you, I need you!"

Hope of Ray

The paramedics spoke as if I were absent, only focused on Ray.

"He has no pulse, he's been like this since arrival, he's asystolic are we agreed?"

"Agreed, time of death 5:17 p.m."

They both withdrew themselves from his body.

I fell to the floor, crawling to his body. I cradled his head against my bulging stomach, I howled, screaming at him not to leave me, we had babies to raise!

"Miss, I'm sorry, I don't know your name."

I looked up at the paramedic, "It's Mrs Bramwell."

"Mrs Bramwell, I have to call the police, it's an unexpected death, I'm so very sorry. Are you with the doctor's in the village?"

I nodded.

I rocked Ray's body in my arms, kissing his forehead, in absolute bewilderment.

Two police cars arrived, with four uniformed officers in attendance. Upon entering the barn they spoke with the paramedics.

I don't know what was said, I just kept holding Ray, I couldn't let go. An officer invited me to leave Ray's body. I ignored him; I wasn't ready to let him go. I was given a few more minutes; then two of them helped me off the floor.

"Can you tell us what's happened?"

I didn't look at them, I was fixated on Ray. "He collapsed; Robson came in the house to raise the alarm."

"Who is Robson?"

"He works for us; he's with my children, in the house."

"How many children do you have, Mrs Bramwell?"

"Four: Hope, Faith, David, and Reuben-Ray. Plus this one, on the way."

"Had your husband been well, health wise?"

"He had a leg injury last week, um, he had reacted to something, his leg was red and inflamed, his left calf; look."

The paramedic went to his body laid out, to confirm what I said. "DVT; pulmonary embolism."

"Mrs Bramwell, can we move you into the house, while we wait. Please?"

They were so delicate in their handling of me, my fragility noted by my protruding belly and four children. I was broken. I had a duty to Ray. Something snapped inside me, my undertaker's head reared itself from an unknown depth.

"I take it you'll now call the local undertaker? And dutifully wait, until he collects Ray's body. I will then have to wait for you to prepare a report for the coroner."

"Mrs Bramwell, out of curiosity, how do you know this procedure?"

"In a former life, before I was a mother and wife, I was an undertaker."

"Well, I didn't expect that! Can I ask where?"

"Fremmington Ayshe. In the South of England.

"Can you ask your questions here? My children are in the house and I…"

Hope of Ray

"Start by telling us his full name, and what happened, in your own time."

"Raymond, Albert, Bramwell...

"His leg got crushed, earlier in the week; concrete blocks fell on his leg. He has been on bed rest since then; today was the first day he was up and about. His leg swelled, and became rashy. He said he must have reacted to something in the hedgerow, and regaled me with a tale from his youth, where similar happened. I trusted his judgement, about how he felt."

"This seems like a tragic incident, I don't believe there needs to be any Police involvement, certainly not an investigation.

"The Coroner will need to determine the cause of death, was Ray on any medication?"

"None."

"We will need to speak to Robson; can we go to the house? P.C. Chalmers, is trained, in child bereavement, would you like her to be with you, when; when you tell the children?"

"Before we leave him, can I go and get his blanket for him? He'd use it in the summer evenings, just to take the edge of the dwindling temperature. It's in the house."

"We'll escort you up to the house. Can I help you find your shoes?"

"I don't have any, um, I ran bare foot. Please let me go on my own. I don't want to alarm the children."

The door was still open, I could hear Robson reading to the children, they adored his story telling, he always made such wonderful voices. Ray's blanket was on the chair, it was orange, brown and white, horizontal and vertical lined pattern. I clenched it to my nose, in an all too familiar way. Like the day Pom died. I'd forgotten, how I felt, the anniversaries had become easier, they weren't all-consuming anymore, like in the first few years, life had continued and taken over. Jacob bought me ice cream the day Pom died, chocolate fudge and honeycomb; yes, they were the flavours.

I hugged his blanket all the way back to the barn. Ray looked sound asleep.

"A little something to keep you warm, my darling. I won't leave you without saying goodbye."

I kissed his red stubbled cheek; Ray always went a couple of days without shaving. He was a rugged, handsome chap to me.

"Where would you like to tell your children?" P.C. Chalmers was a softly-spoken lady.

"I hadn't thought, um; the kitchen. I can give Reuby his bottle, and the children can colour at the table, it's then their choice to interact."

I showed the officers into the kitchen, whilst I went to see the children. Robson took one look at me; I shook my head. His whole demeanour dropped, as he started to shake.

"I need you to meet some friends of mine, babies."

"Mamma, we're not babies." They said in chorus.

Hope continued to clarify, "Well, Reuby is, he still has a bottle."

"Yes, you're right; Reuby does still have a bottle. How about we go to the kitchen, and have a drink? You can sit up at the table with a biscuit, how about that? I need to tell you about daddy."

I started to herd them towards the kitchen, trying to put a brave face on it.

"Has he been naughty, will you throw away the key? Is that why they're here, to put daddy in jail?" Faith was very inquisitive about the police presence.

David kept looking over his shoulder, looking them up and down.

"Hope, Faith, and David, do you remember, how I told you mummy's Pom was poorly once? It's like when you have a special toy and it's broken, you hope they'll get fixed, but sometimes it's not possible. When they can't be fixed, we send them to toy heaven, and they become stars. Pom went to the Moon, didn't he? He was special to mummy, and we hoped he'd be fixed, but couldn't, so he shines bright in the sky now.

"This afternoon, Daddy became poorly, we wanted to fix Daddy, mummy tried her best; I promise you, I did everything I could. I'm so sorry my darlings, I couldn't fix daddy, no one could. Now he's going to have to take a journey, to shine on the moon with Pom.

"In a little while, a special vehicle will come and pick Daddy up. They will take him to the special rocket factory, where he will wait, and in a few weeks time we will have a special party for him. We will then send him to the moon, in his rocket, called a coffin.

"Do you understand, my darlings?"

David ran from the table, screaming "Daddy", all the way to his room.

"Faith, Hope, do you understand?"

"Yes, he's dead, like in our fairytale books; could a magic kiss not save him?"

Hope was pragmatic; she was more like Helen, in that one sentence, than ever before.

They both debated the finer points of a magic kiss, and if the party meant they wore dresses like princesses.

"I need to check on David."

I found David; face down on his bed, broken at the news. Peeling him off the bed, I sat him on my lap, cradling him in my arms, as if he was a tiny baby. He was my baby; he needed me now, no different to the first days of his life. His world had been destroyed. He cried harder than I thought possible. I cried with David, I cried for David. He was going to suffer, Ray had always had a great way of coaxing David out of his shell; he'd always been reserved, and needed his daddy to reassure him.

"Dadda promised me, I could go to the field with him next week, and we can't. 'Saurus was going to come on an adventure with us." He snuffled at his disappointment, not to have his adventure with Ray. David hugged me tight, he couldn't stop crying; I could hear the girls downstairs, giving it chapter and verse. I knew they'd be fine, they were resilient. I swayed him in my arms, as he cried himself to sleep. Gently, I transferred him into his bed, covering him with a crocodile duvet. I knew the initial devastation would impact David more so than the girls.

As I pulled his curtains together, I saw that the gate to the farm was open once more; the undertakers had arrived. P.C. Chalmers met me at the bottom of the stairs.

"Mrs Bramwell, it's time."

I bowed my head in acknowledgement.

Robson continued to watch the girls; he now had to draw rabbits, under a magic tree. Reuby had flaked out on the sofa, with the matching blanket to his daddy's on him.

I was escorted back to the barn, where Ray still lay. It was a good couple of hours since Ray had left this world. P.C. Chalmers introduced the undertaker to me, and took care of the formalities. I stared at his lifeless body, angry with myself, for not insisting he sought medical attention, I should have been more forceful, and now, here I was alone, with no one.

"Are there any personal processions, belonging to Mr Bramwell, you'd like to remove?"

I couldn't quite comprehend the question I was being asked, about three hours ago, my husband was alive and well, walking our farm. Now I was being asked to remove belongings from his dead body.

"Um, his wedding ring."

The younger undertaker, who was fair-haired, went to lean down, to remove the ring; I grabbed his elbow to stop him.

"Can I do it? I need to do this. Please?"

"Really Miss? He won't feel like he did. Are you sure?"

The police officer, who had questioned my knowledge on these proceedings, gave the undertakers the nod to let me go ahead and do so. I knelt down on the right hand side, pulling the blanket back. The clear signs of his death were there, he smelt, he had messed himself, his shorts were damp and the faeces had wept onto the floor, pooling around him. I took his left hand in mine; his fingers had slight signs of stiffening. I wriggled the ring off his finger; it was a golden band, scratched and dented, with the stories of our farm. He felt cold.

I hadn't a clue of our baby's movements that day, I knew she had been kicking in recent hours, but I couldn't determine the regularity since Ray's death. I placed his hand on my belly once more, for our unborn child to say her farewell.

"Our daughter will know of her Daddy, I promise you Ray. You'll walk this path once more, in her."

I took his hand and gave it one last kiss, placing it back down by his side. I wasn't ready to let go, but I knew I had to leave; I had to be with my children, they needed me. I couldn't do any more for Ray. I kissed his forehead once more, wishing him "Good night darling, sleep well." We parted ways temporarily; I took his blanket back to the house with me. It was the last thing to touch him, to have his scent. I wanted to keep it. Through circumstance though, it had to be laundered.

I had a fuzz about me; did this really happen?

"Robson, where are the girls?"

"I know their bedtime is seven, I put them to bed. I didn't know what to do for the best, I hope it's OK? I thought you might need quiet. I took Reuby to his bed as well, with another milk."

I looked out over the farm; I sat myself on the pew, watching his black body bag, as it was loaded into the private ambulance. I'd experienced this a thousand times over. I wasn't living this moment, it was incomprehensible. He was a father of five, and active. He couldn't die, he was too young.

"I'm sorry Sophia, I should have acted quicker. I'm..."

"It's OK." I squeezed Robson's hand to console him, it wasn't his fault. He stood looking out of the window by my side, unsure of what to say or do.

"Mrs Bramwell, is there anyone we can call for you? You shouldn't be alone at a time like this. Can anyone stay with you?"

"My parents, they live in the South of England though. I'll call them."

I took the phone and dialled the number. The last time I broke the news of death to my parents, it was Pom, and I had Jacob by my side. Now I had his children, crushed their daddy had died, oblivious that their father was, in fact, alive and well, I assumed. I felt angry. My children had been robbed of their daddy twice, at the age of four.

"Hello darling."

"Mum..."

"I was only saying to your father today..."

"MUM! It's Ray, he's... He's..."

I dropped the phone down and walked away. I couldn't bring myself to admit it, as soon as I told my mum, I had to acknowledge the truth. He was dead.

"Hello. This is P.C. Chalmers of the local Aileni Police force, I'm very sorry to have to inform you, that Mr Raymond Bramwell passed away this afternoon. Hello. Hello. Hello."

"Hardy. It's Mrs Hardy."

I took the phone back.

"Mum, get Dad.

"Hello Dad, it's Ray he collapsed, there was nothing they could do. Dad, can you come up? I need you Daddy, please. Promise me you'll be here in the morning. I'm all alone. Daddy please. Please Daddy, promise me."

Dad promised me, he and Mum would be here by tomorrow morning, lunchtime at the latest. I just had to hold out until then.

"I'll stay with her." Robson insisted to the police. "I can call my mum to watch the children if needed, she wouldn't mind."

"Thank you, sir. We need to talk to you, ask a couple of questions. Can we have your full name, and address."

"Robson Henry Gable. I live at 6 Moregate Terrace."

"Gable. Any relation to Jenny Gable and kids in the village?"

"Yes, that's my mother."

Robson spent the first night on my sofa, I was grateful he stayed, as I didn't want to feel alone. The children, one by one, migrated to my room, I couldn't sleep and I was so thankful they wanted to feel close to me.

As the first light crept in, I put on his hoodie, it was dirty, but I wanted his smell, to feel him close to me, as I faced the morning alone, knowing he wouldn't share our day. Had I known that yesterday was the last time we'd share breakfast together, I'd have made more of an effort to sit down, savour his words and his love.

Looking at the children, as they sprawled over our bed, they slept peacefully and would wake into a nightmare. I had to hold it together for them, until my parents arrived, then I could grab the five minutes I needed to scream and cry, in the agony I felt.

Robson was my saviour, he fed the children, I couldn't think about food, the thought made me retch.

Hope of Ray

I don't know what happened in the initial days after my parents arrived, they cared for our children, while I shut myself away. I wasn't a good mother, as I pushed the children further and further away.

They were excited to have Granny and Pom spoiling them, they got anything they asked for, Granny made an abundance of cake, it was like a continual party for them.

My parents gave me a couple of days, and then my mother tried to appeal to my better nature, to be a mum once again. I didn't have the strength, I felt tired. My parents had been at the house for about four or five days, I hadn't seen them, unless they were trying to coax me to eat. They had rung the midwife, who suggested a doctor visit, so I could talk to them, I awaited my visit...

My bedroom door knocked, assuming it was the quack, I invited them in. It was Robson.

"Sophia, I'm so sorry, I had to see you. It's my fault; I can't stop thinking of him collapsing. I needed to see you, to tell you I take full responsibility."

"Robson, Ray is the one to blame, he wouldn't look after himself. God, I'm so angry with him."

"Don't be angry with him, he loved you, I wish I could find someone who I felt half of what Ray felt for you. He couldn't talk about anyone but you.

"He told me once, how you saved him, from a very dark place, after his first wife died."

"He told you about his first wife?"

"He told me that, after Helen died, you supported him in his darkest hours, and made him see sense, that he had to accept his new life, and be the best father he could be."

"He told you about Hope?"

Robson nodded.

"I saw Ray as my best friend Sophia, and now I'm telling you the same, follow your own advice, you have to accept that life has changed. You never have to forget him, but you have to honour his memory, by raising your children how you both dreamt."

Robson never said another word, he quietly left my room. I walked over to the window as I heard the front door latch. He looked up at the window as he closed the gate to Lovett's Farm.

He was right. I couldn't be a hypocrite in the face of my husband's death, Robson Gable spoke wise words. I'd spent enough time wallowing in my own self-pity, Ray's death was tragic, and life-changing, but I had plenty of life to live for. I once told him, Hope would heal his raw wounds, and now I had Hope, Faith, David, Reuben-Ray, and our bump to heal me. With all their love and innocence, I couldn't go wrong in life as we moved forward.

Chapter Twenty-Three

Jimmy

After the coroner had filed a report, stating the cause of death to be pulmonary embolism, I had the paper work and was now free to instruct an undertaker. It all came flooding back, I felt rather resilient at this part of the process; I knew exactly *what* I would be dealing with.

I wanted Ray cremated, I was clear on that decision, I wanted to bring him home, so he could roam our farm forever more, and I wanted to commemorate him for the children, in some form of trinket. I couldn't guarantee they'd remember their daddy, so I wanted him to always be close, on their birthdays, weddings, and the special events in their lives that he'd miss. I also wanted him by my side, as I raised the children.

I only trusted one undertaker with my husband. Home was Lovett's Farm, but our story began, individually and together, in Fremmington Ayshe. As reluctant as I was to take the children back there, I knew Ray had to have one last trip. He needed to go back to where he and Helen met, where Helen and I met, where we became friends, best friends in the face of adversity, and where we fell in love. It was the beginning; it should also be the end.

I rang the number for Saunders and Son; I wanted to hear the familiar voice of Joanna.

"Good morning, Powell's and Co., Joanna speaking."

"Powell's? Joanna, it's Sophia. Sophia Hardy."

"Sophia, how lovely to hear from you. It's Powell's now. Jimmy Powell took over about 18 months ago.

"How are you? Life treating you well? It hasn't been the same here without you."

"Joanna, I need you to bring my husband home, he needs to come home to Fremmington Ayshe, and I need to cremate him."

"Sophia, your husband? I don't know what to say, I'm so very sorry."

"Me too Joanna."

"Let me take the details, and I'll ring you back, I need to speak to Jim."

"It's Raymond Albert Bramwell. He died three weeks ago, the coroner has filed his report, and his body has been released."

"Ray? You married him?"

"Yes, I married Ray, we have four children together, and I'm expecting again."

"Sophia, how can I be so happy for you, and yet so heartbroken at the same time? I can't digest this, I'm so, so sorry. I promise you I'll do all it takes to bring Ray home. Can I tell George and Toby you rang? I'd feel terrible hiding it from them, especially George."

"So, after all this time, you and George are an item; I wondered if you ever would, there was always a little chemistry."

Joanna stood by her word, within an hour I had a phone call back; they would liaise with the undertakers here, and then make a trip to collect Ray, on the condition that they could come to the farm and meet us all beforehand. I had many reservations, but to see friendly faces at a time like this was something I hankered for, I felt isolated and lonely.

My parents were relieved to see me up and 'back to normal'. It gave them the courage they needed to leave me, and know I would be able to cope. They made sure I had support in Robson, and he was under strict orders to call them if anything was wrong. A few days after they left I was to receive visitors to the farm.

"Mamma, a car!" A chorus shouted from the garden.

Looking out onto the track, it was Powell's; I'd recognise a vehicle like that any day. I dried my hands and headed out to the gate. I was surprised to see the four of them pulling into the farmyard; I knew Joanna would be here, without a doubt, but there before me she stood with George, Toby, and Jimmy Powell too.

"Welcome to Lovett's Farm, my goodness, it's wonderful to see friendly faces." I said, and immediately burst into tears. I couldn't control how I was feeling, it was a tidal wave of mixed emotions, and I think relief may have been the strongest.

"Jimmy Powell, it's been a long time, thank you for making the journey. Please come in; all of you."

"Hello, I'm Hope."

"And I'm Faith."

The four of them hadn't chance to move before the girls were over.

"Who are you?" asked both girls together.

"Girls, these are some friends of mine, they are going to have tea with us, and make plans for daddy's final party. How about you play, and we'll be boring grownups?"

"Thank you for letting us visit Sophia, I'm so glad you called, I've missed you." Joanna thrust her arms around me.

"Look at the little lad over there, what's his name Sophia?" Toby pointed to David, who had retreated to be in his own company, in the garden, sheltered under the apple tree at the far end, he was a shy boy.

"Who does he look like?" George pondered, "He looks the spitting image of Jacob! Look at the way he's removed himself from the rest of us. We used to spend hours looking for Jacob, he could hide all day! We've never lost a cup since he left."

"Nothing changes with you then George, subtle as ever, I see!" I quipped, trying to change the subject.

"George! How did ever I marry you, with no filter like that?" Joanna was red-faced, mortified as she reprimanded George.

We went into the house, sitting at the table, I laid out the tea set, so that I could still see the children playing outside. I had gone back six years, I'd missed my friends, but we snapped into our working dynamic like nothing had happened in all this time. I felt I trusted them enough to explain what had happened before I left.

"You see the girl with the purple top on, and the older boy, well George, you're right; they do look like Jacob, because they're his children. I left pregnant with twins. The children all think Ray and I are their mum and dad. Coming back to Fremmington Ayshe, I can't have anyone else find out the truth. Hope doesn't know about Helen either, she's too young to understand yet."

"Sophia, I was only making a joke, but bloody hell, he's Jacob's double. I'm sorry."

"You have nothing to be sorry about George. We left so that no one could judge us and ruin our children's lives. I'm a little scared to return, I have to tell you."

Hope of Ray

I was adamant on what I wanted, and Joanna dutifully made notes. I wanted to be in control, I didn't know any different when it came to funeral arrangements, I couldn't switch off the undertaker in me. I wanted to dress Ray, I knew the technique, and he was my husband. I think I felt it would be closure, one last time to touch him; he was so cruelly ripped away from me at a time when I didn't expect it. I saw it as therapy.

Jimmy was adamant that wasn't going to happen; if he let me do it, then it would set a precedent for any Tom, Dick or Harry to make similar requests.

I begged Jimmy to let me do this, I shamefully pleaded. He wouldn't budge. He kept spouting the red tape and insurance lines at me. I was going to do it, even if I had to play dirty with Jimmy, he'd back down eventually.

"Jimmy, I have the utmost respect for you, but I'm not any Tom, Dick or Harry, as you put it. I'm Sophia Hardy, a woman who won several awards in the undertaking business; I was the one who paved the way for women in a man's world. Don't insult my intelligence with 'red tape'.

"This is about your reluctance to cross a boundary, because you are uncomfortable. I made the business in Fremmington Ayshe thrive, not you, and certainly not Jacob, it was me. For Christ's sake, I took on the funeral of Ian Keatan; I survived being mixed up in circles that could have resulted in being blown to smithereens. Did I back down? No, I didn't! That was for a total stranger. Do you really think I'll back down when it concerns my own husband? You knew Ray as my best friend burying his wife. He was the love of my life, and I need to do this Jimmy, if you can't accommodate me, then I'm sure Harry Gilbert, at Larkham and Sons, can!"

I didn't have to say another word, Jimmy backed right down. I knew poor Joanna would have to smooth things over before I came back, the day before the funeral. Jimmy remained ever the professional; it was interesting to see, that in all those years, he still hadn't relaxed.

Chapter Twenty-Four

Joanna

The case stood by the door. It was the last thing I'd put in the car before we left Keeper's Cottage. Six years had gone by in a heartbeat. I'd never intended to return; well, not until such times as my parents would need me. Here I was though, my hand had been forced, how could Ray do this to me?

"Hope, Faith, David, Reuben-Ray, shoes on please, it's time."

"That's my 'lellie Faith, yours have pink ponies, mine are the ooni–corns. Mamma, tell her!"

"Thank you Hope. Faith, please give Hope her 'lellies, look, yours are by the door."

"I don't like your 'lellies anyway Hope!"

Trying to get the children out of the house was no easy task, they bickered terribly; it was their coping mechanism. They rarely travelled off the farm, let alone hundreds of miles into the unknown, to say goodbye to their beloved Dadda.

They were free to roam on the farm; but they would now have to suppress this until we returned.

David spent every waking hour with his Dadda if he could; as soon as he could walk, he'd chase Ray across the yard. Reuben-Ray was now attempting to copy David; he'd put his wellies on the wrong feet, but he didn't care as he was chasing after his big brother, he hadn't a care in the world that all he had on was a nappy and t-shirt. Reuby was our nature boy; he looked just like his daddy, the same warmed complexion and reddened ringlets.

"Reuby-Ray don't chew your welly. Why have you taken your trousers off? Now please, could you act like a little boy, rather than half boy half animal? How about it Reuby, for Mamma, please?"

The children were pretty well behaved, considering what their poor little souls were going through. Some days, they got through the whole day without even thinking of Ray; other days, he was all-consuming. I couldn't plan the future, I hadn't a clue how to wade through this shit storm, I was far too emotional without Ray, I thought with my heart, he was always far more objective, and now no one was by my side to tip the balance more evenly. I felt lost. I was now, and for the duration of parenthood, outnumbered. It was a daunting and empty prospect, that I had no one to share the burden of raising children with me.

As long as the children could run wild in Mum and Dad's garden, that would be a huge bonus. I was sure they'd forgive being cooped up on a long journey if free rein in the garden was compensation. They'd never left North Wales, who knew how they were going to receive Fremmington Ayshe. We had to leave, I could delay all I wanted, but I was just delaying the inevitable. Ray was waiting for me. I had one last wifely duty to fulfil.

"Right girls; are you happy in the back? You have your blankies and your dolls? If you start to bicker, I will split you up. Do you understand?

"Boys, are you happy in the middle? You have your blankies and dinosaurs? Ok then babies; let's go see Granny and Pom."

I was apprehensive, but I couldn't convey my reluctance to the children, who already had enough of a struggle. I had to make the journey an adventure, using the draw of Granny and Pom as the main focus. It was bad enough we were leaving the farm, but when we returned, in a few days time, there would be the finality that their daddy wasn't with us.

"Mamma, we're not babies, and Reuby-Ray has taken his lellies off again."

"OK David, you're right, you're not babies, you are incredibly brave children, and your daddy is so, so proud of you, as am I. I love you all very much." I turned away, so they couldn't see the tears weeping.

Driving through the village, the children quickly spotted Robson; he'd be joining us tomorrow. I felt like Robson and I were friends, but not incredibly close; he spent every day at my lunch table, but I didn't really know him, not like Ray, who definitely had a strong friendship with him, I believe they had become confidants, and I knew Ray had secrets of Robson's. I felt the limited friendship Robson and I had, created a wedge between us at the moment. He wasn't to blame for Ray dying. No one was.

As I wound down the window, Robson came over to the driver's side.

"I'll be down on the first train tomorrow. Are you sure you're OK with this bunch on your own?"

"We'll be fine; you can come with us now, if you like?"

"I have to be here to support mum today. I won't let you down. I will be there tomorrow without fail."

"Take care, we'll see you tomorrow."

Chapter Twenty-Five

Christopher

Joanna and I had rekindled our friendship after I rang about Ray. That evening she rang me from home, we spent a couple hours on the phone, she still had such spirit, she had matured but was still the same Joanna, only more worldly wise than the last time I saw her.

Christopher had retired. He'd started to feel dwindling health, which is when he decided to sell up to Jimmy Powell. About nine months ago, he had a mild stroke, though he had a good recovery, and long-term prognosis.

Hearing the news about Christopher rocked me. Joanna was so cautious about what she divulged; she had a great level of censorship, not wanting to distress me any further, or breach any confidences. Christopher was, like it or not, Faith and David's paternal grandfather; as much as I would like to deny this, the biting reality was still there, they were his blood.

I had known Jimmy Powell since becoming an undertaker. When he visited Lovett's Farm, and I expressed my desire to wash and dress Ray for his final time, Jimmy was not on board with such alternative requests. I was not backing down; I wasn't going to let this go. Joanna had smoothed it all over for me, filling Jimmy in on a detail or two. That I was Helen Bramwell's best friend and this was something I had to do, allowing all events to come full circle.

Jimmy and I had always had a good rapport within the undertaking world, if we could both avoid Harry Gilbert, then we were happy. Jim easily swayed his opinion on my request, and was more than accommodating to my wishes.

I'd made it back to Mum and Dad's by late morning. Having early rising children had its advantages. They slept, from about twenty minutes into the journey, all the way to the front door. I was so thankful; it made an otherwise arduous journey relatively pleasant.

"Darlings, we're here, we're at Granny and Pom's. Come on sleepyheads; look over at the door, who's that on the doorstep?"

"Mamma, look, it's Granny and Pom!" Faith pointed.

As I unloaded the children, they clung to me. Even though Granny and Pom were regular visitors to the farm, the environment was nothing like the place they had been reared. We were lucky if we saw a house from the farm, and the village was sporadic, yet here we were, stood in a cul-de-sac of 15 detached houses. It was quite claustrophobic, by comparison.

Once they realised this was a safe place, they un-tensed and walked towards the house.

"It's OK, Mamma grew up in this house, it's safe my darlings."

Reuby was barefoot and trouser-less, like he always was. Just over the border, I decided to pull into the services for a rest, he stirred, he began to whine and thrash about, I knew one thing would easily remedy the issue, making for a pleasant remainder of the journey. I'd let him be comfortable, and he'd become nature boy again.

"G'anny, Pom." He yelled with glee and excitement, making a beeline straight for them. Hope, Faith, and David followed his cue and all went, full steam ahead, charging towards them. Mum and Dad instinctively knew the children would be shy, they had laid the table with familiar treats, to break the ice, and Granny had made her chocolate cake, just like she did every time they visited the farm.

"Leave me a slice of that, it'll go down well with a cup of tea."

Knowing the children would easily settle with Mum and Dad, I decided it would be best to head towards Powell's as soon as I could, allowing more time with the children in the evening. The task I was about to face, cocktailed with sobbing children, would have been even more heart-wrenching than it was already going to be.

While settling the children in, over a well-earned cup of tea, I looked at them playing together, with my old tea set. David was being bossed around, as always; he just wanted an easy life, rather than being hen-pecked by both his sisters. Reuby was desperate to join in, but he was still very clumsy, Hope was mothering him, and Faith dished up the dinner.

If only Ray could see the girls now; united in grief, and, for once, no power struggle. Dad unpacked the car for me; he brought in the children's backpacks.

"Whose are these?" he questioned.

"They're ours! Stupid Pom!"

"Faith Bramwell! I beg your pardon; that is very rude!"

"Sorry." she bowed her head.

I felt like a bad mother; she didn't mean anything nasty by her comment, but I still had to find a balance between giving them understanding and latitude, and being firm. I feared I misjudged this one, a slight slip.

As the luggage came in, the girls gave my parents a running commentary on the whys and wherefores. They were happy, I only wished their innocence would heal their devastation, and carry them through tomorrow.

Hope of Ray

Driving through the town, seeing some of the old faces I had left, the tired buildings, where nothing and no one changed, I had no regrets. Lovett's Farm was filled with colour and life. I remembered the first day Ray saw the farm; he strode across the yard with such purpose. He made this dream with me, coming back to Fremmington Ayshe had clarified for me, without a doubt, I wasn't giving up our farm, it was still going to be colourful, only now, in Ray's absence, they would be different shades.

I pulled up into the yard, and walked down the side path, edged with blossom, in the spring it boasted the most beautiful baby pink tones. Making my way into the office, my stomach was now apparently in dire need to poo; I knew the feeling would pass, as my nerves calmed. I stood at the door; I opened it; it still had the same creak. I walked in to see Jimmy Powell, sat at my old desk.

"Elbows off my desk, Jim!" I snapped, using humour to deflect my nerves.

"Christ, I never thought I'd end up here again. 15 years ago, I interviewed here with Christopher Saunders, I was 18, and now Jimmy Powell sits at my desk. I suppose I should be grateful it wasn't Harry Gilbert."

"Look who darkens my door again; you're a hard woman Sophia. I always admired your tenacity.

"Come on, I'll take you up to the chapel."

I walked the cobbled path once more.

Chapter Twenty-Six

Raymond Albert Bramwell

"Well Mr Bramwell. Here we are. It's the last thing I will do for you, as your wife, in life and death.

"Why did you do it to me? I love you. We have a life to live. Our babies need their daddy!

"I'm sorry I let you down. I should have looked after you better, I should have known.

"We had so many dreams and ambitions; I promise you my darling, I'll make them come true.

"Never leave me, promise me you'll walk by my side. Even if I can't see you. Promise me.

"I want to hold your hand in mine. How do I raise five children alone? I love you; I need you now more than ever.

"I promise you, with every ounce of strength, every fibre of my being, I'll keep our children safe, and help them grow a bit more each day.

"And, when they are old enough, I'll tell them of your courage.

"I love you darling, show me how to live without you, I'm begging you Ray, show me please?

"I have no regrets.

"Raymond Albert Bramwell.

"NO REGRETS."

Hope of Ray

I let go of his hand, never again to touch him. I kissed his head, he looked like he was asleep, it wasn't a magic kiss, and I couldn't wake him.

Chapter Twenty-Seven

David

David apprehensively came to the kitchen door, Mum had set up the ironing board, ready to iron our clothes, for tomorrow.

"Mumma, I don't want to look like that tomorrow."

"David, sweetheart, what do you mean?" I beckoned him in for hug, and sat him on my lap.

"I want to look like Daddy."

David struck a chord with me, he was right. We were pretending to be something we weren't. We didn't dress up, we spent our days comfortable with who we were, love didn't come with a dress code; crikey, we didn't even dress up on our wedding day.

"You're right David Parker Bramwell. Get Hope and Faith, put your 'lellies on."

We upped and headed to the car. Mum wanted to know what all the fuss was about; she was flapping over the ironing.

"We'll be back in an hour or so. Leave the ironing."

I drove them out to Fremmington Ayshe Country Stores; it was on the outskirts of town. I'd rushed out with so much drive and enthusiasm, from David's statement, that Reuby was only in his nappy and t-shirt, not that he was complaining. Carrying Reuby on my disappearing hips, the children trailed close behind me. The store hadn't changed at all; I went straight to the wellies

"My darlings, you can all have new 'lellies for tomorrow. Daddy would want you to be happy, let's see what you fancy."

I sat Reuby on the stool, he was heavy; they didn't have anything in his size. Already, I knew this was going to result in a trip to Wimpleton, Soles for Souls shoe store. The boots were all dull and green, not what we wanted at all. In my snap judgement, I had made a poor error.

Then David shouted with elation, waving walking boots at me. "Mumma, look; they have them. I'm going to look like Daddy!"

David had found his boots. Nothing could bring Ray back, but it gave David a momentary sense of happiness.

"David, would you like to pay for your boots?"

The girls became very upset, bursting into tears; they thought they wouldn't get new 'lellies now.

"Girls, don't cry; here's what we are going to do. There's a town near here, called Wimpleton, shall we try the shoe shop there? Maybe we could go to Maggy May's Sweets and Treats as well."

I'd just put the fire out, and as we were paying, I heard my name. "Hi Sophia, wow it is you. Are all these children yours?"

I turned around to see Tori Atherton beaming back at me. She took a sharp step back as my baby bump greeted her. I hadn't seen her since that day in the letting agents. I didn't want to speak to her. She was nothing better than a shit-stirring gossip. I had made a tremendous mistake coming back here.

I never wanted anyone to taint the children's lives, which is why I moved, and now I had brought my children into the wolves' den, they were fresh meat. All I could think was that the locals were going to have their pound of flesh, at my children's expense.

Their world was in tatters, hanging on with the barest of threads; the mentality here could very easily blow their whole being apart, with the spiteful bile that certain individuals could spew. The children had mummy and daddy, it was that simple, and they needn't know the rest, just yet.

I replied to Tori, wanting to escape as quickly as I possibly could with four children.

"Hi Tori."

"So, what brings you here?"

Oh God, she wanted a conversation. I didn't even know her, it was only by association, through Helen, and here she was inserting herself in my life like we were old friends.

"We're here on family business."

I tried to be as vague as possible, until Hope and Faith came bounding in like two duelling, verbally incontinent, lonely old ladies. They meant no harm, how could I be cross with them?

"Our daddy's dead."

"Yeah, he's in a rocket."

"Tomorrow, he goes to the moon."

"In a coffin rocket."

"Thank you girls! We have to go. I've got to get to Wimpleton before the shops close."

I scrambled out of the store. There, by the front door of the shop, resting against the wall, was a black-framed bike, with a basket and bell on the handlebars. It was her!

I hurried the children along to the car, opened the doors, and piled them in as rapidly as I could, as if my life depended on it. I'd secured the children, in record time, and just as I was shutting the boot, there she stood, by her bike. I had hoped by now she'd be in the soil, with the bugs eating her flesh. Evidently, no such luck. I wanted to ignore her, but she wasn't going to let that happen.

"They all yours? You didn't let Helen's bed get cold for long, poor girl. There's barely an age between those kids. Taking advantage of poor Ray like that, when he was at his most vulnerable. Shame on you."

I was angry with myself, and such poor judgement in coming back. Maribel was the tip of the iceberg. My children were exposed; I'd do anything to protect them. Maribel had hit a nerve, I couldn't deny that. Helen was my best friend, I'd grappled over the years, if I was being disloyal to her, but I loved Helen, I still did now, I'd do anything for her. Every day of my life I had the gift of Hope's love, and Ray's, he gave me our babies.

In my continued ill-judgement, I decided, this time, to get in Maribel's face. I'd never done it before, but I wanted to warn her off.

"You bile-spewing, sad, old, haggard witch. Come near me or my children again, so help me, I will put you on your backside. Come within a hundred yards of my husband's funeral tomorrow and it'll be yours next. I won't tolerate your vitriol ever again."

I didn't give her the chance to retort. I got into the car, and put the music on to distract the children, we'd have a good old sing-song on the way to Wimpleton. I wanted them to forget what they had just seen.

I promised the children new wellies, Maribel wasn't going to ruin it for them. I didn't want to have to interact with another soul; I'd had my fill of this God-forsaken place. However, my feelings were put aside; I could easily have retreated to Mum and Dad's, but the only ones to suffer then were my babies.

Reuby was put in his buggy, I didn't have the strength to carry him that far. Hope, Faith, and David knew good behaviour would result in sweets. They'd never been to such a large town before.

Shopping for the girls was actually, remarkably easy; they wanted the same as they already had: ponies and unicorns, they knew their minds. I certainly had a couple of headstrong feminists in the family. I felt sorry for the future men in their lives, and heartbroken their daddy would never get to meet those men. The emotions snowballed from one to another. He would miss so many life events, and he'd leave that void, that could never be filled.

Reuby's feet had grown, and he wanted dinosaurs, "RAA". I offered David a new pair of lellies too, the girls started to play their faces at such injustice.

"He already has boots." they protested.

I wasn't going to discuss the politics of it with them. We left with four pairs of boots, and the girls would have to suck it up. We left Soles for Souls, and headed to Maggy May's Sweets and Treats.

Two doors down from Soles was a children's clothes shop, the window display had fairy costumes in it. The girls were absolutely gushing, the window enticed us in. I wanted them to be happy. We went in, pink, blue, purple, green, the whole colour spectrum.

"Can we Mumma?" they sweetly asked.

"Go on then." How could I deny them such a simple pleasure?

"Course, we need wands." Hope insisted.

"Yes, yes, YES." Faith jumped up and down on the spot.

"Daddy's rocket will need sparkles."

I'd bought them all for Ray's funeral, pretty dresses for the girls, and smart trousers for the boys. I now felt incredibly stupid, having done that. The children had to feel in control with how they dealt with tomorrow. I loved David, for showing the error of my ways, and for his courage. David found a shorts and t-shirt set, all in dinosaur print. He was the happiest boy ever,

"Reuby can have the same as me mamma; he likes to be just like me. We're both like daddy now." David gently offered.

I left the shop laden with bags, Ray would have had a pink fit at how much the girls had 'Robbed off us', but the second they smiled he'd have melted. I started towards Maggy May's, when our baby kicked with a thud; she wasn't going to be left out.

"We need to go back to the shop, we need to get our baby an outfit, what do you think?"

We finally got to Maggy May's after much deliberation, on whether the baby would like ducks or not. It reminded me of being in the supermarket, looking for Hope alongside Ray, like a pair of baby dummies, and here I was with another imminent arrival. We settled on ducks, butterflies and flowers.

Maggy May's evoked nothing less than full-blown nostalgia, it was comforting. It hadn't changed since I was a child, and it was now the third generation serving us. We ordered a pound of rhubarb and custard, white chocolate buttons, with hundreds and thousands, and a bar of dark chocolate. They also had free choice up to £1 each; they were elated at such a wonderment of sweets and chocolate.

Our shopping was done. I knew Ray would think I was a right mug for letting the children loose, but he would adore how happy they were. He'd evolved over five years, his introduction to parenthood was somewhat harsh, but by the time he died, he was a natural, better than me, no two ways about it.

The children chattered in the back of the car the entire journey home. Tears ran down the back of my hand as I wiped my eyes. I hadn't comprehended which road I had taken; I had done it automatically, I'd driven these roads for so long, it was still second nature to subconsciously assume a route.

"Mamma, why have we stopped?"

"I... I... I wanted to see this cottage, it's pretty. I like it."

"What's it called?"

"Keeper's Cottage."

Walter must have still been alive, that bike was still propping up the fence there.

Pulling into Mum and Dad's road, a police car was outside their house.

"Who's died Mamma? Someone's died."

David screamed at me, he started to panic, he was beside himself, and he started to thrash in his seat, as he tried to escape the car. He was hysterical, holding his ears and rocking himself, as he cradled his neck and head.

"Mamma, they're dead, they're dead, Mamma, they're dead!"

The girls started to shout his name, as Reuben-Ray joined in the chorus of noise, clearly distressed by David's actions alone. I wrongly shouted at David, and his hysterics. "DAVID! It's the police, they help people!"

David had scarring now; he associated the police with death.

"Oh look, she's a girl." Hope noticed the police officer was female.

I started to unload the children; they needed somewhere they felt safe - the car was not it. The girls I could distract by suggesting they show Granny and Pom their new dresses, the girls held on to everyday life, it was seeing them through; they were coping much better than David.

David struggled to function, blaming himself, I couldn't fathom how he thought he was at fault, but he consistently blamed himself. It was heartbreaking, he barely functioned. He'd always been shy, his daddy gave him a confidence no one else could; not even I could bring him out of his shell like Ray. He was a fragile being. David had a bout of wetting himself since Ray's death, and he lost all control in the car. He was wet again.

"Miss Hardy?"

"Who's Miss Hardy?" Faith questioned.

"Faith Joyce Bramwell, manners please, go on into the house, find Granny."

"She's our Mamma, Sophia Bramwell." Hope corrected them.

"Yes thank you girls, take Reuby on in please."

"Miss Hardy?"

"I don't mean to be rude, is this urgent, or can I take the children in first? He's had an accident."

"It can wait miss."

I took David in and changed him, placing him in the comfort of Pom's arms. I excused myself, heading out of the front door, to speak to the officers, apologising for my initial rudeness.

"I'm sorry, David, my son, associates the police with the death of his father. He has suffered a great trauma."

"We need to speak to you with regard to an incident that happened at Fremmington Ayshe Country Stores, earlier today. It is alleged that you made threats against a Ms Maribel Mackey."

"I told her, in no uncertain terms, to leave me and my children alone. This isn't a new spat; it's resurrected from when I previously lived here, five and a bit years ago. It's the first time I've been back since. She instantly started as soon as she looked at me."

"And what brings you back here?"

"I bury my husband, the children's dad, tomorrow."

"I'm so very sorry Miss Hardy."

"It's Bramwell, I'm Mrs Bramwell now. Maribel wouldn't have known that, she used my maiden name."

"I'll note it down. Can you tell us what happened?"

"I told her to stay away from Ray's funeral, and the children. I tried to end the situation quickly, she initiated it at the store, and I had all four of them in the car. She chose to escalate it, causing unnecessary trouble."

"I think we'll have a word with Ms Mackey. Sorry to have troubled you at such a difficult time."

I heard nothing more and continued with my day.

The girls had all the shopping bags and contents scattered across the living room floor, giving Granny all the ins and outs, chapter and verse.

"Where's David?"

"He's in the shed, with your father. The girls said you told them they can wear their dresses tomorrow?"

"Yeah they can, they just need to feel normal. I appreciate the effort you have gone to mum, David really opened my eyes earlier. I couldn't have done this today without you."

I broke down in tears, propping myself on a kitchen chair. I remembered the first time I told my mum about Jacob, sat here at this very table, and now, here I was with his secret children, grieving another man they called and loved as daddy. I had screwed my children up.

"We've never been able to do it without you, and now I'm alone. Why did he leave me mum? Why did he push himself so hard? I'd do anything to have him back. How do I bring up five babies alone?"

"Sophia, he pushed himself to build your future as a family. DON'T ever be angry with him. He loved you. It was always so easy to see, he'd light the room up when he came in and saw you!

"How do you raise these children? Well my darling, you carry on doing what you're doing now. One day at a time. Don't change your life because Ray has gone; follow the dreams you had as husband and wife still. In time the wounds will slowly heal."

"I'm all alone mum, I'm so lonely."

"Look at those babies of yours! Reuby is the spitting image of Ray. You'll never be lonely with these children by your side; and in a few weeks time, as bittersweet as it'll be, Dad and I will be there to support you, as you welcome a new bundle of joy into your life. She will signify that there is a chance for new beginnings."

Dad came back in with David. He was smiling; dad had given him some nuts and bolts, which he could tighten and loosen, attached to an off-cut of wood, like a fidget board. I dried my eyes; I didn't want the children seeing I was upset. They needed to see their Mamma was strong.

"Well David, did Pom give you a drink in an old honey jar? The first time your daddy went to the shed with Pom, they drank from honey jars. Shall we see if Granny has a jar you could have a little juice in, just like your Daddy?"

Reuby was pretty clueless to all that was going on, it was all a grand adventure to him. David seemed relatively calm about tomorrow, he told me every night he'd look out for the moon, when it was shining full he'd know daddy had landed. He'd always say hello when he shone bright.

Hope and Faith came crashing down to earth with an almighty thud.

"Daddy doesn't love us, he left and he won't tell us how pretty we look in our dresses tomorrow."

"We were too loud the last time he looked after us, he said he couldn't stand the noise and now he's left forever. I was shouting Mamma. I made Daddy leave!" Hope was in pieces, hitting the floor with her fist.

My daughter was hurting herself as an expression of the pain she felt, I couldn't rationalise with her though; all I could do was comfort her, and support her as she went through her own grieving process.

Hope of Ray

Picking her up, and holding her firmly, so she knew she was safe, was the only thing I could think to do, I felt like I was treating her like a baby, but she was our baby, so fragile and in need of my attention.

"My darling Hope, none of this is your fault, not even Mummy knew what was going to happen to Daddy. Please don't ever blame yourself. It was a very sad accident."

As I rocked her, it didn't take long for her to nod off in my arms. I wanted to wrap them all in cotton wool; everything in life was an abstract lie, to keep them safe, not even I could protect them.

Chapter Twenty-Eight

Hubert Parry

The morning of the funeral ran smoothly, the children played like any other day, my parents helped the children dress, whilst they gave me time to ready myself, gain my composure. I had changed so much in the years we had spent on the farm; I left a girl and returned a woman. I was certain of who I was; the farm had put perspective in my life. I straightened the elastic on my skirt, and headed back down stairs, ready for the questioning as to my chosen attire.

"Darling, is there a problem, you're not dressed yet?"

"Mum, I'm wearing this, this skirt is the patchwork of mine and Ray's life together, and I refuse to pretend I am anything other than Ray's wife and the mother to our children. Love doesn't have a dress code. Neither does grief."

With that, mum didn't say another word. I loaded the children up into our car as I always did, and we made our way to the Church, where we were met by Powell's.

The church was full, standing room only, I couldn't differentiate faces.

I stood up - legs like jelly, well, more like a trembling gelatinous mess, in absolute honesty.

I stood up, hollow, numb with agony; my stomach was knotting, I could feel my rectum cramping, I was gripped with nerves. It was as if I was six years old again, the weight of the world upon my shoulders; I was that shy little girl playing Mary, only this wasn't a rehearsal.

Hope of Ray

I couldn't get the words out; in what seemed to be, an ever descending reality; the teacher wasn't there to prompt me, I couldn't escape the fact that this wasn't the Nativity, it was my life.

The words moulded into a large mess, I kept staring at the paper – wishing, hoping, he was going to walk into the Chapel, but nothing. How could he? When the harsh reality was right there. He was cold, in the box, even as I clumsily attempted to articulate about the love of my life, all the while our children sat in the pew, unaware that Daddy was never coming home, and all they had now was his picture staring back at them.

Our story had me illustrated as this strong, formidable woman, today I was about to crash and burn, I just wanted to hide in my bed and pretend I was a fairy, doing all the silly voices to my babies, as I read their favourite story. The story I read today however, was one I never wanted to open the pages of again.

I was smacking back down to Earth with a crashing sensation, as I now used my reserves to fulfil my last wifely duty. I couldn't survive under this facade of strength, I knew for us to survive now, as a family of five, and for me to ride the storm of four children five years old and under, I would have to openly admit my vulnerability.

This, running through my mind for what must have been seconds, felt like hours, I looked down at the paper for inspiration once more. Nothing. It was still a blur, the sea of words were just a black hole.

As I looked up, I drew a breath; the wave of colour, worn to honour him, gave me the clarity I needed, this was my final chance to tell him I loved him, with everyone else to share the emotion with me. These people, who had taken time out of their day to show my family sympathy and respect.

"Ray, my darling, you walked into my life thirteen years ago. The day we met, I vowed I'd never forget those boots. I never knew if I'd see you again.

"The friendship we built, and the sorrow we shared. In the times of hardship, the comfort we sought in each other. Never in my life did I imagine, the life we built together, the patience and understanding we had for one another and histories past. Never in my life did I imagine I would be your wife, and a mother to our children.

"Today, tomorrow, and always, I vow I will never forget those boots, the boots you wore carrying me over the threshold to Lovett's Farm, our forever family home. The boots you wore the day of our wedding. The boots you wore the day you delivered our Reuben-Ray.

"Your boots will forever walk the farm, in the footprints of our children. I promised you our home would be forever, our children will one day spread their wings and fly. Your boots will forever walk our farm, with our children and our grandchildren.

"A piece of you will forever be in my life, as it will Hope, Faith, David, and Reuben-Ray's. Every time we sing we will look back in fondness of you. And when the moon shines bright, I know you will be looking down on us.

"I love you Ray, I have no idea how to do any of this without you, but one day I will make you proud once more. Until death us do part, and it parts us today. I'm hollow without you my darling."

I stepped down from the lectern, and I beckoned the children to join me from the first pew, where my mum, dad, and Robson, held the children. My dad handed me Reuby, and we all crouched down by the side of Ray's coffin, adorned in the flowers we'd picked from our farm, which I had hand tied, just like I did for Helen.

The three older children held each other's hands and I was mesmerised by their unity. David put his hand out for Reuby to join them, which he did, and I stood up behind them.

"Let's all sing, for daddy, one last time."

They nodded their heads.

"Ready...?"

"And did those feet in ancient time,

"Walk up on England's mountains green:"

My dad joined in from his seat, and one by one, the congregation stood and joined us. By the end, most were struggling for the lyrics. I'd spent so much of my life singing it at funerals, and singing it at the rugby, I knew it intimately; we had always sung it to the children, Ray and I appreciated it on varied levels. It was a song that defined our family. By the end, the children were struggling too. I carried on. I could hear only one other voice, out of sight behind me, its sonorous baritone filled the room.

"In England's green and pleasant Land."

The final note harmonised with mine. The last time I heard such splendour reverberate was... But it couldn't be... Could it...?

Hope of Ray

Acknowledgements

His Chelsea boots trampled all over my heart. While I spent a lifetime trying to naively move on. It wasn't until I wrote this book, mainly for cathartic reasons. As I hit 30, I realised how lost he'd made me feel, the mistakes I endured to compensate.

As I spent many nights crying at my self-discovery, there was one man unconditionally by my side, with cups of tea and a hug to make me feel secure. I could finally say goodbye to the man who stole my heart, my body, my soul; laying that chapter of my life in its final resting place.

Now I can freely love the man I call my husband.

For your unconditional love, through every tantrum, every self doubt, every... everything.

Always and forever, I am your wife, Mr Vee.

Printed in Great Britain
by Amazon